P9-CDK-722

PRAISE FOR **LES ROBERTS** AND
THE MILAN JACOVICH MYSTERY SERIES:

"A clever plot, a vibrant Cleveland and rural Ohio setting, and a realistically drawn hero make this series one to watch. It exudes much the same sort of charm as the early Spenser novels did."

—*Booklist (on Pepper Pike)*

"Roberts handles the private-eye format with aplomb and takes full advantage of his Cleveland scene . . . Best of all is his Slovenian sleuth, vulnerable and fallible, whom we are likely (and would like) to see more of."

—*San Diego Union (Pepper Pike)*

"Fast-paced and smoothly narrated."

—*Washington Post Book World (Full Cleveland)*

"Another smooth page-turner from Roberts, who keeps the action moving and still fits in some wry observations on parenthood, teenagers, and marriage."

—*Kirkus Reviews (Deep Shaker)*

"Roberts combines a strong character and a clever plot with the ethnic diversity that Cleveland provides. He proves that Midwest private eyes can hold their own with the best ones from either coast."

—*Des Moines Register (Deep Shaker)*

"There's an affection for Cleveland and an insistence on its ethnic, working-class life that gives vividness to the detection. Roberts writes with sharp wit, creates action scenes that are drawn with flair, and puts emotional life into a range of people."

—*Washington Post Book World (The Cleveland Connection)*

"Roberts is one of the best crime writers around, and *The Cleveland Connection* is his best effort yet. The plot has all the right ingredients—danger, suspense, intrigue, action—in all the right amounts; Milan Jacovich is the kind of guy we want on our side when the chips are down; and Roberts even makes Cleveland sound like a swell place to live. Don't miss this one."

—*Booklist*

"Packed with unusual heroes, villains, and political twists and turns . . . a mystery that defies predictability."

—*Midwest Book Review (The Lake Effect)*

"A real treat . . . If you've somehow missed this series, definitely give it a try . . . If you're already a fan, this book will delight you even further."

—*Mystery News (The Lake Effect)*

"A corker of a whodunit . . . Gritty, grim, humorous, sentimental—a perfect
10." —*Chicago Sun-Times* (*The Duke of Cleveland*)

"Roberts affectionately weaves in the history and rich ethnic mix of Milan
Jacovich's Cleveland turf." —*Publishers Weekly* (*Collision Bend*)

"Roberts is a wordsmith of high order, and *Collision Bend* is a terrific novel
of the mean streets." —*Meritorious Mysteries*

"Roberts certainly creates a sense of place. Cleveland rings true—and he's
especially skillful in creating real moral and ethical choices for his characters." —*The Plain Dealer* (*The Cleveland Local*)

"Jacovich [is] one of the most fully realized characters in modern crime
fiction . . . Roberts is a confident writer who knows his character well and
who has made him complex enough to be interesting."
—*Mostly Murder* (*The Cleveland Local*)

"A series that gets better and better . . . strongly recommended for those
who like their detectives cut from the classic mold."
—*Booklist* (*A Shoot in Cleveland*)

"[Milan Jacovich] is a hero one can't help but like. Roberts's polished
prose, inventive plots, and pleasantly low-key style add extra appeal to his
long-running series." —*Booklist* (*The Best-Kept Secret*)

"Page turner of the week . . . narrative comfort food . . . a nifty spin on a
classic P.I. formula." —*People magazine* (*The Indian Sign*)

"Brilliantly plotted, with a powerhouse climax." —*Booklist* (*The Dutch*)

"[A] roller coaster ride of a mystery . . . Roberts speeds the reader through
an investigation offering plenty of delicious twists and turns without ever
compromising credibility." —*Publishers Weekly* (*The Irish Sports Pages*)

"An enjoyable whodunit with a deep realistic look at Cleveland now and a
nostalgic surreal look at the city in the 1960s though the distorted lens of
memories." —*Midwest Book Review* (*King of the Holly Hop*)

"Solid prose and a consistent hard edge."
—*Publishers Weekly* (*The Cleveland Creep*)

"A fast paced and riveting read of fiction . . . a much recommended addition
to mystery and thriller collections."
—*Midwest Book Review* (*Whiskey Island*)

SPEAKING OF MURDER

The Milan Jacovich mysteries
by Les Roberts:

Pepper Pike

Full Cleveland

Deep Shaker

The Cleveland Connection

The Lake Effect

The Duke of Cleveland

Collision Bend

The Cleveland Local

A Shoot in Cleveland

The Best-Kept Secret

The Indian Sign

The Dutch

The Irish Sports Pages

King of the Holly Hop

The Cleveland Creep

Whiskey Island

Win, Place, or Die

The Ashtabula Hat Trick

Speaking of Murder

SPEAKING OF MURDER

A MILAN JACOVICH MYSTERY

LES ROBERTS
WITH DAN S. KENNEDY

GRAY & COMPANY, PUBLISHERS
CLEVELAND

Iosco - Arenac District Library
East Tawas, Michigan

Copyright © 2016 by Les Roberts and Dan S. Kennedy

All rights reserved. No part of this book may be reproduced
or transmitted in any form or by any means, electronic or
mechanical, including photocopying, recording, or by any
information storage and retrieval system, without written
permission of the publisher.

This book is a work of fiction. Names, characters, places,
and incidents either are products of the author's imagination
or are used fictitiously, and any resemblance to actual events
or locales or persons, living or dead, is entirely coincidental.

Gray & Company, Publishers
www.grayco.com

ISBN 978-1-938441-84-4

Printed in the United States of America
First printing

*To Josh Pachter and his brilliant wife,
Laurie—great friends who live too far away.
And to Holly Albin—always and
forever to Holly Albin.*

SPEAKING OF MURDER

PROLOGUE

MILAN

Do you ever get the feeling that you really need help?

I don't mean help to open a jar of peanut butter, clean your garage, hold the ladder while you clean the gutters, or tell you what ingredient is missing when you're cooking pasta sauce from scratch.

I don't even mean if you're elderly and some Boy Scout helps you cross the street, as wonderful as that might be.

No—the question is, do you need help to be a better human being so you can make more money, a lot more money, get promoted, be more successful, be more popular, make friends, get laid, or find The One and fall in love and make it stick?

Thousands of people—salesmen, athletes, ministers, ex-politicians, fading movie stars, academics and others—have become motivational speakers, metaphysical thought leaders, life coaches, self-appointed gurus, personal performance trainers, even cult leaders. They are ready to help change who you are—as long as your pockets are deep enough or your credit card limits are high enough to pay them well for their time.

Some are members of SHAM, the Self-Help and Actualization Movement; others, of the Get Rich Fast crowd. They crossbreed. Many you know by name—from real TV shows or bought-and-paid-for infomercials, public appearances, best-selling books, CDs, and lapel buttons and photos and bumper stickers, souvenirs and bobblehead dolls.

The Movement, so-called as if it were holy, might have gained its first foothold in America almost a century ago, when Dale Carnegie's book, *How to Win Friends and Influence People,* became a blueprint for those losing their way on the path of life, and in need of scattered Hansel-and-Gretel breadcrumbs to help them on their journey.

I read that book as a teen, thinking the answer was far too simple for such a long book. I offer it without charging you an arm and leg: If you want to win friends and influence people, stop being an asshole.

Why am I talking about this industry, which earns nearly ten *billion* dollars every year? Because recently my business company, Milan Security, did a job for the GMSA—the Global Motivational Speakers Association, chock-full of the few who can successfully give self-help speeches.

The GMSA holds its major convention in a different city each year. A third of the speakers talk professionally for a living— sometimes a most handsome living, especially if they appear regularly on television, raking in six-figure speaking fees once only reserved for former United States presidents. Their shtick is telling everyone how they can become uber-rich, famous, popular, or adored. The other two-thirds are wannabe speakers and gurus hoping that if they just brush shoulders with superstars, some magic might stick to them. More likely, it'll be bullshit rubbing off.

Most speakers tell you how to be successful in business, in life, in sports, and in love. Of course, if they just flat-out told you not to be an asshole, and you listened to them, they'd all be out of business.

Their most recent GMSA whoop-de-do was held in Cleveland, which is why I got involved—hauled on board for an entire weekend and getting paid nowhere near what top-rung speakers earn for fifty minutes' work—to augment the security of the venerable Renaissance Hotel, looming over Public Square. It's one hundred years old, within walking distance of Lake Erie, the Rock and Roll Hall of Fame, the Cuyahoga River that twists and turns its way through downtown, and just steps away from the Horseshoe Casino. The facilities are spacious and pleasant, the rooms clean, with the most spectacular views either of the square itself, the Cuyahoga River, or the lake, and close to some of the Midwest's best restaurants.

My assistant came along with me. He's Kevin O'Bannion, preferring to be called K.O., both for his initials and for his ability to score knockouts frequently whenever he gets physical with others who only *look* bigger and stronger than he does. That's one of the reasons I keep him around. He fights better than I ever did, and if he happens to get tagged a time or two, his youth heals him quickly. Thirty years my junior, his teenage captivity in juvenile detention and three army combat tours in the Middle East taught him to handle any situations that might arise.

The Global Motivational Speakers Association is rife with self-anointed superstars, desperate wannabes, and a scruffy crew of never-gonna-bes all milling around the hotel, along with the glassy-eyed attendees looking for the fairy dust to change them from losers in business and life into wealthy entrepreneurs because they're told nobody, but *nobody*, works for someone else—hoping some maven notices them, buys them a drink, or takes them to bed.

Or perhaps all three.

When hosting a large convention of celebrities and hangers-on, the Renaissance Hotel goes through a great deal of planning and preparation before anything happens.

And that's where I came in.

CHAPTER ONE

MILAN

Ask Americans what they're afraid of, and one fear is head and shoulders above the others. Not heights, snakes, germs, fire, claustrophobia, the dark, or even the terror of lack of sanitation that sends you outside behind a bush rather than daring to sit down on a public toilet.

Most people are scared stiff of public speaking.

It doesn't frighten me—six foot three and two hundred thirty pounds on a good day—but then I rarely speak to more than six people at one time. I'm a private investigator, emphasis on "private." I'm also discreet, if you need someone quietly poking around in anything you're too nervous to examine on your own.

I was explaining all this nervousness of speaking in public to my "significant other." I call her that because we aren't married, so I can't say "wife" or "spouse," and at our ages, there's no way we can refer to one another as "boyfriend and girlfriend" without sounding like teenagers on a corny TV sitcom. In any event, her name is Tobe Blaine, and she is a homicide detective sergeant with the Cleveland Police Department.

The evening after I'd been interviewed for the job, Tobe and I were having dinner at Corleone's, on the West Side, a restaurant situated at one corner of a strip mall. Just driving by it, you'd never know how elegant it is inside, nor how good the food is. Both the manager and the waitress greeted Tobe by name, so I knew she'd been there several times before.

Corleone's also boasts a superb wine list.

I'm not yet a wine-drinker. For most of my adult years I was a beer guy—Cleveland is one of the best beer towns in America—until Tobe came along and started introducing me to beverages with which I'd had little or no experience. Single malt scotch, hand-tended bourbon made in very small batches, and gin martinis that are delicious but too hard to handle.

"I don't understand," Tobe was saying. She had little problem with martinis and was sipping hers, garnished as usual with a lemon peel twist and not the standard olive. "When hotels have big conventions, they have their own security department, and if they need more, they hire local police departments to look out for them, so nobody gets totally shitfaced in the bar and then trashes their room like they were twenty-year-old rock stars."

I said, "They have celebrities coming, too."

"Kanye West?"

"Who?"

She snickered. "I forgot you never even heard of the Kardashians, so you sure wouldn't know Kanye West."

"I do know who the Kardashians are," I said. "I just can't tell them apart."

"Nobody can," she said. "So the P.D. protects the peasants who show up there to spend money, and you take care of the big shots who make the money?"

"Something like that."

"Interesting job, Milan—kissing the tushies of famous celebrities. I only have to butt heads with stone-cold killers."

"Lucky you, Tobe. Whoever butts heads with you loses."

"That," Tobe Blaine said, "is why I get the big bucks." She opened her menu. "I'm starved. Let's eat."

We had a great dinner, but I kept running over in my head the meeting I'd had that morning in my office with the head of security at the Renaissance Cleveland Hotel.

Her name was Swati S. Sathe, a handsome fifty-ish woman of East Indian descent who had a classy hairdo and subtle but attractive make-up, and if she'd ever smoked a fifty-cent cigar in her life like the hotel dicks in old movies used to, I doubt anyone ever saw her do it.

"I was a police detective in India—Bangalore," she said when I asked how she wound up with her present job. "When my husband and I moved here for his business, I applied to the Renaissance Hotel. They were interested in a security boss, and the position sounded easier to handle than a city of more than five million people."

K.O., seated at his desk near the window, observed, "Nobody ever said Cleveland is easy."

She looked at him. "That's why I'm here. The Global Motivational Speakers Association's having its convention here next month, with some of the biggest names in the business. We expect at least two thousand people, and we'll need extra support."

"Are you expecting trouble, Ms. Sathe?"

"I'm expecting there won't *be* any trouble, thanks to extra security." She cleared her throat. "If you take this assignment, Mr. Jacovich, you'll have to watch some of those prestigious guests more closely than others."

"Why is that? Have any of them had death threats?"

"If you're famous," Swati Sathe shrugged, "*really* famous, there's always a small fringe group that hates your guts, mostly because of your success and their lack of it. The biggest name scheduled to show up," she said, removing a list from her jacket pocket, "is Tommy Triller."

I said, "He's a singer?"

That made K.O. laugh. "Have you been living in a coal mine, Milan? Tommy Triller is a motivational speaker. He's huge!"

"Nobody made any speeches in my coal mine, K.O."

Ms. Sathe hid her smile with her hand. "Triller has written fifteen books, he's made six yearly half-hour infomercials that air everywhere, and also a few real TV specials a year. He packs tens of thousands of fans into seminars all over the country and in Canada, too, and sells five- and seven-day retreats, coaching programs, and other events where there are all sorts of inspiring things to do—and he charges about seven thousand dollars to be there."

K.O. looked disappointed. "No T-shirts?"

"Tons of them with his picture on them," Ms. Sathe said seriously. "Also buttons, bumper stickers, photographs, ballpoint pens, and sayings of his, framed or on plaques that are supposed to magically change you from a washout into a superhero. The celebrities want to create a feeding frenzy—a stampede to the vendors' room at the Center to draw convention-goers with money to them like moths to a flame. It's all meant as a *transformation*."

"I'm wondering, Ms. Sathe," I said, "how you came to us for what's little more than bodyguarding. There are plenty of companies in town that provide that."

"Frankly, the company we'd contacted first chose to bow out."

"Why?"

She shrugged. "I didn't ask why. I started looking around for a replacement—and it's you."

"Again, why us?"

"Frankly, a high-up in your police department highly recommended you."

"A high-up? Not the police chief?"

"No, Mr. Jacovich. They turned me on to someone in the homicide division, and she gave us your name."

"Detective Sergeant Blaine?"

"No—someone higher up than that," she said. "Lieutenant McHargue, I believe."

That caught me off-guard. Lieutenant Florence McHargue, Tobe's boss, wouldn't recommend me for anything except a one-way ticket to Timbuktu.

"And you want us for all four days?" I said.

"That's correct."

"And," K.O. broke in, "to pay special attention to Tommy Triller?"

"He's the one speaker who is most successful—he banks approximately a hundred million dollars annually."

"That's more than I make in a week," K.O. said. "For selling T-shirts?"

"For selling hope," Ms. Sathe said, "and marketing skills. *And* T-shirts."

I said, "Is this extra security all about him?"

"For the most part. He's asked the convention for extra security—and nobody has explained why to me."

"If I made a hundred mil a year," K.O. said, "I'd want extra security, too."

"True," she said, checking her list again. "But there are others. You have a TV set—so you know who Dr. Ben is."

Naturally I knew who Dr. Ben is. Doesn't everybody? Dr. Ben Mayo, sporting a gleaming pate and overdoing an old-boy yahoo drawl, has his own eponymous daily TV show, now in its twelfth year, featuring an endless parade of guests whining about their problems, hoping that within sixty minutes he'll identify the cause of their misery and pompously pronounce a four-sentence cure that makes them feel better about themselves so they can go home and sin or suffer no more. This is the driving force behind his inspirational self-help books, courses, web sites, apps, and YouTube videos, and his fees for endorsing everything from weight loss pills to rehab centers to used cars.

Mayo, with a master's degree from the University of North Carolina and a doctorate from Michigan State, had been a psychologist for several years, zeroing in on marriage issues. But once battling his way onto television and with the multi-millions he pockets annually, he now deals with business entrepreneurs whose careers are threatened, hotshot salesmen stuck in no-sell slumps, obnoxious neighbors with barking dogs, meddling in-laws, drugs and booze and anorexics and bulimics, dysfunctional families, out-of-control children, and people who weigh nine hundred pounds and can't haul themselves out of bed.

I said, "Will Triller and Dr. Mayo need more protection than the other two thousand attendees?"

"Everyone calls him Dr. Ben," she went on. "He and Triller are the biggest celebrities in this particular field." She made a note on her paper. "I've brought you a complete list of the attendees and a separate list of—"

"The big shots?" K.O. asked.

"Mr. O'Bannion, there are many so-called 'big shots' in this group if you happen to be in the self-help business." She studied K.O. "You don't look like you need any help."

"Mr. O'Bannion," I said with more weight than necessary, since his under-thirty smart-assness gets on my nerves on a daily basis, "needs all the help he can get—but not from spending his last nickel on snake-oil salesmen."

"Maybe," Swati Sathe said, "but you won't be paying them; they'll pay you."

"I thought the hotel was hiring us."

She shook her head. "Triller asked the Global Motivational Speakers for extra security—and since the organization's head-quarters are in Minneapolis and nowhere near Cleveland, they asked me to do their legwork." She raised her eyebrows. "Asked isn't quite right. They're bringing a lot of business to this hotel, so they demanded we find someone. But you'll be working for them, not us—watching over the biggest of the big shots." She picked her purse up and pushed her chair back from across my desk. "The executive director of the GMSA will be in town the day after tomorrow to meet you. He'll be more specific."

"About what?" K.O. asked.

"About everything," Sathe said, "including how much he's going to pay you."

The Cuyahoga River—*Cuyahoga* is an Indian word meaning Crooked River, which means it's the Crooked River River—flows right by my second-floor office in The Flats. During all but the worst weather, enormous ore boats navigate the hairpin turn where my building is, Collision Bend. It's so named because in the old days, big boats heading in opposite directions to and from Lake Erie, nearly a mile farther north, would often crash into each other. Now, though it's infrequent, they still do.

My view encompasses where the Cleveland Indians play base-ball, Progressive Field, which used to be called Jacobs Field, more popularly "The Jake," and the Quicken Loans Arena, "The Q," where the Cavaliers play basketball, which was built as the Gund Arena. I miss the old "Jake" name, as everyone else does—and most still call it that.

It's a good idea they changed the Gund Arena's name, though. Saying "Gund Arena" aloud, quickly, always sounded like a sexu-ally transmitted disease.

I was at the window enjoying the brightness of mid-October when K.O. came out of the john. "Ever been inside the Renais-sance Hotel?" I said.

"Never had a reason to go there."

"Well, you'll get a good look at it the day after tomorrow."

"Will I have to wear a tie?"

"Wear what you want—if you prefer looking like a bum."

"Well, *you* hardly ever wear a tie." He slid behind his desk. "But considering your ties, I wouldn't blame you."

He's correct; my ties are awful. Tobe Blaine gave me a beautiful Jerry Garcia tie for my birthday, but so far I've had no occasion to wear it. Tomorrow might be its lucky day.

Tobe and I have been together for a year and a half—my longest romance since my marriage, which ended badly a quarter century ago. It works because she understands that what I do for a living sometimes gets sticky. She's a Cleveland cop, but unlikely to be involved in the GMSA's annual get-together. Her area is murder.

And nobody ever gets murdered at a GMSA convention—unless they get talked to death.

CHAPTER TWO

K.O.

K.O. had never been inside a luxury hotel like the Renaissance. He'd overnighted at motels, and in Iraq and Afghanistan, his week-long army leaves to Cairo and the United Arab Republic had been spent in third-rate hotels catering to the U.S. enlisted military. So when he and Milan climbed the sweeping staircase into the main lobby, he was struck by the lavish decorations, the ornamental drapes, and the beautiful fountain at the front of the lobby, carved by a master sculptor from flawless white marble from the same quarry in Italy that Michelangelo used to sculpt the statue of David.

Outside the day was gray autumn, but the sweeping view of Public Square, including the looming Soldiers and Sailors Monument, the Old Stone Church, and a slim peek at the entrance to the busy Horseshoe Casino right next door, caught K.O.'s attention.

"This is some hotel. You come here frequently, Milan?"

"A few times. We'll be here a lot if this convention job works out."

K.O. said, "What about this job? We aren't cops or bodyguards. When we see something wrong about Tommy Triller, do we run and tattle to the teacher?"

"The guy paying our bills can tell us what he expects. His name is Fesmire. Reeve Fesmire."

K.O.'s eyes opened wide. "Someone really named him Reeve?"

Milan said, "I doubt he picked it out himself."

K.O. continued looking outside. "Look at all those people out there. It's like a carnival."

He turned to watch Swati Sathe approach, this morning in a gray skirt and a white blouse. She juggled a short stack of files in the crook of her arm that looked like they might drop all over the floor at any moment.

"Are we late?" Milan asked.

"No, Mr. Fesmire was early—and he's twitching already. Come on, I've set up a meeting room on the second floor."

They took one of the elevators up, then followed her down the hallway to a meeting room named after a forgotten long-ago governor of Ohio.

At the small conference table sat an annoyed man Swati introduced as Reeve Fesmire, the executive director of the GMSA. Bad comb-over, horn-rimmed glasses, a moderately expensive but wrinkled suit, and a nose crinkled in distaste as though something had died three days ago in his handkerchief pocket.

No handshake, which always told Milan something, as did the contemptuous look. "Are you kidding me, Swati? Is *this* your added security?" Fesmire snapped. "They don't look very impressive to me."

"They're the best," Swati replied. "I researched before I contacted them."

Fesmire looked both men up and down as if they were low-rent hookers in a Tijuana brothel. "They don't look like they're the best. A father-and-son team?"

Milan said, "Mr. Fesmire, we aren't father and son—and if you continue talking about us like we're not here—just like magic, we won't *be* here. Abracadabra."

"Is this how you apply for a job?" Fesmire asked. "Is that how it works in Cleveland? Or is it just you?"

"How about," Milan continued, "you tell us what you want us to do for you—and if *we* think it's a good idea, we'll hang around. If we don't like it, we'll tell *you* we're not taking the assignment."

Swati leaned on the back of a chair. "Cool down, gentlemen. This convention is nearly on top of us; let's not start off on a bad footing. Let's discuss what's mutually beneficial for everyone."

Milan and K.O. gave it a few moments' thought before sitting down across the table from Fesmire.

Swati asked, "Shall I order some coffee and rolls for you?"

"Tea for me," Milan said.

"Tea," Fesmire muttered. "Jesus!"

She went to one end of the room and quietly ordered breakfast snacks over the phone. Then she smiled as she sat down on Milan and K.O.'s side of the table. "Mr. Fesmire, why don't you explain to Mr. Jacovich and Mr. O'Bannion exactly what you *do*—and then tell them what you want from them."

Reeve Fesmire primly folded his hands in front of him, like a grade-schooler. "The GMSA is the oldest and largest association of leading speakers—and the most successful speakers' bureau as well. Nowhere else can you find such a spectacular and diverse array of great public speakers. Most companies or groups searching for entertainment that informs can't just call up a speechifier and make a deal. We're the go-between with a large staff that marries the right speaker with the right client, audience, and venue, and works out the contract."

"And they all talk about one form or another of self-help?" K.O. asked.

Fesmire leaned back in his chair and sighed, impatient with explaining something he thought everyone should know. "If you have a large corporation, and you want a speaker at an event, you'd want your employees to learn something, to be inspired. Of course, some speakers are amusing as well—but that's frosting on the cake."

"And your agency takes a percentage?" Milan asked.

"Movie stars, millionaire athletes, best-selling authors—their agents all take a percentage off the top. Why shouldn't I have the same benefit?" His smile turned smug. "I put together *the* agency for speakers, and every year I hold this convention and showcase. Speakers from all over the world compete, fight to secure an opportunity to sell their books and courses and entice people to sign up for one of their programs or retreats. Especially Tommy Triller's weekend, where everyone pays a high fee for the Firewalk Experience. To walk barefoot, confidently, over a bed of hot coals."

K.O. was incredulous. *"What?"*

"That's Triller's thing—people walking over hot coals. Supposedly it proves mind-over-body ability, that every ordinary Jack or Jane has extraordinary powers. I suppose—and this comment doesn't leave this room—it's sophomoric. But it sells."

"Why do you need extra security?" Milan said.

"The hotel security will generally keep things in order," Reeve Fesmire said, nodding at Swati. "City police officers will be present in case there are drunken squabbles, arguments over who sits where, crowd-control issues—but, unfortunately, there aren't enough cops in Cleveland to fill the job properly. Your responsibility—assuming we come to an agreement—is to watch over the famous speakers, the really big ones, to keep them safe from the fans." He chuckled. "And from each other."

K.O. found that hard to believe. "There's bad blood between them?"

Swati spoke up. "Like in any other business, it's a question of who's on top. Who is Number One? Who makes the most money? Who gets the best convention opportunities?" She covered her mouth with her hand again to hide her smile. "And who's the most famous?"

"My guess," K.O. said, "would be Dr. Ben Mayo."

"Perhaps," Fesmire said, "except that, forgetting TV for a moment, Tommy Triller makes the most in-person appearances, sells the most—resources. Gewgaws. He makes twice as much money as Dr. Ben. Did you ever see that really successful documentary they called *The Secret Power?* It was huge! Aired in every big city in America and in Europe, in theaters and arenas. Now it's on cable TV all the time. It made Triller so damn famous! People credit him with starting the whole firewalking thing to unleash his clients' secret power. He's gotten thousands of people to do that."

K.O. said, "Nobody burned their feet?"

"Triller says no, because they've freed themselves from their hang-ups and found their power—thanks to his training."

"A miracle?"

Swati said, "I see no miracle about walking barefoot over hot coals—especially if it costs me seven thousand dollars."

"That's an expensive way to toast your toes," Milan said. "Speaking of money, Mr. Fesmire—are you making us an offer?"

Fesmire shifted in his chair as if it were uncomfortable. "It's important. In some ways these star speakers are children, with giant, demanding egos—and Tommy Triller has the most giant ego of all of them. My reputation, my entire business depends on him being—managed carefully. Since Ms. Sathe recommends you highly, I'm prepared to be extremely generous."

"How generous?"

"It's just the two of you?"

"You're looking at my entire organization," Milan said.

Fesmire played Beethoven on the tabletop with his fingers, considering it. Milan stayed silent, poker-faced, tapping K.O. under the table with his foot to make him keep quiet. Finally: "Three and a half days, from Thursday morning until Sunday noon, I propose a fee of fifteen thousand dollars."

Milan did the math in his head, dividing by total hours—not as big a number as it sounded. But it was a good number. To K.O., it seemed a very big number.

Milan said, "Agreeable."

"It's a damn good thing," Reeve Fesmire said, "because I wouldn't pay you a nickel more."

CHAPTER THREE

MILAN

Tobe and I had eaten dinner at Nighttown, about three blocks from my apartment, and had returned for a postprandial drink so we could spend some time with my dog, Herbie. I'd never owned a dog, and wound up with Herbie because his original owner died unexpectedly when I was on a case. Adoption from a shelter would have been unlikely, as he was the least attractive dog I'd ever seen—a combination of a mini-German shepherd from the neck up, and a Welsh corgi body for the rest of him. So I brought him home with me. After a year, I find myself becoming more attached to him every day, which is why Tobe and I spend more time in my apartment on the Cedar-Fairmount triangle in Cleveland Heights than in hers, which is on the West Side near the lake. Herbie wags what there is of his tail almost constantly and looks up at me with unconditional love. I feed him regularly and walk him three or four times a day. Often, I take him with me to my office so he doesn't get lonely.

Nevertheless, Herbie is a world champion gas-passer—so if you meet him in person, try to stay upwind.

Tobe and I sipped on Courvoisier. Before her, I'd never bought a bottle of Courvoisier in my life. I laid out our meeting with Fesmire that morning for her, since it involved her police department. Finally she said, "When a big convention comes to town, Cleveland cops crawl all over the joint. Why do they need you?"

I picked up a VIP list and several pages I'd printed from Google.

"There are big-deal names on here who need to be nannied while they're in town."

"Nannied? Washing out their undies, or finding them hookers or something else?"

"You know who Dr. Ben is?"

"I'd rather get a root canal than watch his television show—but sure, I know who he is," Tobe said. "Is he the big-deal name?"

"One of them. Then there's Tommy Triller."

"The walking-on-fire man who starred in that *Secret Power* movie rip-off? What does he do for an encore? Change water into wine?"

"Whatever it is, he's only slightly less rich than the Sultan of Brunei." I scanned the list. "How about Dr. Lorelei Singleton?"

Tobe shook her head. "I've heard about this Dr. Lorelei, but I've never seen her."

"Well, she's no physician or psychologist—she doesn't even have an honorary doctorate in anything."

Tobe laughed. "'I'm not a doctor, but I play one on TV.' That's one way to make a buck."

"She makes her money by hating gays, abortion, atheists, and putting down just about everyone who calls her show with a problem. She's not the richest speaker at this convention, but she does OK, writing books about everything she hates, and knocks down about twenty grand every time she goes somewhere to give a talk."

"Hell, *I* could earn twenty grand in one night," Tobe said. "Robbing a bank."

"These so-called celebrities all cheerfully loathe each other— jealous with a capital *J*. Most speakers on the second or third level, or even lower, hate them, too."

"There's a difference," Tobe pointed out, "between jealousy and envy. You're envious when other guys try to hit on me—but I don't think you're jealous."

"Not when they see your badge, I'm not. Maybe you've even arrested this next guy," I said, putting another sheet of paper on top. "Street killer turned millionaire hip hop star—Hy Jinx."

"Never heard of him," Tobe said, "not being a rapper fan."

"His real name is Hakim Washington—a native Angeleno. By

the time he was eighteen, he was a maven in a powerful drug gang that had weekly shoot-outs. Google says Hakim killed not only a rival gang member, but an eight-year-old who happened to be standing on the sidewalk."

"Could they prove it?"

"The local D.A. went after him for Murder One, but his lawyer was better."

Tobe sighed. "Drug dealers always afford the best lawyers—and the little shit walked, too! Why's he making self-improvement speeches? Found Jesus, did he?"

"Bingo. He rapped all week long and preached in a neighborhood church on Sundays, until somebody told him he was more motivational than religious and hooked him up with the GMSA."

"They still call him Jinx?"

"Calling him Hy Jinx draws bigger crowds than Hakim Washington. He just shows up, gives a forty-minute talk, and hangs around all weekend selling his books and his albums. So this convention is stuck with him—and K.O. and I are stuck with Tommy Triller."

"You have movie stars at this piss-up, too?"

"John Wayne was a movie star. Everybody since him is a wannabe. No, our biggest film name is Siddartha West. She's been in movies forever."

"I read she's into Ouija boards and tarot cards and astrology—and every day she throws three pennies in feng shui so she can learn about her own existence, if you can believe that. She swears she's living her eighth life already. Does that mean she only has one life left to go?"

"Nine lives are for cats, Tobe. She gives spooky, woo-woo talks, telling people to take control of their next life as well as the current one. It pays her more money than the movies. I read this all on Google."

"So you're telling me that now I can just look up all my murder suspects, and Google will tell me the right one to arrest?"

"That's why," I said, "you have private eyes."

"They're paying you a lot?"

"They made a generous offer—and supplying hotel rooms for us for all three days of the convention."

"I can't believe you want me spending three nights at the Renaissance with you while you float through the hallways looking for would-be assassins. We did that hotel-buddy stuff last year in Ashtabula County. That was enough for me."

"That was a crappy motel. This one is elegant."

She frowned. "Seriously—extra round-the-clock security sounds like Triller expects trouble."

"There'll be some. Micro-mini celebrities are targets for the love-struck and the wannabes. Besides, if there wasn't any trouble, I'd be out of business."

CHAPTER FOUR

K.O.

K.O. hung around the main desk in the hotel lobby on the first day of the Global Motivational Speakers Association convention, observing the attendees checking in. It appeared to be a room full of ballpoint pens and plastic pocket protectors. Early birds were either eager listeners hoping to change their lives or low-grade speakers trying to pick up a follower or two before the big shots arrived and sucked up everyone's attention.

Most convention-goers were considerably older than K.O.— mid-to-late forties, he guessed, with a few downright elderly. He wondered whether, in twenty years, he'd also cough up a hearty attendance fee to improve himself.

One balding, potbellied man was making a minor fuss at the check-in, unhappy he'd been given a fifth-floor room when he'd wanted to be up higher, with a better view. Raising his voice and pointing an accusing finger at the reservations clerk, he drew more negative attention than he'd wanted from others milling around the desk.

"According to your reservation, Mr. Paulin," the desk clerk was saying, "you made no request for a specific floor. Your room has a nice view of the Square and part of Lake Erie—but this is a convention, sir, we're all booked up. I'm sorry but there's nothing more I can do."

Mr. Paulin whipped out a notebook and clicked a ballpoint pen almost in her face. "Well, I can do something," he snapped. "I want your name when I contact the owner of this hotel! And it's *Reverend* Paulin, young woman."

K.O. gritted his teeth to keep from walking up to Paulin, whoever he was, and kicking his ass out onto the street. It constantly amazed him that bullies invariably pick on those with low-paying salaries and who were most vulnerable.

K.O. wore a tie and jacket—an outfit he'd never get used to—and hanging from his belt was a short-range walkie-talkie that poofed out his jacket at his right hip. He'd used a similar device while on patrol in Iraq, courtesy of the United States Army, but the one he now wore had been issued by Swati Sathe, which made him feel like a damn fool in the lobby of the Renaissance Cleveland Hotel.

More awkward had been listening to a Reeve Fesmire lecture in Swati's office when he and Milan reported for work.

"Introduce yourselves to the VIPs," Fesmire said. "Show them your badges and let them know you're here. But—and this is very important, gentlemen—you are *not* their buddies. I don't want you hanging around or chatting with them. You're not their pals—you're servants."

K.O. said, "I'm no goddamn servant, Mr. Fesmire—and you better remember that. We're professionals."

Fesmire ran his fingers through his thinning hair, breathing heavily. "I'm going goddamn crazy here already, and the convention hasn't even started yet. Don't give me crap, okay?"

"And vice-versa," K.O. said.

As soon as the meeting ended and they were back down in the lobby, Milan backed K.O. into a corner and, without raising his voice, became very intense. "You are aware that we're in business to make money, aren't you?"

"I don't work for you because I think you're a charity."

"Well, why do you insist on insulting our employer?"

"Reeve? Because he's an asshole."

"An asshole with a checkbook. You've gotta knock it off, K.O. I understand you've got—attitude. I listen to it every day, and I usually ignore it because you're good at what you do. But I can't ignore it when we're on the job. So keep your trap shut. If you can't say anything nice, don't talk."

"What if somebody comes at me with a gun? Should I respect them?"

Milan sighed. "Don't push me , K.O."

That was an hour earlier. Now K.O. was on watch in the lobby while Milan patrolled from the vendors' room to the overcrowded ground-level coffee shop to the meeting rooms and the Grand Ballroom on the mezzanine, wearing a dark gray suit and the vivid, colorful Jerry Garcia tie Tobe had bought him.

The first question for K.O. came from an older gentleman wearing a toupee he probably ordered on the Internet, and a sporty outfit nearly thirty years too young for him. "Where's the men's room?" he wanted to know.

Just south of the marble fountain, a uniformed Cleveland cop stood against the railing of the steps, tall and visually imposing. K.O. felt a twinge of guilt. As outside security, he was being paid three times what the officer earned in an everyday job. His walkie-talkie crackled. He stepped behind a large pillar in the lobby and unhooked it from his belt.

Milan's voice sounded as if he were in Antarctica. "I'm at the street entrance. Dr. Ben is on his way up. Look sharp."

"Copy," K.O. said. "It's like being back in the army again!"

He strolled over to the sweeping staircase and moved to the side as Dr. Ben Mayo marched up the broad steps into the lobby, leading the charge like Julius Caesar crossing the Rubicon. He was wearing a gray trench coat, a jaunty driver's cap, and a pair of black leather gloves. *Nobody* in Cleveland wears gloves in early October.

One step behind him but keeping close was Dr. Ben's wife, Caroline—vibrant, blond, pretty, with blue eyes reflecting an early summer sky and a subtle eroticism none would miss. A husky linebacker-looking guy walked almost beside Mayo, just in case anyone wanted to jump in and actually touch the revered personage.

Scattered applause of recognition broke out as he headed toward the check-in desk; most attendees were too interested in getting themselves settled and in the proper rooms so they could begin their kiss-ass mission and post-lunchtime drinking and schmoozing in the bar to bother giving Dr. Ben a big hand.

Besides, Mayo only had a *daytime* TV show.

But he didn't approach the desk directly; one of his "people" did, a harassed-looking young woman clutching a clipboard close to her chest as though she slept with it, explaining that there were four in Dr. Ben's party, requiring two separate rooms in addition to a large suite for the doctor and his wife. Two reservation clerks went momentarily loco trying to find everyone's names on the computer and figure out what rooms they'd been assigned.

Nobodies who'd come in after the Mayo party stood around waiting, shifting impatiently, juggling their luggage. The convention hadn't even begun yet, and already people were cheesed off about feeling less important.

K.O. couldn't blame them. Mayo had *that* look, "smug" tattooed across his forehead for all to see. Those who never missed his TV show wouldn't notice, hanging as they were on his every word. In their minds, as in his own, he was a major star.

This seemed as good a time as any to introduce himself, but K.O. didn't get within twenty feet of the latest VIP when the linebacker guy planted himself in his path. "You can't bother Dr. Ben right now," he said firmly.

K.O. showed his special ID badge. "O'Bannion, special security."

Linebacker nodded. "You still can't talk to him."

"It's my job to talk to him."

"And it's my job to make sure you don't." Forty-eight inch chest expanding. "If everybody just walked up to talk to Dr. Ben, he'd be standing in the lobby until a week from next Tuesday. You're a security guy, go be secure someplace else."

K.O. glanced at the clock behind the reservation desk. He'd been on duty less than an hour, and already he wanted to punch two people. This would be *some* assignment.

No one else was allowed in the elevator as Dr. Ben, his wife Caroline, the linebacker guy, and the flustered young woman with the clipboard entered along with a bellman with a cart overloaded with their personal luggage.

Just then another doctor—not really a doctor at all—came sweeping up the stairs with a hanging bag slung over her shoulder. Lorelei Singleton wasn't quite five feet tall, her hair was long and black, her toned body was that of an athlete, and her eyes were dark chocolate brown. She moved with a specific confidence, but being a radio personality, she knew she wasn't as big a star as Mayo. She had a lot of clout, though; every day, hundreds of masochistic sad sacks called her show to be maligned and insulted, and millions listened—to feel better about themselves by comparison. Those millions bought every advertised product Lorelei endorsed—and Lorelei skimmed a little off the top, too.

K.O. waited until she checked in and then got on the elevator with her. When she stepped out on the sixth floor, he did, too, and introduced himself, showing his ID.

"Special security?" she said, eyes twinkling.

Her suite was just opposite the elevator, so she went over and unlocked it. "And what if I need you?"

"You call Security," he said, "and they'll call me."

She swung the door open. Her windows faced north toward the lake, though another office building across the square was in her way. She stood in the open doorway. "Coming in?" she twinkled. Flirty-flirty.

"I'm on duty. I just wanted you to know we're here for you."

"Aw, that's sweet. Do you listen to my radio show?"

"I'm usually working," he said.

"Then I hope you come hear my talk on Saturday."

"Maybe—if I can."

She took a five-dollar bill from her purse. "Thanks so much, sweetness."

"I don't take tips, Dr. Singleton." He handed her a business card with Swati Sathe's name on it. "If you have problems, call this number. They'll reach me."

She batted her eyelashes. "Day or night? Oh, wait!" she said as K.O. moved across the hallway. "I haven't been in Cleveland for years. Is there any restaurant nearby that's really fabulous?"

"There's a packet for you inside. It has all the information you'll need."

She pouted, lower lip extended. "Aww—I was hoping you'd show me exactly where to go." Then, coyly: "I'll buy your dinner, naturally."

"Working," K.O. said. "Sorry. Have a good convention."

Escaping on the elevator and exiting at the lobby, he literally bumped into the man who, five years earlier, had tried fruitlessly to win his party's nomination for the Presidency of the United States.

Jonah Clary, former governor of a solidly red southern state, was tall, curly-haired, ruggedly handsome, a man rarely seen without a broad smile. His campaign manager who had gotten him elected to the governorship in the first place didn't have a clue as how to shut him up whenever he spoke on national television about what disasters he'd likely cause in the Oval Office.

Not only falling short of the nomination but enraging his state constituents who promptly voted him out of office in favor of a Tea Party religious fanatic who'd really like to bomb *everybody*, Jonah Clary was out of a job, out of the public eye, and out of extended hands to shake—until Fesmire discovered and signed him, making him a traveling public speaker pulling down thirty thousand bucks for a one-hour speech.

The two ghostwritten books, with movie-star photographs of him on the cover, were full of homespun homilies, similar to books by Tommy Triller, except Clary's were mostly about winning in politics and making money. The formation of a right-wing group lauding the virtues of pre-marital abstinence, openly hateful towards gays, violently opposed to abortion but not caring a tinker's dam about what comes after birth, and the mantra of profit-no-matter-what, helped him stay visible.

"Excuse me," K.O. said after the bump.

It wasn't a violent bump—barely shoulders brushing—but it irritated Clary. "Just watch it there, boy! Don't be pushing people! Do you know who I am?"

K.O. was about to tell him what he thought, but remembering Milan's admonition, he bit his tongue and moved away as the elevator doors shut on a flummoxed ex-governor.

I did say "Excuse me," he thought. *What a rude sonofabitch!*

It had been a difficult fifteen minutes, making K.O. painfully aware it was only the start of one hell of a weekend.

CHAPTER FIVE

MILAN

'd only been standing on my feet for six hours or so, and they hurt like hell. I've spent too many stake-out nights sitting in a car, hunched down to avoid being noticed, with so-called healthy snack bars in the glove compartment, and an empty coffee can if I needed a potty break and there was no john handy. This convention was different; a busy, bustling hotel lobby, people to look at—but no place to sit down.

For my entire life, I'd loved Cleveland. I especially relate to the downtown area, the vibrant restaurants and bars and clubs, the elegant sports arenas I could see out my office window, and the beautiful, historic Public Square with its Soldiers and Sailors Monument dating from just after the Civil War, and the ancient Old Stone Church nestled between new and imposing skyscrapers. On this job, I didn't get to see any of it, ensconced as I was inside the hotel.

Ah, well, I thought, Monday was coming and life would go back to normal.

I noticed a slim young woman get off the elevator. Her blondish hair was puffed out in a beehive not worn by anyone since the 1960s—an era in which she hadn't yet been born. She wore a truly ugly dress of baby-shit green, and heels several inches too high. She stopped, plastered on a faux smile, and rubbernecked around for a celebrity to talk to. Not recognizing anyone, her over-bright façade slipped into what might have been the beginning of panic.

She peered into the lobby bar, then moved away. Finally, at loose ends, she headed down the stairway to Tower City and the shops, not wasting a smile on the uniformed cop at the head of the stairs.

All those who had already arrived kept checking out everyone else, dying to ask, "Are you anybody?" All were there either to buy something or sell something—and all were up for a good time. Nevertheless, a desperate expectation hovered over them. They'd paid a hell of a lot just to be here.

The normal crowd buzz suddenly grew intense as most people sidled toward the top of the stairs. Tommy Triller was making a grand entrance, and no one wanted to miss it. Screw TV personalities and washed-up politicians and quasi-spiritual gurus; this was the megastar of the moment everyone had waited for.

He'd been chauffeured to the main entrance in a black limousine. I learned later that all megastars had arrived in a high level of motorized luxury, like a rented Rolls or a Bentley, believing what they were constantly telling the crowds that listened to their speeches—that if they acted famous and successful and super-rich, everyone would believe they *were* famous and successful and super-rich.

Tommy Triller was nearly a giant. I'm six-three, or used to be until age and bad posture had probably shaved half an inch or more from my height, but he towered over me by six inches. His salon-tanned skin gleamed from a recent facial, his curly hair was artfully mussed, his shiny nails were manicured, and he rewarded everyone with a wide smile, showing a mouthful of huge teeth I'd only seen before on a horse.

Reeve Fesmire had to trot beside him to keep up with his long strides. Swati Sathe greeted him, but Triller blew past her as if she were invisible. Three big men in off-the-rack suits followed him, with two bellmen carrying enough luggage for a trip around the world, rather than three days in a Cleveland hotel.

Fesmire pantomimed "fifteen minutes" at me, jerking his head toward Triller and then pointing upward. The whole Triller group disappeared into an elevator, and I watched the floor indicator until it stopped on number 12.

In the crowded bar, attendees enjoyed mid-afternoon drinks, dressed slightly better than those wandering the lobby, figuring what to do until the opening ceremonies in the ballroom later that evening. The rest were up in their rooms studying the sheets of instructions they'd been issued and trying to decide where in the neighborhood they should go to dinner.

That's when I heard my name called.

The last person I thought I'd meet at an GMSA convention was Victor Gaimari—hedge fund manager, rainmaker, man about town, perennial bachelor, and the undisputed godfather of the Greater Cleveland Mafia, a job inherited from his late uncle, Giancarlo D'Allessandro.

On some level, I'd loved Don Giancarlo, who'd always been honest with me—but Victor and I have a long, checkered history. We began as mortal enemies a quarter-century earlier, found a platform of relative civility, and became sort-of friends, and then former friends, apparently because I'd pushed him too hard about his questionable pals in the mob. We're now no longer friends or foes; what we are, I'm not sure. Frenemies, maybe, if such a word really exists. I wondered why he was at the Renaissance Hotel bar, better dressed than everyone, in a suit without a wrinkle, a blinding white shirt, and a flowered gray tie that must have cost a hundred dollars.

He nodded and waved me over. I hadn't seen him for the better part of a year, and it took me a while to adjust to him being clean-shaven. Ever since I'd met him, he'd sported a mustache. No longer; I gather he figured that a mustache made him look older.

"I heard you've been hired as outside security," he said. Victor has informants everywhere. "Or maybe just an overgrown babysitter."

"And you came here to watch me work?"

"Hardly." He nudged the elbow of the man next to him. "Milan, say hello to Tony Nardoianni."

Nardoianni was in his late fifties. I remembered him vaguely, dressed in his Colorado Rockies uniform, a baseball team he'd managed for at least ten years. Now he was a mid-level motivational speaker—nowhere near as big an earner as Tommy Triller or Dr. Ben, but he made a good living, showing up here as a minor draw. Several of his ghostwritten books would be on sale—about his sports career and what motivations brought him to where he is today—as well as baseballs and photos to autograph for his fans at thirty bucks a pop. Mostly, like everyone else, he was selling his own book, *How to Hit One Out Every Time*, morphing into *Be Your Own Best Coach*. He and Victor Gaimari seemed like an odd match.

"I didn't know you two were friends."

Nardoianni said, "I managed the Rockies back in the day—but now I'm a public speaker, and Victor here manages *me*." He laughed aloud as if it were his first humorous remark and not the five hundredth time he'd said it. I wondered why Victor managed him, and how they had originally connected. "You gonna come hear me talk?"

I said, "I'm working. Security."

He pointed at the walkie-talkie at my waist. "That's a cute little gizmo. Can you call some general on that?"

"Generals have second lieutenants answer their walkie-talkies for them."

Nardoianni guffawed again, bending over and slapping his own thighs. "Man, I love this guy! Hey, listen, is anyone gonna throw a beer bottle at me here? Somebody actually did in Philadelphia."

"Because your team was winning," I reminded him.

His chest puffed with pride. "I always win—doesn't matter what the score is."

"Milan will take good care of you," Victor said. "He's good at what he does."

"I do my job, Victor."

"So I remember. I'll be here for Tony's speech. Afterwards, maybe we can have a drink together?"

"Depends on if someone throws a beer bottle," I said, which made Nardoianni laugh some more. Damn near everything amused him.

"I hope you won't shoot anybody, Milan," Victor said.

I patted my pockets. "I'm not carrying."

"I'm not either. I don't have to."

"That's right," I said. Then I added, "Don Victor."

"Oh, yeah," Nardoianni crowed. "He's The Man!"

Victor tilted his head, accepting that so-called title with a certain grace.

Ready to welcome me back into his outer circle of friends because now he *was* "The Man"? Or was it because it had been years since I'd had a problem with anyone Italian?

I finally excused myself, and took the elevator up to the twelfth floor to the suite where Tommy Triller now held court.

Along with Reeve Fesmire, the three musclemen were in the suite with him, unpacking his clothes. None were as tall as Triller, but all were all built like monsters in an X-Men movie.

Fesmire, though, was quick to explain me to Tommy Triller, who bestowed on me a nod and a tooth-flashing smile in place of a handshake. He did stand up, for no particular reason except he liked to remind everyone he was taller than them.

"You're private security?"

"That's right."

"I'm not sure I'm comfortable with that. I have a private life," Triller told me, "even at a convention."

It must have been hard to talk like that when he was grinning, and it put a rock in my path for a moment. He was the one, as I was told, who'd asked for extra security in the first place. It took me a moment to find a comeback. "We all have private lives, Mr. Triller."

"Fine and dandy, but I remind you that my private life is just a tiny bit more important than yours. So I won't appreciate you poking into my space every second I'm here."

I took a step backward to behold the man whose life was more important than mine. No wonder I had taken a dislike to him on first sight.

Triller tried a calmer tone, palms down like a symphony conductor during a particularly soft movement. "Okay, now—we're all friends here, right? I just think we should get a few rules in place up front." Another horse-smile. "After all, I teach the power of clarity and the drawing of boundaries—to unleash the power within."

"I know the rules," I said. "I used to play football, and I'd rather be on your team than us glaring at each other across the line."

Now Triller was interested, seeing an opening for his charm offense. Show a genuine interest in what interests the other person. If you can fake sincerity, you've got it made. "Played football, did you? NFL?"

"College. Kent State."

"Celebrated? Successful?"

"I was a nose tackle. Not the most glamorous job in the world."

Now he shifted into practiced shtick. "I can make you successful and respected," Triller assured me. "Right here, this weekend. I can give you the kind of motivation you wouldn't believe! Success is a mystery to many, but leaves clues for those who seek them. Sit in on my talk Saturday, and I'll reveal the clues to success. Fortune. Fame. You'll probably want to sign up for one of my courses."

"I'll be there," I said, "because I'm getting paid for it."

"You don't have to like me, Jacovich." Triller pointed his finger at me—nails neatly clipped, with clear polish. I hate fingers pointed at me. "Just keep people the hell away from me—unless I want them close."

I waved a hand at the movie monsters who were obviously on his payroll. "What are these men here for, then? To iron your underwear?"

The monsters looked worried that now they *would* have to iron his underwear.

Fifteen minutes later, coming out of the men's room down on the lobby floor, I ran into Swati Sathe on her way into the women's room, still looking harried, still juggling her security duties, but amused, too.

"About every half hour," she said, "I hear from Reeve Fesmire that you or K.O. have insulted someone else. I give you credit, Milan, you went straight to the top with Triller."

"Who else here has a bigger ego?"

"That's not what Fesmire hired you for. And he has the biggest ego of all."

"I don't think so," I said. "Underneath the bravado, he's a little man with a bad comb-over, terrified someone will spit in the punch bowl and ruin everything."

"He doesn't expect a cowboy gunfight. But some speakers are famous. They make enemies—or worse, strangers becoming stalkers because they can't be best friends."

"I've been stalked myself on occasion."

"Damn!" Swati Sathe said, heading into the women's restroom. "Now who will I have to hire to protect *you?*"

CHAPTER SIX

K.O.

K.O. was at a table in the Tower City Food Court, staring out the window at the Cuyahoga River. He'd never seen Collision Bend at this angle and from this side of the river. He'd not had a minute to himself since morning, and it was good to get away for a while. Tower City was crowded, too, with shoppers, movie-goers, or workers from the attached buildings—and no one had yet asked him a silly question.

He hadn't ordered anything from the circle of over-commercialized food stands, nor would he—he'd had enough nasty army food to last a lifetime, and he held no fast food restaurant in high regard. He'd had breakfast early, before leaving the apartment he shared with Carli Wysocki. She'd awakened with him and cooked a breakfast to last him all day. Bacon and eggs, pancakes, grapefruit juice, and bagels she'd bought the day before at Bialy's, in University Heights—known by every Cleveland maven as the best bagel joint in town.

They'd made love, too—once in bed and again when they had shared a shower. Their relationship, heading toward its two-year anniversary, was still in the "brand-new-dating" setting, as romantic now as it had been the first time they'd had sex. Carli had been a cosmetics clerk in an upscale Beachwood Place shop when they met; now she was learning the finer points of public relations at an agency specializing in making its clients look better than if they only wore the make-up she had once sold.

As K.O. glanced from the view outside to the Tower City visitors, he saw a different crowd from those who wrote big checks to hear lectures on how to improve their lives. These were mostly working people, bargain shoppers, or those who simply hung around downtown. Conventioneers, though, might be bankers, stockbrokers, lawyers, sales reps—those who took making money seriously.

Big money.

Since the weekend assignment had been offered, K.O. had read up on the so-called "success" philosophy, and figured it boiled down to the same things: work hard, be confident, and don't be a jerk. He'd learned it at the Beachwood Public Library much less expensively than taking any series of high-priced seminars from the strange tribe of "success experts" he was watching over at the convention. The real question was whether the "success" philosophy would work for him or anyone else.

Finally he returned to the hotel, looking at the crowd anxiously awaiting the opening ceremony in the ballroom that evening in preparation for the big, gaudy, noisy public event beginning the next morning. Nearly everyone was talking into their cell phones and not making eye contact with anyone. K.O. almost felt sorry for them.

Almost. Unless it was an animal—*any* animal—in trouble, K.O. was missing the empathy gene. The speakers were sharks, and those who paid a fortune to listen to them were simply minnows frightened of being swallowed up, whole. He hoped the convention would be this quiet the next few days—but he'd toiled at Milan Security long enough to know that things rarely go well. Taking a quick reconnaissance of the speakers and those who hoped to be touched and healed of their troubles during the weekend, he wondered which of them would go postal and shoot up the place.

Would it be the asshat Tommy Triller, or killer-millionaire Hy Jinx, or Tony Nardoianni, who never could coach baseball worth a damn, or Governor Clary, who'd been insulting with his first sentence, or even Dr. Lorelei, possibly more interested in fucking him than causing trouble for anyone? Of course, he hadn't met any of the other self-helpers yet, the big deals who made more in a month than he did in a decade; they might be even loonier.

Turning back for another slow patrol through the hotel, he

noticed a young woman looking miserable as she stood alone near the marble fountain. Short and slim, her movie-star make-up made her seem cheap. Her chin was hardly there at all, and her puffed-out hairdo had not been seen since early Elvis movies.

She saw him looking at her, and her face lit up with slight hope. "Hey," she said, "I'm sorry, but—do you work here?"

"At the moment, yes." Just like every other attendee who'd showed up, there was a name tag, pinned at the top of her left breast, on which she'd scrawled: KYLEE GRAVES. Kylee, with two *e*'s. K.O. wondered if her parents had chosen the two *e*'s themselves or if it was her idea.

"Um—can you tell me what room Tommy Triller is in?"

"I'm not allowed to tell you."

Her last hope for survival clearly swirled down the drain, and he thought she might cry. "They won't tell me at the desk, either. They were nasty about it."

"You wouldn't want everyone knowing your room number, would you? Just ask the phone operator to ring him."

"I did—but some man answered and said Tommy's not taking calls."

"VIPs never take calls from people they don't know."

"But he *does* know me! We . . . " Kylee's cheeks flushed red. She prattled over a few words he couldn't decipher, looked around in what seemed to be panic, and then whispered, "Sorry I bothered you," and scooted off, quickly getting lost in the crowd.

The ridiculous beehive hair vanished among the jostle. K.O. thought the longer he worked for Milan, the stranger people became. Kylee-with-two-*ee*'s seemed nervous and frightened. She and Tommy Triller knew one another. Triller was taller than people should be unless they played center for the Cleveland Cavaliers. Perhaps his size intimidated.

But it was none of K.O.'s business—unless Kaylee had a deadly weapon hidden in her hairdo.

Something unusual was happening at the check-in desk. Approaching, he couldn't miss one of the major film stars of the last century, Siddartha West, stirring up a fuss with the reservations clerk and drawing a coterie of gawkers. West, now well into her seventies, had some years earlier loudly switched her well-earned fame from award-winning actress to well-known off-the-wall spiritualist and channeler. A half-hour personal reading from her cost ten times as much as sitting through her movies in a theater. Unlike most fading film stars who paid for ghostwritten autobiographies, West's seven transcendental, flower-power published books were self-written, claiming her current incarnation on Earth was not her first. Had the books appeared fifty years earlier, she would have been labeled "hippie kook." Now she was *grande dame* of the aging weirdo set. Onlookers wanted her autograph, but she gave them small cards instead, featuring her photo ads for her newest tome. The title: *Have the Life of Your Times.*

Former Governor Jonah Clary exited the elevator, having changed from a business suit to an old-fashioned cowboy outfit—fringed leather jacket, string tie anchored by a hunk of turquoise the size of a ping-pong ball, and a cowboy hat so big that it probably *could* have held ten gallons. No one could miss him; he looked like a doofus. Still, he marched around, beaming, shaking hands as if still running for president.

Clary spotted Siddartha West at once, and pushed his way through her clamoring followers to tip his hat and bend over to kiss her hand. Siddartha's politics were one hundred eighty degrees from Clary's; she regarded him as an outer-space enemy alien and wiped the back of her hand on her skirt.

K.O. approached her as soon as Clary walked away, and introduced himself. "Special security," he said, giving her one of his own cards. "I'm here all weekend—so if you need me for any reason at all, call the desk. I'll get to you within minutes."

"That's good to hear," she said. Then she looked twice at his name on the card. "K.O. Like in knockout."

"Yes, ma'am."

"Cute."

"Some don't think so."

"I'll bet not. Has Ben Mayo showed up yet?"

"Dr. Ben? Yes, he already checked in."

"Shit," she said. "I was on his TV show eight months ago. He told America I was crazy, and I made him look foolish for saying it—but those shows are taped in advance, and by the time it hit the air, it was edited to make him look like a bald wise man instead of the weasel he is. I hope I run into him this weekend so I can tell him what I really think of him."

"You'll both be there for the opening ceremonies tonight. I'll keep my eye on you if you want."

"Good boy," she said, and softly touched his cheek. "You're sensitive and kind. I can tell just by looking at you." Then she became top sergeant, squaring her shoulders and jutting out her chin. "Meantime, just get me up to my room so I can kick off these shoes that are killing me, light a candle, and meditate."

K.O. took Siddartha's elbow and led her through the yammering crowd. Most were too young to remember her great movie performances, but they somehow intuited this was a bona fide, Oscar-winning movie star.

He guided her into the elevator. "Do you meditate a lot?"

"Every day—and I'll really need to at this convention." She sighed. "What the hell am I doing here, anyway?"

"Tell me about it," K.O. said.

CHAPTER SEVEN

MILAN

Even tough guys get hungry.

It was now close to five p.m., and all I'd eaten was a handful of crackers, grown stale in the dispensing machine. The opening event would begin at seven-thirty; if I didn't have some food, I wouldn't make it through the evening.

I used my walkie-talkie to tell Swati Sathe I was heading up to the snack food at the VIP lounge.

When I arrived there, though, someone else was sucking up all the attention.

Dr. Ben Mayo was lecturing those who'd stumbled in for a chicken sandwich, telling them to "take control of your own life," holding a large paper plate filled with goodies in one gloved hand, and a bottle of Sprite in the other.

He saw me and waved. "Come in, join us," he assured me. "I won't bite." Under the strong fluorescent lights, he looked as though he practically lived in suntan parlors. A closer glance revealed his TV make-up, from the open collar of his shirt up to his shiny bald dome.

He came over, juggling the Sprite bottle with his forearm against his ribs while he bit a slice of ham right off the plate. Alert: Don't eat from a paper plate while standing up and trying not to spill anything from a bottle.

"Nice tie you're wearing," he said jovially.

I reached for the knot. "You want to buy it?"

He laughed. "Thought I saw you hangin' out when I was registering."

"Security," I told him. I offered him one of my business cards, but both his hands were busy so I tucked it into the breast pocket of his sports jacket. "If you have problems, let me know."

"Oh, I've got problems!" he said too loudly. When his munching listeners looked over at him, he looked uncomfortable and motioned me over to one corner.

"I've got problems," he repeated, more softly. "Anyone gets problems when they're as famous as I am."

As famous as I am. I'll write that one down in my memory book.

"It's jealousy. More people watch me in any given week than used to watch Johnny Carson. When they get jealous of my success, they try to hurt me. Since you're the security guy, be careful who hangs around me this weekend and keep the weirdos away."

"I'll keep my eye on you, Dr. Mayo."

"Dr. Ben. Nobody ever calls me Dr. Mayo. The first name makes them think I'm one of them."

I wonder how many people would think he's one of them if they heard him say things like "as famous as I am."

"Make sure you hear me talk tomorrow. Tell me where you're sitting—I'll introduce you to the crowd."

"Don't introduce me," I said firmly. Private investigators are supposed to be private. "It's your show, not mine."

He nearly whispered, "Is Jonah Clary going to be at lunch tomorrow? He's so jealous of me—of my show and my blog. I hate how he walks around looking like some faggot cowboy. I don't want him in there when I'm giving my big talk."

"I can't keep him out. He belongs at this convention, too."

"Oh, shit!" He rubbed his hand across his shiny head. "Ha! I'm not s'posed to say that word on television."

"You're not supposed to say faggot, either. Look, it doesn't matter to me," I said. "I just came in for a fast sandwich."

Mayo looked surprised. "I thought you were working."

"I am," I said, moving over to the table and selecting some rye bread, turkey, lettuce, and a tiny bag of chips. "Working people eat, too."

He scowled. "My TV staff damn well eats when I tell 'em to eat."

I squirted mustard on one slice of bread. I'd rather eat the local brown, spicy Stadium Mustard than yellow mustard, but I had no choice. "That's the second reason I wouldn't want to work for you."

Belligerent, now. "And what's the first one?"

"You don't want to hear it, Doctor." I headed for the door. I'd have preferred sitting at a table to eat in peace, but that wasn't happening; I'd have to scarf my sandwich in the elevator. "And I *will* be looking after you," I said, "whether you like it or not."

By the time I got downstairs, Reeve Fesmire buzzed my walkie-talkie, demanding we meet immediately near the fountain. I dislike anyone making demands, and I'd been annoyed all day by almost everyone.

Fesmire had a clipboard in the crook of his arm. "I've had nothing but complaints about you," he said angrily, shifting into attack mode. "You and O'Bannion, too."

"High-level security isn't a walk in the park. If you want politeness and having to swallow all the crap being shoveled on you, hire apple-cheeked altar boys trained by old-fashioned nuns wearing habits and wimples."

He looked puzzled. "What are wimples?"

"Look it up."

"You're rude! If everybody at this con gets cheesed off at me, I'll never be able to stage another one. Can't you be nice to the VIPs I hired you to keep safe?"

"I'll do my best to keep them safe. The 'nice' part might be something else again. This hotel is full of uniformed police, and they're not all that 'nice,' either."

"How do you know?" Fesmire was growing frustrated—like I cared.

"I used to be on 'the job.' My significant other is a Cleveland police detective."

"Really? Are you gay?"

"Why? Is this a pick-up?"

He rolled his eyes. "I was implying all police officers are male. It was a joke."

"Very amusing. By the way, it's *police detective sergeant, homicide.* Pray you don't have to get to know her—in case there's a murder here in the next three days."

"A broad who's a homicide cop?"

"And if you *do* meet her, be sure you call her a broad."

K.O. and I connected outside the Grand Ballroom on the mezzanine floor, where fancy parties were typically held—high-end charity benefits at which everyone wore tuxedos or evening gowns with glittering bling, and big corporate meetings, with hired third-rate entertainers who hadn't worked on television in fifteen years.

No dinner tonight, though—just chairs set up, row after row, and a podium onstage in front of a gigantic white banner spelling out MAKE IT HAPPEN in enormous letters, green like the color of money. The attendees, filing in like lemmings to find a seat, mostly fell midway between K.O.'s age and mine.

I said, "Have you met all the megastars we're supposed to protect?"

"Almost," K.O. replied. "I never saw a bigger crowd of egomaniacs in my life."

"That's just VIPs," I said.

"Who wins the asshole-of-the-week award?"

"I'm torn. Reeve Fesmire gets an honorable mention."

K.O. said, "I'm still worried about Dr. Lorelei; she wants my body."

I laughed. "You're getting to be a real sex object."

"Lorelei is lots older than me. There's something—I can't put my finger on it, but she reminds me of a wolverine. And I don't mean the Michigan football team."

"You mean she's rapacious?"

He shook his head. "I'll have to look up that word when I get home." He sighed. "*If* I get home. This weekend hasn't even started yet."

"It will in about five minutes. Let's go inside."

Chairs filled up rapidly, the energy increasing like a Las Vegas crowd assembled for a heavyweight championship fight. The front row seats were reserved for the lucky few who either had enough money or the right connections to hook them up. K.O was stationed in the back of the room near a cash bar; I stood inside the doors, looking severe, hoping nobody'd realize that despite my Jerry Garcia tie, I was not a dynamic, charismatic, super-successful Somebody.

At a few minutes past seven, the celebrities began filing in from the wings of the stage and carefully managing the few steps downward to the main floor. With each step, the buzz grew louder. Dr. Lorelei came first, inclining her head to the applause as if she were the queen of England, followed closely by former governor Jonah Clary, raising both hands above his head in V-for-victory signs. Clary had ditched his cowboy Stetson in his room.

Then came Siddartha West, acting surprised and awed that she was being applauded, and blowing two-handed kisses to the assembled before sitting.

The clapping trickled down for Tony Nardoianni, not many recognizing him until he took an awkward batting stance and swung for the bleachers. Still, he beamed, more at the other speakers in the front row than at the audience. Being a so-called celebrity is really just one way to surround oneself with other celebrities.

Hy Jinx sported a shiny black leather jacket, dark glasses, and leather fingerless driving gloves, yet he didn't get much applause when he bounced over to his seat. This was a 98 percent Caucasian throng in the Renaissance ballroom—unusual for Cleveland.

Jinx sat down, legs sprawled into the front aisle, as Dr. and Mrs. Ben Mayo slithered from behind a curtain. Every TV watcher was thrilled, and Dr. Ben acknowledged their "love"—but the crowd was probably cheering Caroline Mayo, who'd changed into a tight red sleeveless dress that drew attention to her body. Dr. Ben waved until the acclaim waned as Caroline slipped into a chair. Then, ears red, he sat down, staring straight ahead, not acknowledging his wife and not reacting to the entrance of the most important celebrity of this conference.

When Tommy Triller finally appeared—he knew how to stretch that wait for drama—the crowd's roar shook the hotel. He accepted it graciously, his toothy smile dazzling, his eyes radiating faux-sincere appreciation with a humble tilt of his head. After two minutes, he gestured for his fans to quiet down. Finally he sat three seats away from everyone else, clueing in folks that he wasn't just *any* old luminary, but the Big Kahuna. In Hawaii, *kahuna* means wise man, or shaman, one who knows all; on the mainland, it means the biggest of big cheeses.

Then Reeve Fesmire made his own entrance onto the stage. He held onto the podium's sides as if he might otherwise fall over. Wearing an awkward smile he hadn't practiced, he introduced himself as the guy had who made it possible for everyone else to be there, welcoming them to the annual convocation of the Global Motivational Speakers Association.

He reminded the crowd who would speak during the weekend, a waste of breath since everyone had a schedule with them. He introduced the celebrity speakers, and everyone clapped again as they'd done just moments before. He also named many restaurants within walking distance in downtown Cleveland, all of which had paid for listings in the schedule. Fesmire told no lies; there were many great eateries a few blocks away, on East Fourth Street or West Sixth Street, depressed areas until a few years ago, when someone figured out downtown had to sparkle and shine. Now they're busy and happy—especially when hotels are crowded with conventioneers.

Then Fesmire got serious, speaking not from his heart but his wallet, and told the crowd about the sales center, which he called the Resources Room, where speakers' books, CDs, DVDs, courses, events and coaching programs would be available, with a nice piece off the top going to the GMSA, and Fesmire's pocket.

"Don't forget," he said, "you're here for success transformation—in business, money, love, life as a human being." He gestured at the sign behind him. "To make *it* happen, whatever *it* is for you, you need knowledge—insider knowledge, expert knowledge, success knowledge from the super-successful here that I've assembled for you. Secondly, you need *commitment*, which is demonstrated by *investment*—investment in yourself, your mind, your skills. Investment in take-home resources that will keep you on track and motivate you every morning. Everyone wants success, but only a few invest in getting it. And third: Take *action!*" He took a deep breath that inflated his chest. "This is *your* right place at the right time. When the student is ready, the Master Teacher will appear. Open your heart. Open your mind. Be transformed. Make *it* happen!"

Polite applause. It occurred to me that Fesmire himself was a frustrated motivational speaker, but he didn't look the part of Master Teacher: short, pudgy, pedantic, with a squeaky voice. Instead, he scurried about, kowtowing to the likes of Triller and Dr. Ben and Dr. Lorelei. I wondered how he really felt about his precious GMSA stars.

I knew that K.O., near the bar, hadn't been listening to Fesmire, but was evaluating everyone in the audience. An excellent P.I. who could also spot the poisonous weeds among all the pretty flowers, he was getting good at his job. If only he'd stop being angry at everyone.

I'd been watching all day, and had many more years of experience, but I hadn't noticed anyone who seemed prone to violence. Snarky, maybe. Jealous? For sure. Insecure. Bitchy. But violent? That would never happen here.

Then again—what do *I* know?

CHAPTER EIGHT

K.O.

K.O. fidgeted at the back of the ballroom, shifting feet as he checked out the crowd—mostly middle-aged, dressed casually but neatly, more interested in the schedule and packets of information they'd been issued than whatever Reeve Fesmire had to say. But K.O.'s attention kept returning to Kylee Graves, sitting halfway back from the stage, one leg coiled tightly over the other as if to take up as little space as possible, her bright red lipstick fading, her solidly sprayed beehive wilting. She ignored the jabbering Fesmire, instead riveting on Tommy Triller in the front row, three empty seats from Dr. Ben.

He observed the other paid admissions, barely paying attention to Reeve Fesmire promoting himself and the sales. Tommy Triller wasn't listening, either, turned in his chair and looking back at all the faces, waving and grinning, although arrogance and contempt lurked behind his eyes. He could turn mean within seconds—and K.O. guessed he'd more likely bite you than hit you.

Fesmire was loving the sound of his own voice, though no one else seemed to. The audience shifted nervously in their seats, like someone who's gone to the movies to see *The Hateful Eight*, not realizing it would take almost three hours to watch it. Fesmire didn't talk that long; it just seemed like it.

A few people left, probably heading for the bar or for a walk around downtown, and Fesmire saw he had to do something to keep them there a while longer.

"All our wonderful leaders," he said, making a sweeping gesture at the front row, "will speak to you throughout the weekend, and you don't want to miss a single sentence. But if we can coax Tommy Triller to come up here and say a few words of welcome . . . "

He didn't have to plead. The audience did it for him—hooting, hollering, cheering and clapping. Triller stood, faux-embarrassed, and climbed the steps to the stage, where Fesmire hugged him as though connecting with his long-lost father.

Dr. Ben didn't seem happy, though, and next to him Caroline Mayo scowled, lips slightly apart to show her clenched teeth. Nor were Dr. Lorelei, Governor Jonah Clary, Hy Jinx, or Siddartha West entranced, either. Tony Nardoianni looked slightly annoyed, and Hy Jinx appeared bored. They were accustomed to being big stars wherever they went, and Triller outshining them all twisted them out of shape.

"Hey, everybody," Triller said when the noise finally died down. "This took me by surprise. I didn't expect to talk tonight, but unaccustomed as I am to public speaking . . . " Pause for the expected laughter. "I'll share a few thoughts now—to help you make the most of this conference so you can make the most of *your life*."

Holding a hand mike, he strode from side to side, body and voice in a rhythm. "Listen, I'm just a regular guy. I'm no *doctor*. I'm no movie star, no rapper, no politician, no ex-athlete or coach. I started out in a one-room apartment, washing my dirty dishes, my drip-dry suit and me in the same little bathtub, and raised myself from a nobody to a somebody. But that's not what's important. *You* are what's important."

Triller seemed to make eye contact with every single person, even as he made it with no one. "Make choices!" he ordered. "Either let the world make you, or you make your own world. To be a product of *evo*lution, or create your own *revo*lution. To be controlled or to *take* control. To be invisible and unimportant, or to be seen and heard and respected. These are choices, friends. I've led more than a million people out of the shadow of ordinariness and into the sunlight of exceptional, exciting lives. These are your choices. I can lead you to the sunlight, too, if you'll let me. But just as you can't go east by looking west, you can't get to your future by looking at your past. It's a new day for a new you. Unleash the secret powers of that new you. Think differently about yourself and the world." A pause—then: *"Are you ready to think differently?"*

Except for the other star speakers, whom he'd just dissed, the crowd yelled, *"Yes!"*

He cupped his free hand behind his ear. "That sounds too cautious. *Are you ready to think differently?"*

This time they leapt up in unison, and their *"Yes!"* actually vibrated the room.

Both Milan and K.O. recognized it as echoing Fesmire, from whom Triller was unabashedly stealing, planting the "invest yourself" trigger to pull later when he wanted to pitch his five-day Life Transformation Retreat—at seven thousand dollars a pop.

"Then yell Yes and Yes and Yes as you follow me to your future. Tomorrow we begin the revolution of your new life. *Yes! Yes! Yes!"*

He shot his fist skyward with each Yes, and the crowd mimicked him. He marched up the center aisle and they all fell in behind him, a frenetic parade of entranced zombies, raising their arms, yelling *Yes! Yes! Yes!*

His own handler-monsters were already at the back of the hall, apparently expecting what had taken the rest of us by surprise. Providing security to this clown wouldn't be easy.

The other VIP speakers shuffled out the back stage door, each turning back to see the orgiastic mob led away by Tommy Triller. If looks could kill . . .

Fesmire stood to one side of the stage. His notes were still on the podium, his announcements unread, his closing remarks unsaid. For the first time, the blustery, bossy little bastard looked sad and dejected. Triller had stolen the show—the other speakers' show. Fesmire's show.

And K.O. had a frightening premonition: something violent and even deadly might happen here this weekend.

Unless he and Milan stopped it.

"We ought to get paid more," K.O. said when the two of them met by the double doors. "This is going to get worse."

"Pay attention, K.O., and learn something."

"Three years in the army didn't make me Secretary of Defense. So now what? We're supposed to watch over the VIPs, and we don't even know where they went."

"Maybe they want to experience Cleveland in the flesh—possibly inexpensive flesh. Most likely they're retiring to their suites to order dinner from room service." .

"We should melt away, too?"

"We're supposed to hang around until eleven," Milan said. "You go have dinner now and I'll wander around, looking for trouble. We can change places in an hour—unless you'd prefer eating with Dr. Lorelei."

"Now you're scaring me, Milan."

After one more quick look around the lobby, K.O. headed out the door. There was little ambient light left in the sky, and the square wasn't nearly as crowded as during the day. Heading east on Euclid Avenue, he found a string of small restaurants close to the Horseshoe Casino, and chose one at random.

When he walked through the door and looked around, he recognized one of the speakers, eating dinner all by himself, munching on a burger and fries.

"Excuse me," K.O. said when he approached the booth. "Mr. Jinx . . . "

"I don't sign autographs while I'm eating," Hy Jinx said, barely looking up.

"I don't want your autograph. I'm one of the security people at the con." He handed over his business card. "I didn't follow you here, I just came in for a quick bite. Nice meeting you." He started to walk away.

"Hey," Jinx said. "Mr.—uh—Bannion?"

"*O*'Bannion. Yes?"

The rapper re-checked K.O.'s card. "Right—with an O up front. If you're alone, why don't you sit down here and join me?"

"That's nice of you." K.O. slid into the booth opposite him. "You're one of the big stars at this con. Are you here by yourself?"

"Yeah. I hired a model from around here to run the booth in the sales room. She'll probably sell more books and stuff than if I sat there myself." Wink! "She's got *some* rack, too."

K.O. studied the menu. "You're eating alone?"

"Yeah—no homeboys here. That opening skit didn't exactly remind me of Harlem."

"I noticed. But Cleveland's a diverse city."

"Not at this event. People comin' to hear these speakers—for the most part they're lily-white, unless it's about religion. That's why I'm the only brother on the list. Fesmire should've corralled a few more blacks, just for the hell of it."

"Don't you make lots of speeches, Mr. Jinx?"

"Jesus, I'm no Mr. Jinx! Call me Hack—my first name's really Hakim. Yeah, I give fancy talks, but mostly to a black crowd. And if I do TV at all, it's when I rap, usually *Saturday Night Live.*"

"I thought Dr. Ben had a variety of speakers on his show."

Jinx shook his head. "He has people with big problems, and they come on to whine and piss and moan so he can solve them in an hour. And he always does, too."

"Sounds more like *Law and Order SVU.* You can't get on his show?"

"Like I give a shit. I don't make as much money as Ben—or Tommy Triller, either. But I'm a big-deal rapper, and last year I put away about eighteen mil. I do just fine."

"You don't do Tommy Triller's TV specials?"

"They been lying to my manager for years that they're booked up. Fact is, his followers are white, his show is white, and him? He might as well wear a white sheet and a pillowcase with eye holes." He dipped a french fry into ketchup.

"Triller is racist?"

"Not where everybody can see it. He's the only big-shot celebrity speaker who didn't even say hello to me today. Shithook!" He shook his head ruefully. "Well, you're one white guy who bothered to talk to me."

K.O. felt his face go warm. It wasn't a blush—it was something else. "In Iraq," he said "when my buddy's legs got blown off next to me in the truck, I didn't think about his skin color—just the color of his blood."

"I hear you," Jinx said. "Tough shit over there, man. Well, maybe Cleveland's not so bad at that." He waved a hand at the passing waitress. "Order whatever you want, my brother. It's on me."

CHAPTER NINE

MILAN

Many who'd sat through the opening ceremonies and Tommy Triller's I-can-make-you-rich speech had repaired to the lobby bar. The only times I drank in such a crowded place was at Nighttown, my neighborhood Irish drinking joint, on St. Patrick's Day. Back in the day, I'd always hung out at Vuk's Bar on St. Clair Avenue, where many other Cleveland Slovenians stopped for a shot and a beer, but now, with Tobe, I've stepped up a class or two whenever I want a drink.

Besides, Vukovich, the owner-bartender who'd served me my first legal alcoholic drink, was now in his eighties and didn't come around much anymore.

I wished I could sneak a drink, too—the whole con bored the socks off me. None of the celebs hung around, but had dissolved into the wings behind the stage. Their day was officially over. Mine wasn't, however. The bigshots might come back down and trade palaver with the paying guests. So until eleven p.m., I couldn't even leave to grab a bite somewhere until K.O. came back.

At the Global Motivational Speakers Association gathering, no one looked potentially dangerous, but I couldn't explain an invisible tension. No expectations to be entertained as they might at a rock concert, nor a sports event, where there was a winner and a loser. Here, everyone was anxious to the point of desperation to somehow be given a miracle that would make them grow rich and successful.

I considered the VIP speakers. Siddartha West's big career was well behind her—but she *had* won an Oscar. Hy Jinx had collected a record-breaking number of awards from various musical organizations as the best entertainer of the year, best rapper, best African-American musician, and a load of others. Tony Nardoianni's baseball team never won a World Series, but he'd captured two National League championships and was once voted Manager of the Year. The puffed-up Jonah Clary had been the most important guy in his entire state for eight years before fumbling a nomination for the presidency of the United States. Dr. Lorelei was highly rated on her syndicated radio show, having combined five-minute solutions for everyone's tragedies with an unpleasant Tea Party twist that made her revered on the far right and loathed on the left. Dr. Ben was a TV icon—one of the few Americans immediately recognized on the street. And Tommy Triller? Tall, toothy, infomercial superstar, and the richest and most successful of them all.

Beside a large grand piano in one corner of the lobby, Victor Gaimari and Tony Nardoianni had pulled two armchairs closer together and were talking quietly, sipping on drinks. I didn't know whether to interrupt them—but then again, I *did* work here, and sitting down would be a welcome reprieve.

Nardoianni started to rise as I approached. "Don't get up," I said.

"You look tired, Milan," Victor observed. "Long day?"

"Join us," Nardoianni said. "Pull that chair over here and take a load off."

"Thanks—as long as I can sit facing the lobby."

"Milan," Victor said, "wouldn't want to miss a murder in here."

I pulled a chair over from another table and turned it so I could see the entire lobby. "I don't deal with murders, Victor. I'm just an extra security guy."

"Ha ha." Victor never laughed—he just said "Ha ha." It got on my last nerve. Then he added, "Murders happen when you're around, though. I know this from experience."

"True. But I'm getting older now. You, too."

Nardoianni laughed this time, but it was real. "I'm sayin', Vic, I love this guy!"

Vic? I'd known Victor for a quarter of a century. I had never heard anyone, friend or foe, Italian or Irish or anything else, refer to him as "Vic."

"Tony," I said, "how was it that you met—Vic?" Victor turned away so I couldn't see him smile.

The baseball manager shrugged. "Mutual friends. I knew people he knew, so we got together."

"And he's your manager?"

Victor nodded.

"Victor, that means you own a piece of him."

"Where'd you hear that?" Victor demanded. "In a Marlon Brando movie? It's an investment—like pork bellies."

"Yeah, Vic," Tony said, "but you saved my life."

A soft, quiet warning: "Tony . . . "

Tony shut up. "All these years, Milan, and you still don't stay out of people's business."

"At the moment," I said, "I'm just curious."

"Well, Tony was in heavy debt a few years ago—we've all been there, haven't we? We made a deal that works for both of us. Now he makes more money as a public speaker than he did sitting in a baseball dugout, chewing tobacco and spitting." Victor shifted around to look at me. "Does that satisfy your—curiosity, Milan?"

"For the moment."

"How long a moment is that?"

"Until something else makes me more curious. For instance, I'm curious why you're both here this weekend. This group isn't on the same page as you." I stood up.

"Hey, you're not gonna stay and have a drink?" Tony said.

I shook my head. "I'm working."

"Did Fesmire hire you?" Victor asked.

"Indirectly, yes. He's the boss man of the GMSA."

"He's also a *cafone*."

"Should I look that one up in my Italian-American dictionary?"

"You won't find it in the dictionary."

Nardoianni looked puzzled. "I'm Italian, and I don't even know what that means."

"You don't know what bunting with two outs means either," Victor said, his jocular tone growing sharp teeth.

"You don't like Reeve Fesmire?" I asked.

"I have little use for him."

Apparently, conversation regarding Fesmire made Tony Nardoianni uncomfortable. He looked around to discern whether anyone else was listening. "Let it go, Vic."

"Tony, you have no use for anyone here this weekend," Victor said.

"Greedy, money-grubbing Jell-O heads, you ask me. All except that Hy Jinx guy. Watch how he moves when he raps? He could play second base for me anytime."

"And you hate the rest of them?"

The baseball manager coughed nervously. "Hate's a pretty big word. Let's just say I think they're all shits—especially that Triller guy."

"What's wrong with him?" I said.

"He yells at people and gets 'em to walk barefoot on fire! What kind of fuckin' nutburger does that? Besides, it'll cost your left nut to burn your tootsies."

I said, "Tony—your thing for Triller seems more personal than not liking his act."

Tony looked at Victor before answering. "It's no secret. The prick got me to testify in one of his infomercials. He had me say he helped me move from baseball to business. He promised me speaking gigs at his events in eight cities that year. Then he stiffed me."

Victor wasn't smiling, but there was a twinkle in his eye. "You didn't know this job would put you into a den of thieves, did you, Milan?"

"I didn't know I'd run into you, either."

I shouldn't have said it, but he ignored it. "It's a big small town. No one goes anywhere in Cleveland without seeing somebody they know—or know *of.* The Rock and Roll Hall of Fame, the Art Museum, the Cleveland Orchestra, the West Side Market . . . "

"You hang out at the West Side Market, Victor?" I said.

"Some of my cousins have a produce stall there."

"Not a surprise. But you know everybody, Cleveland or not."

"I haven't had the pleasure of meeting Dr. Lorelei," he said. "But by the time this thing is over on Sunday, I will."

"You think she's hot, Victor?" Nardoianni asked.

"Hot—but too old," Victor answered.

The baseball manager wasn't a bit upset, though; he just laughed. "Okay, fine. Maybe I should go check her out myself again, just to make sure." He leaned in to me. "These out-of-town get-togethers get pretty wild sometimes. Don't say anything to my old lady, though."

"Is your wife with you?"

"Fuck no, she wouldn't come to anything like this. She's home in Denver."

"Then," I promised, "I won't say a word about it to her."

"You da man!" he announced again, standing up. He shook both our hands, and then faded away toward the bar.

"He never stops yakking!" Victor said. "He wears me out in a couple of minutes. I wish I weren't involved."

"Cut him loose, then."

"It's more complicated than that. It always is."

"I'm a good listener, Victor."

"Especially if it's none of your business." He sipped his drink. "That's always been your problem."

"It's my job—paying attention to what goes on at this convention."

"Then do it. Watch out that some fruit loop with an arsenal on his hip doesn't go crazy and shoot everyone he sees."

"Hasn't happened in Cleveland," I said. "Yet."

"Tony owed money to Chicago people. I paid it off and worked up a contract giving me a percentage of all speeches he makes around the country. It's a good thing he's such a talker—otherwise he'd be like one of those ballplayers from the 1940s, opening a bar and grill someplace."

"How much of a percentage, Victor?"

He shook his head sadly. "Milan, Milan . . . "

"Okay. How'd you manage to talk Reeve Fesmire into bringing him aboard this weekend?"

Victor waved an airy hand, studying the lobby ceiling. "I'm a good salesman."

That's what I figured. Most who worked in the Renaissance Hotel belong to a union. So do taxi and limo drivers—and the Cleveland police. The regular working union guys do their work well and efficiently and then go home to their wives, but those who run the unions are more political than any politician—and Victor's mob family generally pulled strings to get all the members to dance, which meant he had a tremendous amount of power in Greater Cleveland. I'm certain Fesmire, expecting nearly two thousand people or more before the weekend ended, would hate it if all the workers decided to go on strike the day his convention started.

Even more than his old-fashioned uncle, Don Giancarlo D'Allessandro—who did everything, including the many illegal activities in which he engaged, with gentleness and understanding—Victor Gaimari was some piece of work.

Victor finished his drink and said he was going home and wouldn't come back until Tony Nardoianni's speech. After he left, I planted myself at the top of the main stairway until K.O. returned from his dinner break—with a surprising dinner partner. He and Hy Jinx had apparently become friends.

"K.O. told me a lot about you," Hy said. "You're the boss, right?"

"I'm K.O.'s boss," I said.

"Then who's your boss?"

"Nobody. I'm like you, Hy—I pretty much do things my way."

He cocked his head at me. "K.O. says your main squeeze is a sister. Is that right?"

"She's also a cop."

"Whoa!"

"You've had experience with cops, haven't you?"

"Every black man in this country has experience with cops!" A certain vinegar taste crept into his hip hop voice. "But you know what? I'm still here."

We talked a bit more until Hy Jinx said goodnight and headed for the elevator.

K.O. told me about the place he'd eaten and suggested I go there, but it was late, almost ten o'clock, and I wasn't that hungry anymore. We took one more sweep through the public parts of the hotel and then headed to our rooms.

They were about one-fifth the size of the hotel rooms occupied by Tommy Triller and Dr. Mayo and the others—but we weren't planning to throw a big party. I kicked off my clothes, got into bed, and was asleep within five minutes.

Shortly after two-thirty in the morning, my phone jangled, and after my sleepy hello, Swati S. Sathe, sounding more frazzled than I'd ever heard her before, informed me that I'd better get dressed right away.

There'd been a murder.

CHAPTER TEN

K.O.

One bleat of the phone had K.O. sitting bolt upright in bed, sweating, breathing hard. He hadn't been dreaming of Carli— it saddened him that he never dreamed about the woman he loved, the woman usually sleeping right next to him. But dreams are tough sometimes, especially after three Middle East combat tours, and the telephone ring reminded him of the sirens that got him and his buddies out of the rack and into combat gear within seconds.

When he answered and Swati Sathe told him there'd been a murder, he found himself calming down. Murders were scary, but nothing like a bomb detonating under a truck full of American GIs.

No time for a shower, so he did what he could with a wet wash-cloth, jumped into the pants and shirt he'd worn the previous day, and went out the door. At two-thirty a.m., the elevators in the hotel typically weren't busy—but this was no normal early morning. After ninety seconds of waiting, K.O. found the stairway and climbed up to the twelfth floor.

Milan was there already, along with Reeve Fesmire in wrinkled Dockers and a sweatshirt, Swati Sathe wearing baggy jeans and a pullover sweater that had messed up her hair, and two uniformed Cleveland policemen. Dr. Lorelei Singleton, with no make-up and a robe over her flannel jammies and her black hair in pigtails, Tommy Triller's three assistants or bodyguards, and several people in various forms of sleepwear who also had rooms on the twelfth floor, were also standing around. One of the cops stood in the doorway of the room in question, scowling, arms crossed over his chest like a eunuch guarding a seraglio. From inside the suite, the noise from the TV was blaring too loudly.

Milan spoke to the cop, flashed his Convention Security badge, and motioned K.O. to accompany him over the threshold and into the suite of Tommy Triller. Two more uniformed policemen were waiting inside, and one pointed toward the open door of the bedroom. "In there," he said. "Don't touch anything."

Tommy Triller, in a white dress shirt with rolled-up sleeves and suit pants, lay on his back, a nickel-sized hole between his eyes. The bullet had blown off the top of his head and continued traveling into the ceiling.

What made the setting much more dramatic, though, was that one of his CDs had been forced into Triller's mouth, ripping both corners, pulling his face into a horrifying clown's grimace.

K.O. suppressed a shudder and walked around the body to look at Triller from a different angle. He said to Milan, "Any idea what time this happened?"

"The coroner's office will know."

"I can tell from here that whoever shot him was shorter than he was."

"Everyone around here is shorter than he was."

"Then he was standing up when he got it because the hole in his head looks like the gun was fired upward." He glanced around. "Nothing's broken in here. No struggle."

"The CD was an afterthought." Milan pointed to the dresser top. "There's his wallet. I'm betting it's full of cash."

"That means this wasn't a robbery."

"Holy crap!" A voice cut through the rest of the noise and the overly loud TV. K.O. didn't recognize it, but saw that Milan did. "Two civilians pretending to be cops."

Milan didn't bother turning around. "Good evening, Lieutenant McHargue. Or should I say, good morning?"

"Try goodbye." Florence McHargue marched into the bedroom, dressed more casually than usual—black slacks and a lightweight zippered jacket over a white T-shirt. She looked at Triller's face and then at the hole in the ceiling. "Whenever someone is iced in my town, Jacovich, you're never more than two minutes away. Why is that?"

"You were the one who recommended us for this job, Lieutenant," Milan said.

"Probably because it was the only way I could get you away from pawing my top detective, even for three days. Besides, in addition to being a royal pain in the ass, you're good at what you do and you're a big guy who can supposedly keep order." She jerked her head toward what used to be Tommy Triller. "Nice job you did."

"I didn't know we were supposed to sit on the edge of his bed all weekend."

"They told you wrong." She walked around the bed, checking the deceased from every angle. "From what I hear, this vic was a sleazebag, but his infomercials will still be playing ten years from now." She looked at Milan. "You knew him?"

"I talked to him briefly when he arrived. That was it."

"Who called you to come up here?"

"Ms. Sathe," K.O. said. "Hotel head of security."

"The Indian woman out in the hallway?" McHargue rolled her eyes ceilingward, as she often did. "Goody! At least one other person besides me in this whole joint who's not a WASP. I'll talk to her—and then I want you two."

Milan said, "I'm surprised to see you, Lieutenant. Doesn't Detective Sergeant Blaine handle most of the homicides?"

McHargue narrowed one eye. "You're involved in this case, just like you are in too many others, so Blaine doesn't get anywhere near you this time, to flutter around you like a high school sophomore. You'll do all your talking to me."

"Homicide lieutenant handling a murder case personally?"

She nodded. "Don't think when I pinned on a gold badge, I stopped being a good cop." She turned from Milan to K.O. "Get a key to one of those conference rooms so I don't run you over the coals in public."

K.O. said, "That was Tommy Triller's thing."

"What?"

"Part of his program—having people run barefoot on a bed of hot coals to show themselves how tough they can be."

"You're joking!"

"True," Milan said. "And people paid gobs of money for the chance to do that over a long weekend."

"Supervised, naturally," K.O. added.

"Think somebody shot him because they burned their feet?"

"There are plenty of people mad at him," K.O. said. "All the speakers. Mad—or jealous."

McHargue pulled out her notebook and jotted something down. "I want to hear more, O'Bannion. In the meantime, this is a crime scene; we haven't had time to put up the yellow tape."

"So?"

"So beat it."

They beat it, but Swati Sathe caught them in the hall as they waited for the elevator. "I can't believe it. Nothing like this ever happened here before."

"Nearly everyone who came to this convention wanted to see Tommy Triller—but just one came to kill him." Milan looked around at the ceilings in the hallway. "No security cameras up here?"

Sathe shook her head. "There are cameras all over the lobby, in the parking garages, and out on the street in front of both entrances to the hotel. They're in the elevators, too, in case you hadn't noticed."

"That means," Milan said, "somebody came up through the stairway in the middle of the night."

K.O. said, "I'd look at the other speakers first. They're all ticked off at him."

"Even if the cops examine every room for trace evidence," Milan added, "they're more likely to pick up prints or strands of hair that've been on the floor or the furniture for years."

Swati said, "Can't they check to see who has a gun?"

"You really think," K.O. said, "somebody commits a murder and then sticks their gun back in their underwear drawer for the police to find?"

She shook her head, shoulders slumping. "I'm not thinking at all. I'm not even sleeping in my own bed, and it's the middle of the night."

"That's the best time for a murder," Milan said, "when everyone is still sleepy."

Reeve Fesmire came charging over to them. "Jacovich! You and O'Bannion were supposed to protect Tommy Triller, goddamn it—not stand around while he gets shot! Why do you think I was paying you?"

"We weren't expecting a murder, Fesmire."

"Is that right, Jacovich? You thought this was just a fuck-off job?"

Swati said, "Take it easy, Reeve."

"The hell with that!" Reeve almost roared. Then he stuck his face as close to Milan's as he could get, considering the difference in their height. "Get the hell out of here so I don't have to look at you again! You're fired!"

Heading down in the elevator, K.O. laughed. "*You're fired.* Fesmire doesn't even have the Donald Trump hair."

Milan nodded. "Or the Trump money, either."

The lobby was normally deserted at this hour. Now it was a sea of dark blue uniforms and plainclothes guys flashing their badges and acting important. The night clerk behind the counter seemed teetering on the edge of shock; his hands shook, and he kept waving them in front of his face. K.O. explained to him who they were and snagged the key to a conference room overlooking the Square.

Milan said, "When the sun rises, there'll be media here, too. Newspapers, TV—and not just the local crew, either."

"Are we going to get our mugs on television, Milan?" K.O. said plaintively.

"Not if we can help it."

"Right—I forgot, we're fired. Fesmire doesn't want the best part of us."

"Probably not. But he's not the boss of bosses."

"Who is?"

Milan considered. "The boss of bosses—the *capo di tutti capi* is what the mob used to call it. The godfather. The don."

"That Victor guy? You think he'll hire us, then?"

Milan shrugged. "Who knows?"

*   *   *

In the conference room, both K.O. and Milan rubbed at their sleepy eyes and yawned. Lieutenant Flo McHargue, though, was awake and angry; only her casual outfit indicated that she hadn't just come from her office but from her bed.

She sat at the head of the conference table. It was a meeting room, all right—as long as there were no more than eight people at a meeting. No windows, either. "Damn near every detective in town is here asking questions," she said, annoyed, "taking statements, diagramming blood spatters. The coroner's lab boys are here, too."

K.O. tried not to smile. Whenever some TV cop called the coroner's assistants "lab boys," he always thought of ten-year-old kids in too-large white laboratory coats.

"Nobody on the twelfth floor heard the shot?" Milan said.

"Someone would've said so by now."

Milan said, "No forced entry?"

"No—but the shooter left in a hurry and the door wasn't all the way closed."

"Who found the body?"

"One of Triller's assistants had been in the bar for much of the evening. Heading back to his own room he saw the door ajar, looked in, and let out a holler they could hear in Akron."

"He called the cops?"

"He called Sathe. She called HQ. HQ got me out of bed." McHargue sighed. "Too damn many people in this hotel."

"Between us," K.O. said, "we've talked to all the big-name speakers."

"Then," she said, "stay out of my way. This is my investigation, not yours."

"We're completely out of your way, Lieutenant. We got fired."

That set McHargue back a step or two. "Good. When?"

"Right outside Triller's room just now."

"By?"

"Reeve Fesmire," Milan said. "He's the boss-man at this convention."

"And," K.O. chimed in, "he's an asshole."

"I met him briefly; I agree with you." McHargue leaned back in her chair. "Okay, gentlemen. You dealt with all the famous and sort-of-famous here at this get-together. I want to hear all of it, every bit." She looked briefly at her wristwatch. "We've got the rest of the night, so take all the time you need." She pointed a red-tipped finger at K.O. "You first, sonny-boy. Go!"

CHAPTER ELEVEN

MILAN

I t took us about twenty minutes to pack our clothes, and another half hour trying to get out of there, waiting for the valets to fetch my car while showing our credentials to every cop in Cleveland milling around on Public Square. It was a chilly autumn morning, the not-so-subtle hint that winter was waiting just around the corner. We didn't officially check out, though. Reeve Fesmire's organization had rented our rooms in the first place, and we both hoped he'd get charged for an extra day for each of us.

Driving the few minutes across the Cuyahoga to my office with all the windows down, K.O. wondered aloud whether we were still going to get paid.

"I don't know, K.O. I'll check with my lawyer."

"What would've happened if we'd been bodyguarding Triller while some other speaker got offed?"

"Same thing. Fesmire would've canned us."

"That sucks."

"Work for someone—anyone—and you can get fired any time. That's why you should work for yourself. But if your business falls apart, you'll be out of a job anyway."

"You mean you can fire me whenever you want to?" K.O. asked.

"I can, legally—but we've worked together for two years, and except for pissing me off on occasion and insulting our clients, you do a great job." I parked the car in my usual spot. "Speaking of which, you're racking up lots of hours. Are you still interested in getting your own P.I. license?"

"I count the hours every night after work."

"And?"

K.O. grinned. "When the time comes, I'll let you know."

Before going upstairs we strolled around the side of the building and looked across the easy-flowing river at Progressive Field and the rest of downtown, shimmering in the early-morning sun. I regretted losing the job, but was glad to be outside catching a breath of good old-fashioned Cleveland air.

"Pretty soon," I said, "Cleveland will be this frosty every morning for months."

"Don't they call this temperature 'bracing'?"

"That's why we're tough—and you might be tougher than all of us, K.O."

He waved it away. "That's just another word for surviving." He shoved his hands in his pockets. "We just got fired, damn it, so I don't give a damn who the perp is."

"Maybe." I turned, my back to the river. "We'd better get upstairs." My instinct was to clap him on the shoulder, but unless it's his girlfriend, Carli, K.O. doesn't like to be touched unnecessarily—by anyone.

With another look at the river, we turned around and headed inside. When I unlocked the front door, all was quiet. The wrought-iron company on the ground floor that manufactures gates and barred doors and windows, and made a certain amount of noise all day, hadn't yet opened, and the downtown traffic hadn't kicked into high gear, as it was only six-thirty in the morning. We went upstairs. I'd slept little before had Swati Sathe called me to the crime scene, and my eyeballs were itching.

I didn't check my messages. Clevelanders rarely call anyone before breakfast, unless they're trying to sell you something. K.O. opened his smartphone, checked his email, and apparently found something from Carli, as his face took on that silly, dreamy look. He immediately typed a response. I rarely type on my smartphone, as my fingers are too big and I make dozens of mistakes. Texting doesn't much appeal to me.

I spent the next two hours checking the progress of my other assignments, hating being cashiered off a homicide case before I could even poke around.

At a quarter past eight, Tobe Blaine walked in. She rarely comes to my office, and I stay away from the homicide squad at the old federal rock pile on Payne Avenue. Why complicate a beautiful relationship?

"I'm so ticked off at you!" she said in place of a hello.

"Nice entrance line, Tobe."

"McHargue called me in the middle of the night," she said, "to tell me I had to stay away from the Triller murder because *you* were all over the place."

"So?"

"So—then you got fired, and now it's *my* case. Damn it, Milan!" She glared at K.O. "You, too!"

"I didn't do anything," K.O. said.

"The director of the convention sacked you both. What's his name again?"

"Fesmire," I said. "Reeve Fesmire."

"Reeves Fesmire?"

"Reeve. Singular, not plural."

"Like I give a damn." She plopped into a visitor's chair. "McHargue de-briefed you before you left, but boil it down quickly for me. Who done it?"

"Triller was the richest, most successful guy there," I said. "Everybody either thinks he changed loaves into fishes, or they hate his guts."

"I don't suppose you have two lists of who loves and who hates him?"

"Left it in my other pants. But the other speakers all have problems with him, so I'd probably look there first."

"There are some weirdo attendees too," K.O. said. "One woman, Kylee Graves, I think, was stalking Triller. You can't miss her; look for the beehive hairdo."

Tobe took out her notebook.

"And another guy," K.O. said, "who didn't have a thing for Triller, specifically, but a hard-on for everybody."

"Name?"

"Paulin. Jesse Paulin. Some sort of reverend, or so he says. Chunky, balding . . . "

"Let's watch the balding stuff," I said, running my fingers through my ever-rising, ever-thinning hairline. "I can't help it— it's a Slovenian thing."

Tobe said, "What's Paulin's problem?"

"You can always spot a prick like that when they're picking on someone who can't defend themselves."

Tobe wrote it down. "So you got canned because you didn't know a murder was about to happen and weren't there to prevent it."

"Reeve Fesmire," K.O. said, "is a first-rate asshole."

"Really? Who is a *second-rate* asshole?" Tobe pushed herself to a standing position, reminding me my visitors' chairs are very uncomfortable. "Since I can't get a lousy cup of coffee in this joint, I'll head over to the Renaissance and look for murderers. Count yourselves lucky to be out of it."

I got up from my seat, too, and walked around the desk to embrace her. She gave me an unromantic kiss, then leaned back and looked at me. "Don't you shave in the mornings anymore, Milan, or are you going for that 1980s *Miami Vice* look?"

"Sure," I said. "Next week I'll be wearing a pastel-colored suit."

K.O. said, "What's *Miami Vice?*"

Sometimes it's hard talking to young people.

After she left, K.O. and I worked independently until a few minutes before nine. Over the racket of the wrought iron guys who began at eight, the door opened downstairs and I heard footsteps ascending.

"Fesmire here to apologize and beg us to come back?" K.O. said.

"That'll be the day."

Moments later, Victor Gaimari made one of his more dramatic entrances. His suit was the same shade of the gold on a palomino horse, as was his silk tie, scintillating against a light beige shirt. His cologne was one of the least subtle things about him. Tobe Blaine, whose hyperosmia condition picks up and identifies almost any scent in the world, would develop an instant headache around Victor Gaimari.

"You're here early," he said. "Industrious."

"We never went to bed, Victor."

He nodded. "I heard. Tony Nardoianni called at six a.m. to tell me all about it."

"Did all your sleepovers go home after that?"

Most people would've missed his infinitesimal smile. "Just the one."

"Well, we're plumb out of beautiful women around here this morning."

"And out of a job, too." Victor considered sitting, then changed his mind and went to look out the window. "You suppose they'd allow you back in that hotel?"

"We didn't work for the hotel," K.O. said. "We worked for the convention—and Reeve Fesmire."

"Reeve Fesmire. Ha ha." Victor pressed the side of his knuckle softly against his lips, a sure sign he was making a decision. Finally: "Interested in working for me?"

K.O. and I traded looks. "It's been—decades since I worked for you, Victor."

"Surprises can be nice," Victor said.

"Doing what?"

"I manage Tony, as you know. He wouldn't kill a fly—but if his—history gets exploited, his reputation will cost both of us money."

K.O. said, "What history?"

"You don't need to know that."

"I think we do, Victor," I told him, "or we might end up looking stupid. I've always respected your confidentiality."

He glanced at K.O. "What about him?"

K.O. beat me to an answer. "I'm right here—don't talk about me as if I weren't. I know who you are, Mr. Gaimari, and you don't scare me for shit."

Victor looked amused. "I don't?"

"Not unless you were an Iraqi soldier with guns and bombs and mortars."

I gave K.O. a warning look. The kid just couldn't keep his mouth shut.

"No mortars, so relax," Victor said, moving to a spot in the room equidistant between our desks. "Tony's a gambling addict—even when he managed the Rockies. At the time, my uncle made Tony's debts his business. To whom do you think he owed all this gambling loss?"

That wasn't hard for me to wrap my head around. Don D'Allessandro always refused to have anything to do with drugs, even when other Mafia families had gone into it big-time. He never ran a prostitution ring, being a very moral Catholic. Gambling, however, and money laundering and the infamous Sugar Wars of Cleveland during Prohibition were altogether different.

"Nardoianni owed money to your family, Victor?"

"Owes to The Outfit in Chicago. My family is distantly related. If he had gotten busted for gambling on baseball while still involved in it, he'd be out on his ass. No more baseball, no more jobs, no more speeches, and a good chunk of the country hating his guts for what lots of Americans do weekly—bet on sports. If that had happened, I'd be screwed out of all the money he owes us. So I took him on, legally, as manager and partner. Our lawyers drew up contracts longer than a Stephen King novel, and whenever he gets to talk at one of these conventions, we take a big juicy bite of it."

"So," I said, "you want us to . . . ?"

"Keep the police and the media from digging up his past."

"I have no clout with the police."

"I hear differently."

"Then forget it, Victor." My voice took on a razor edge, making me remember why Victor and I hardly ever got along.

"If Tony's exposed, there's big money at stake."

"How big?"

Victor almost sighed; I'd never known him to sigh before. "The amount is important to you, Milan?"

"If we take your case, we'll need to know how important it is."

"If you insist. Give or take, a few bucks shy of five hundred thousand."

"A half million?" I said. "That's big betting."

"He's already paid off close to fifty—and I'm discounting the vig."

I stood up, finally. I was taller than Victor by a few inches, and though he's never mentioned it, I think it's always bothered him. "Who else knows about this contract? Is it on Cleveland's books?"

"Completely private. Still, if the media gets desperate enough to find out . . . " Victor cocked his head.

"So you're telling us to find who really killed Tommy Triller."

"You can't investigate capital crimes, Milan—that's against the law. But in the process of protecting the ass of a beloved former baseball manager, you just might stumble over the murderer, too." Then he added, "If that's what you choose to think."

"Because of the money?"

"Partly."

"What's the other part?"

Victor removed a very slim checkbook from his jacket pocket, and took a ballpoint pen from the mug on my desk. "Anthony Nardoianni."

"So?"

"So," Victor said, filling out the check, a reluctant smile turning up some otherwise invisible dimples, "he's *Italian*."

K.O. and I went to our respective homes, showered, changed into fresh, informal clothes, and met in Public Square just outside the hotel. There were twice as many cops than usual, and I informed K.O. that although we had been hired as private investigators now, we had no badges, walkie-talkies or name tags, and that we could rightfully be forbidden to enter many of the GMSA convention exhibits.

There were video trucks from the major local TV stations—and because of Tommy Triller's nationwide presence, national network news crews as well, along with reporters and photographers from the newspapers, and one of the sexy blond second-string hairdos from Fox News. There's something avaricious about crime reporters.

"Are we allowed in the lobby?" K.O. asked.

"It's public. So is the bar."

"And we can talk to the speechifiers?"

"We're not employees of GMSA, so the speakers could tell us

to go to hell. We should tell Swati Sathe we're working private so she doesn't throw us out."

"How about Reeve Fesmire?"

I gave my fast two-word answer no thought at all.

He asked, "How are we supposed to protect Nardoianni's ass?"

"Nobody's tried to kill him—that we know of. Our job is to keep his profile low."

"How do we do that?"

"Eliminate him as a suspect," I said. "So let's gird up our loins and start asking questions."

"Gird up our loins?" K.O. wondered. "Does that mean when some guys wear their pants low so their underwear shows?"

I shook my head and instead warned him, "Rule Number One: No beating the crap out of someone to make them talk."

K.O. shook his head almost sadly. "That's not even close to *my* Number One."

We went into the hotel. In semi-shock, many conventioneers wandered the lobby. The only purpose for the low-rent morning lecturers was to get people into the vendors' room. Reporters from the *Plain Dealer* and the *Akron Beacon-Journal* approached anyone who might be completely jazzed at being quoted in the paper. The place crawled with cops; civilians are intimidated by a blue uniform and a badge.

It took ten minutes until we spotted Tobe Blaine standing near the front reservations desk, talking to another plainclothes cop I didn't recognize. She seemed surprised to see us; annoyed was more like it.

"Why the hell are you here?" she demanded. "You don't have a job anymore."

"We do," I said. "A private job."

She rolled her eyes. "When McHargue hears this, she'll shit a brick."

"We'll try to stay out of your way, Tobe."

"Don't try; do it! I don't need your help."

"You asked for my help before—in Ashtabula."

"I looked at that as a working vacation. But this is no Ashtabula—and you're already all over my toes." She suggested, "Go home and let me catch a killer, okay?"

"We can't go home," I said. "We're getting paid."

"By?"

I felt silly saying it to the woman I love. "It's confidential. That's why they call us *private* investigators."

She shook her head more in sadness than frustration. "It's no wonder McHargue hits the ceiling every time she sees you."

"Don't you go postal on me, too, Tobe," I said.

"I can't promise that. Are you carrying?"

"No." I raised my arms shoulder-high. "I'll be happy if you searched me."

Tobe's eyes narrowed as she moved off. "Go away, Milan."

I'm crazy about her—strong, robust, and good at what she does. I admire that and the way she can ignore me and go about her business. Meantime, K.O. and I had other work to do. I found a house phone and asked for Tony Nardoianni. Apparently he didn't have a cadre of assistants banging into each other in his room, trying to hang up his clothes, because he answered the phone himself, seeming glad to hear my voice. He gave me the room number, and we headed upstairs.

"Fifth floor," K.O. remarked as the elevator rose slowly. "Triller was a household name so they had him in a big suite up on the twelfth. But not Nardoianni."

"Well, Tony's no Somebody—but he isn't exactly a Nobody, either."

"What is he, then?"

I thought about it until the elevator door whooshed open at the fifth floor. "Tony Nardoianni," I said, "is an in-betweener. And that's the saddest thing of all."

CHAPTER TWELVE

K.O.

Nardoianni was still in his hotel bathrobe. Under it he wore bright red parachute pants from the old M.C. Hammer days, white socks with no slippers, and a vivid purple T-shirt from the team Tony once managed, the Colorado Rockies.

"Hey, come on in, come on in, good to see you. Hey, you guys want some o.j. or something? I can call down . . ."

Milan shook his head. "Thanks, we're fine. This is my associate, K.O. O'Bannion."

Tony grinned. "K.O. Like in boxing, right? Us Italians had some great fighters. Tony Janeiro—he was from Youngstown, y' know. Willie Pep, Jake LaMotta, Rocky Graziano . . ."

"Rocky Marciano," K.O. added.

"Oh, man, fantastic! You must be a fighter yourself."

"I'm not Italian," K.O. said. "The last name is O'Bannion."

Tony looked chagrined and almost waved K.O. away. "Ah, well—Irishmen can't fight worth a damn. At least when they're sober."

K.O. said quietly, "The first heavyweight boxing champion of the world was John L. Sullivan—and he lost that title to another Irishman, Jim Corbett. And oh yeah, there was a third Irish champ in that division, too—Jim Braddock. They called him the Cinderella Man. And you know what? They made movies about all three of them."

"Whoa!" Tony pumped K.O.'s hand once more. "Heavyweight champs and movie stars, too. Hey, come on in, siddown, siddown." He resumed his seat, half-hidden behind the detritus of his recent breakfast, and Milan and K.O. took seats opposite him at the table.

"So," he said, "Vic wants you to prove I'm innocent of this Tommy Triller thing."

"That's not exactly what he said," Milan told him. "It's to keep your past mistakes from getting leaked out."

Tony drew himself up as full as his chair allowed him to. "What are you talking about?"

"You gambled back in the day."

Nardoianni's head shook almost violently. "A long time ago. Another lifetime."

"People forgive sometimes," K.O. said, "but not on the Internet."

"That means your income might fall right off the edge of the table," Milan added. "And if it stays there long enough, your name might be forgotten altogether."

"That's why we're here," K.O. said.

"Hey, I never got arrested, never got busted over the gambling."

"Victor might disagree," Milan said.

"Vic—uh—he got involved. So now I pay off the debt. You guys have cars, right? Houses? Credit cards? And you pay 'em off every month? I do the same thing." He calmed down. "I know, gambling's illegal," making quote marks in the air, "unless at a casino, or the race track. But everybody gambles. On something." Nardoianni put his hand over his heart. "I never bet against my own team. Not once. You can ask anybody."

"Did the other owners know that, Mr. Nardoianni?" K.O. asked.

"Even if I did, I'd bet on them to win! Why would I bet on myself to lose, for Christ's sakes?" Then the color fled from his cheeks. "Uh—like I said, I never bet on any games my team was playing."

"No accusations," Milan said. "Victor knows about it, he told us—and we're pretty sure your bookies aren't going to blab. Who else knows?"

Nardoianni shrugged, looking vulnerable. "Who knows? Word gets around."

"Gets around where?"

"The speaker business. These big talkers are famous, they know a lot of people. And when people know people . . . "

"Bullshit," Milan said. "It's not even an answer. The police'll knock on your door any minute. They expect answers to their questions—now! Triller's been killed—and their job is to find out who."

"Well—I think Governor Clary knows all about me."

"That dipshit?" K.O. exploded.

"K.O.," Milan warned, "watch your mouth."

Nardoianni said, "He used to—bet with the same people I did."

"With the mob?"

"Unless you're at an Indian casino," Nardoianni said, "everybody who bets eventually bets with the guys. That's how this country is run."

Milan rubbed his tired eyes. "All right, who else?"

"Owners?" K.O. said.

"Not the major owners. But some people owned little pieces of ball teams that didn't brag about it." He shook his head. "You know who owns about five percent of the Pittsburgh Pirates? Just as an investment?"

"Are we supposed to guess?" Milan said.

"It was Triller," Nardoianni said with wonder. "Tommy Triller."

After their meeting with Nardoianni, Milan and K.O. had a quick conversation in a quiet corner of the lobby ."Unless the police ask straight out, Nardoianni shouldn't mention his involvement with Triller, or with Governor Clary." He looked at his watch. "I should probably talk to Clary now."

"Let me go," K.O. said. "I've talked to him already."

"You insulted him."

"Yeah—and if he gets mad, he might spill the beans." He frowned. "Where did that expression come from? Who spills their beans, anyway?"

"Everyone in Boston. All right, go for it. Meantime, I'll visit Dr. Ben again."

"Stick around," K.O. said. "You can see him today on TV."

"I don't get paid," Milan said, "for watching him on TV."

"True—but in person you don't get to hit the MUTE button."

"Watch me," Milan said as he headed for the elevator. K.O went down to the free breakfast room (for convention attendees only) to get a large coffee before he headed back up to talk to Clary.

Jonah Clary opened the door to his hotel room, wearing a blinding white cowboy outfit with studs all over where his heart was supposed to be, long cattle horns sewn in by hand, and high-heeled white leather boots. A bizarre Roy Rogers look. When he saw K.O., he glowered.

"What the hell *you* want here, boy?"

K.O. offered him the tall coffee. "Peace offering, Governor. Sorry if I insulted you. Too much sarcasm, not enough brains. Can I come in?"

"Well, you can't stand in the hall drinking my coffee." He stepped aside and K.O entered. The suite wasn't as elegant as the one in which Tommy Triller died, and its view was of the sprawling Cleveland steel mills to the south. Even so, it was pleasant enough for an ex-governor and publicly humiliated presidential wannabe.

"I figured you'd like the coffee hot and black. Hope it's okay. Nice outfit, by the way," K.O. smiled when he spoke.

Clary preened. "Thanks. I got a matching Stetson."

"You have a sidearm, too, Governor? A Colt, or a Smith and Wesson?"

"I have eight of 'em. And a whole case full a hunting rifles, too." K.O. winced, thinking of this man killing animals for fun. "But I didn't bring 'em with me. Can't take a handgun on an airplane without a whole lotta rigamarole." Then he became grave. "A damn good thing, too, after what happened last night." Clary made a gun with his thumb and forefinger, pointed it at his head, and pulled the trigger, supplying the sound effect to go with it. "Glad I didn't bring a weapon."

"Would you have shot Triller if you were packing?"

Clary took off the cap of his cardboard cup and sipped his coffee. "Don't be a damn fool again. I don't shoot people."

"Then why so many handguns?"

"It's my Second Amendment right. Yours too, boy."

"Are you friends with Tony Nardoianni, Governor?"

"I wouldn't call him a friend. We know each other—have for years. But he's a sports guy, and I'm a politics guy."

"You've never been involved in sports?"

Jonah Clary almost blushed and stuck his chest out a little. "I played football in college. Strong safety." Then he looked at K.O. with just a hint of contempt. "Bet you didn't play football in college, huh?"

"No. I threw hand grenades instead. Did you get along with Tommy Triller?"

"Used to. He videotaped some programs in my state. Took me to dinner a time or two while he was there—and then stabbed me in the back."

"How?"

"Well—I ran for president last election. I guess you knew that already, huh? Triller was in my state so often, I figured he'd be on my side—but he came out against me before the primaries and supported the other guy."

"Which other guy?"

Clary's lower jaw became pugnacious. "The guy who got the nomination and then didn't win." He clenched one fist. "Triller did *The Larry King Show* one night—that son of a bitch was everywhere! Anyway, there he was, right on TV, saying I wasn't smart enough to sit in the Oval Office. That was pretty shitty, don'tcha think?"

"Pretty shitty," K.O. said. "It also gives you a motive, Governor."

"Motive? For what?"

"For killing him."

For a millisecond, fear flashed across Jonah Clary's face. Then he squared his shoulders into his usual arrogant posture. "Listen, boy, if I shot everybody who said I shouldn't be president, we'd be living in a lonely wilderness."

"How about if you shot every adult male you call 'boy?'"

Clary laughed. "That don't mean nothin'. Down south, it's just the way we talk."

"Black males don't like being referred to as 'boy.'"

"Well, yeah—but you're a white man."

K.O. clenched his teeth. "Thanks for noticing. I guess I'm through here."

"Was there something specific you wanted to ask me?" Jonah Clary said.

"Sure. Did you kill Tommy Triller?"

Clary's face turned into an angry thundercloud, and he took a few steps toward K.O. Evidently he thought better of it and jerked open the door. "Thanks for the coffee," he said, and then added, "boy."

In the elevator going down to the lobby, K.O. unexpectedly found himself face-to-face with Kylee Graves. The beehive hairdo was the same, but this time she wore a white blouse with dark blue slacks and low-heeled shoes. Her eyes, though, were red, and what little eye-liner she wore below them had been washed away by tears.

"Ooh." Her voice quavered. "I've been looking for you."

"For me?"

"We have to talk. There's no place in the lobby. Can you come up to my room?"

"Not a good idea," he said.

"No, I don't want to . . . —God, no! I just need to talk to you."

While he didn't find her particularly attractive, K.O. was stung by the "God, no!" line. He said, "We can walk for a few minutes, maybe around the Square. Then I'll have to get back."

Kylee looked disappointed, but she agreed. They stepped out of the elevator at street level and ran into Tobe Blaine. Tobe didn't say anything, but her eyebrows climbed almost to her hairline.

K.O. stammered, "Hi, we're—uh—going for a walk."

"How lovely for you." Tobe's tone was dry as dust as she moved into the hotel. She was friendly with the much-younger Carli, and it made her uncomfortable seeing K.O. with another woman.

"Who's she?" Kylee asked. "Friend of yours?"

"She's a homicide cop."

Kylee shuddered. "I guess that's what I need to talk to you about. The—homicide. Tommy. I mean, you're a security person, so . . . " She put on sunglasses as they walked by the Soldiers and Sailors Monument, a huge edifice with statues and plaques that has been on Public Square since just after the Civil War, honoring Ohioans who gave their lives in that particular bloodshed.

He almost explained to her what the monument was, like a tour guide, but thought better of it.

They crossed the street, passing the skyscraper that used to be the British Petroleum Building until British Petroleum packed up and moved elsewhere. Kylee said, "I'm heartbroken. Tommy and I were very close. We were thinking about getting married."

"You're kidding!" K.O. said it before thinking. "Sorry, that surprised me. Where did you meet him?"

"I live in Charlotte, North Carolina. He came there to give one of his programs. We took one look at each other and—well, bells rang."

"When was this?"

Kylee counted on her fingers. "Eight months ago—in February." She gasped, swallowing a sob. "The day before Valentine's Day." As they turned left and walked toward the Old Stone Church, the second-oldest building in all of Cleveland, she rummaged in her small purse for a tissue.

"He didn't live in Charlotte," K.O. said.

She dabbed at her nose. "No—but he promised he'd visit."

"Did he?"

"He was very busy."

K.O. tried not to look at her. "You mean you only saw him that one day?"

"And night," Kaylee whimpered.

"And he asked you to marry him?"

"Not in so many words. But he told me he loved me."

"He did?"

She blushed, her head down.

At the corner they turned left and headed back toward the hotel. K.O. said, "So you came here to Cleveland to be with him at this convention?"

"Oh, yes. I wrote him I was coming. But those terrible people wouldn't put me through when I called his room," she pouted. "And I couldn't get to see him, either, like face to face. Now he's gone." She sobbed, sniffled. "Gone for good."

"Kylee," K.O. said as gently as he could, "don't you realize Triller just used you back in Charlotte?"

"That's not true!" she gasped.

"If not, why wouldn't he see you again? He's got a reputation as a swinger. He was a famous celebrity—women threw themselves at him every night of the week. That's why he wasn't interested in you anymore. I'm sorry, Kylee, but you were the day before yesterday's news."

"You mean he didn't love me?"

K.O. shook his head, and Kylee began crying quietly as they walked, hidden by her large sunglasses, which covered the reddening eyes but not the tears running down her cheeks. "I needed someone to love me. I still do."

"That's—very sad, Kylee."

Her next sniffle was loud, ponderous. Then she whispered, "Do you think *you* could love me?"

After he dropped her back at the hotel, K.O. took off for Tower City, needing a break from the convention. Maybe, he thought, he was too soft to be in a profession that brought him in contact with some of the most pitiful people in the world. Everyone wants to be loved—that part was true—but not necessarily by the first person who meets their eyes and smiles.

He didn't think Kylee Graves was Tommy Triller's executioner, but one never knew. She had one hell of a motive. Soft or no, he would report this conversation to Milan—part of his job.

Whether or not Milan mentioned it to Tobe Blaine was not K.O.'s problem.

CHAPTER THIRTEEN

MILAN

We have many acquaintances in our lives, but few really good friends. One of mine is Ed Stahl—a daily columnist for the *Plain Dealer* since the Pleistocene Era. His columns are often angry because he is, too. Constantly cranky, glum, and over-weight, he drinks Jim Beam nightly to medicate his serious ulcer and smokes a smelly pipe. Nobody's gotten him to stop, despite the laws against it. In his bottom drawer is a Pulitzer Prize medal won so many years ago that he doesn't remember what it was for. He never mentions it, even when asked.

Yet anywhere in town, if you happen to blow your nose, Ed knows about it—and if you blow it twice, he'll put it in his column. Mention any politician, social leader, star athlete, bartender, media presence, local author, or the guys from a twice-weekly bowling league in Parma, and Ed knows all about them. Tough guys shake in their boots when he appears, notebook in hand, glasses down near the end of his nose and a pipe clutched between his teeth, rocking slightly when he walks because the weight he's never managed to lose sometimes throws him off balance.

I never expected to find him in the Renaissance Hotel lobby during a Global Motivational Speakers Association convention.

"Nice to see an old face, Ed," I said as we shook hands.

"Not so damn old. I came here to put a column together. Now that Triller got iced, it'll be a way better column."

"Cynical."

"I'm a journalist, not the Archbishop of Canterbury." Ed tried lowering his voice. "I came to poke holes in this whole set-up—this multi-billion-dollar industry that just loves people at the end of their rope. But all these speakers, vendors, hangers-on, the self-help book writers—they're selling exactly the same thing: bullshit. They tart it up, put colored ribbons on it, and call it other names, but it's all the same bullshit."

"You think any of them will give you the time of day?"

"Doubtful. I have appointments with a few third-level speakers nobody's ever heard of. Then I'll mingle with the bourgeoisie for comments. By the time it hits my column on Monday, everybody'll be out of Cleveland, and I won't get my ass kicked." Ed shifted the stem of his pipe from one corner of his mouth to the other. "A woman from Florida named Lianna Hicks is the first one. You might have seen her wandering around. Middle-aged blond bombshell, sexy-looking—and nobody in the speechmaking business takes her seriously. But behind all the peroxide and powder and sexy outfits, Hicks is very successful, rich from her own motivational business—and the testicles of all these hotshot speakers are tucked tightly away in her little beaded purse."

I nodded. "Let me know what she says. I don't work for GMSA anymore, but I do have a private client here."

"I won't bother asking who it is; you'll tell me to go fuck myself."

"I'm too fond of you, Ed. I'll just tell you to go fly a kite."

He almost laughed—almost. "I haven't heard that line for fifty years. But if you promise to sit quietly during my interview with Hicks, you can tag along. You'd like meeting a fifty-year-old blond bombshell." Ed checked the time. "Let's go."

Lianna's room—nowhere near a suite—was on a lower floor. She was made up like a middle-city blond news reporter, sporting a relatively low-cut scoop-necked white blouse and the rest of her outfit—jacket, long billowy pants, and stockings—was jet black. Her high-heeled shoes, however, were lipstick red.

"I heard your name from somebody yesterday," she said to me when Ed Stahl introduced us. "You're security, right—or you used to be?"

"Same basic job," I said. "Different boss. I appreciate you letting me sit in on Ed's interview. He's a Pulitzer Prize winner, you know."

Her face lit up and her eyelids fluttered madly. I think that in her mind, Pulitzer Prize recipients were all rich. "Well, then, I'm glad I accepted this date with you, Ed."

Date? Strange word, especially since Ed Stahl hasn't had a real "date" with a woman for decades.

We took chairs and Lianna sat on the bed, hands planted firmly on the mattress at her hips, her breasts straining at the blouse. Or maybe not straining; maybe she was just made that way.

"You want to hear all about my business?" she continued. "I train individuals—and some of the biggest companies in America—in all the ways they can make even more money." She proceeded to name them, though Ed didn't write them down. "I've been on loads of TV shows and worked with all the name-above-the-title speakers. I give about a hundred talks a year, like the one I'll give later today."

"About developing potential?" Ed said.

She smiled, licking her reddened lips, and leaned toward him. "I see you did your homework. Good boy—you get an *A*."

I felt like a geek at a high school dance. Was she coming on to Ed? I jumped in. "You worked with Tony Nardoianni?"

She didn't even turn her head to look at me. "A few times. Baseball bores the bejesus out of me. He doesn't have much to say, anyway; he's just trying to sell his out-of-date book."

"How about Dr. Ben?"

She nodded. "I've been on his show. Also *The View* and Maury Povich."

"Siddartha West?"

"Before my time."

"Hy Jinx?"

She sighed. Her breasts sighed, too. "Are you kidding?"

"Dr. Lorelei Singleton?"

Her face turned into that of a crazy-eyed zombie. "That dizzy little bitch! I can't stand the sight of her."

"Lianna—you worked with Tommy Triller, didn't you?" Ed said.

The zombie look morphed into sad and sorrowful. "Oh, poor Tommy. I don't even want to think about that. We were close. Two peas in a pod. We were almost partners."

"Partners?" Ed flipped a page in his notebook. "Partners in what?"

"We were negotiating—discussing the idea of the two of us bringing our companies together. He and I talked about the same thing—and if our two companies became one ... "

I jumped in again. "Even though you earn good money, Triller made fifty—even a hundred times that much, every year. Why would he want you as an equal partner?"

Her nostrils flared. "That's not the point!"

"That's exactly the point," Ed said, "but let's move on. Now Triller's gone, your future partnership is over before it starts."

In a matter of seconds, she turned sly. "Not—necessarily," she teased. She waited for us to ask her to elaborate. We didn't—but she elaborated anyway. "Let's just say the Triller Organization has good reason to welcome me with open arms, like Tommy himself did."

"I'd love," Ed Stahl said, "to share this with my readers. It sounds exciting."

Now came the negative finger-shake like a kindergarten teacher. "No no no," she said. "I don't tell tales out of school."

"But you have so much to brag about," Ed said. "All the corporations who have you straighten things out for their employees and make them work harder."

"Well, yes," Lianna said. "Big corporations—big! And of course, the biggest corporation of all—the United States government."

Ed turned back to a page on which he'd scribbled something. "Let's talk about partnerships some more. Several years ago—in Stuart, Florida ... "

She laughed a tinkly come-fuck-me laugh. "You're saying it wrong. Ed. It's not *Stew*-art. In Florida, everybody calls it *Stoort*. One syllable."

"If you say so. You had a partnership in—Stoort, back in 2004. Your business was very similar to the one you have today. Your partner, though—a Mr. Melvin Tarver ... "

"Mel-*ville*," she said, and her voice turned icy, her lips almost disappearing. "Like the *Moby Dick* guy. Melville."

"Sorry, Melville. Shortly after you and Melville Tarver formed a partnership, he was murdered."

She put a hand over her chest, hiding her cleavage. "Yes?"

"For a while, you were what they call a person of interest."

She wet her lips again "Someone shot him. We were all persons of interest. Mel's wife, his son, his next-door neighbor, me. Everyone who had anything to do with him was a person of interest."

"And as his partner, you got everything, a hundred percent."

"That's how the deal was set up. If it'd gone the other way, if I'd died, he would've gotten everything."

"The Stuart—Stoort police," Ed said, "couldn't find enough evidence to charge anyone. The case is still unsolved."

Lianna shrugged. "If they did solve it, they forgot to tell me."

"You were on the verge of a big-money partnership with Tommy Triller," I said. "Now that he's been shot, will you be a person of interest in Cleveland, too?"

She let her polished, carefully controlled performance slip for an instant, revealing coarseness, and a temper as hot as Triller's coals. Her eyes blazed and her voice hardened. "We didn't sign any partnership agreement. Why would I kill him *before* he was my partner?"

Ed clicked his ballpoint shut and put it in his pocket, closing his notepad. "I think we have enough here, Lianna. Thank you very . . . "

"Wait a minute! I hope you'll make me look good, Ed. I'm terrific at what I do, and it'd be wonderful if everybody knew that." Now the seductress returned—come-hither smile, lip-licking, eye-fluttering. "I'd really—*really*—be appreciative."

As we headed down in the elevator, I said, "I guess I'm a dumb shit."

"Nowhere near, Milan. Remember she said the Triller people have good reason to like her partnership?"

"What's the reason?"

"If I knew," Ed said, "you'd read it in my column on Monday. But since you're on good terms with the police department, if I were you, I'd mention all this to Tobe Blaine."

"I'm way ahead of you. You have someone else to talk to?"

"Naturally. A Mister—check me, *Reverend*—Jesse Paulin, of some church or other in Independence, Missouri."

"I've had a gutful of reverends lately, Ed."

"Oh, you'll love this guy. He's a crazy-ass like Pat Robertson."

"Why would you want to talk to a loony-tunes like that?"

Ed said, "He's a speaker, though he doesn't usually show up at big conventions like this. He has about a hundred employees, his own home that cost him a couple mil, a fleet of cars—and his own airplane."

"Wow."

"And he hated Tommy Triller's guts!"

When we got to his room, Reverend Jesse Paulin was in shirtsleeves, suit pants held up by suspenders. When he began talking, he might have been addressing the masses in St. Peter's Square.

"Yes, indeed, I did dislike Tommy Triller. But I wish no one's death. Our Lord and Savior Jesus Christ commands that we love all our neighbors, even those who blaspheme," Reverend Jesse Paulin preached. He didn't just speak; he *preached*. "So there's hope in my heart for the redemption of any person, even Triller."

"Still," Ed pushed on, "it's well-known you despised Triller. Why? Specifically."

Paulin sighed. "He seduced people into walking on hot coals, which symbolizes man-made power over even Hell itself. For his own obscene profiteering, he taught humanism and self-determination, as if mortals should be gods. He spoke of personal power, not God-given talent. He was an agent of Satan. One cannot mourn his departure."

"Satan?" Ed said, scribbling. "Seriously? All he did was *talk*."

"*All?*" the Reverend thundered. "All? Proverbs 18:21, Solomon: Death and life are in the power of the tongue. What Triller did, what I do—it's serious business. He lived a life of unmitigated greed. But I've been the Lord's Number One salesman for six decades. I've never known a more satanic influencer. In his death, God has smitten him. God has spoken!"

"Most people at this con want to hear about making money," Ed said.

Paulin shook his finger. "Prosperity is God's will. God wants your success! When you tithe—when you donate ten percent of your money to Our Lord and Savior—it is multiplied tenfold for you."

Ed Stahl, always an atheist, got angrier than usual when debating religion, and this was too good for him to pass up. "So,

Reverend, how come Triller's preaching about money is evil when you're here, too, selling the same snake oil with a different label?"

"You try my patience, Mr. Stahl. I preach the Gospel of Prosperity—for the whole person and for the glory of God."

"So," Ed said, "when I want to tithe to Jesus, do I write him a check? Call his 800 number and put it on my Visa? Slip him cash to tuck into his tunic? Oh wait, I get it. I give the money to *you*."

Now that things had gone completely sour, I saw no harm in getting to the point. "I just wonder, Reverend, if you and Triller competing for the same speaking engagements and audiences—and his popularity soaring while yours isn't—might have tempted you to step up and do God's work here for him?"

"That is a gross insult! Triller was a flavor of the month. I was here before him, and I'll be here after him. In the great scheme of things he was—*inconsequential*."

Ed said, "He was the headliner, and you're speaking late on the second day, in a breakout session against three other much-lesser-known speakers. That doesn't strike me as inconsequential. Not to anyone here, and not to you."

Paulin stood up, indicating the interview was over. "If Triller had heeded God's warnings he might be alive. In Matthew 12:36, Jesus said, 'Every one of these careless words will come back to haunt you. There will be a time of reckoning. Words can be your salvation. Words can be your *damnation*.'" He took a deep breath. "Triller's demise, sirs, had nothing to do with me and everything to do with God's will. But even God isn't infinitely patient." He waved a finger at Ed. "You might consider the same warning if you write about this conversation."

Going down in the elevator after we'd been frostily asked to leave, I took a moment to enjoy something I'd seen rarely in the past forty years. Ed was almost smiling. "I can't wait for your column," I said. "It'll be a doozy. But for me, things got messier."

"How's that?"

I slouched against the rear of the elevator. "I just found another person with one hell of a motive for wanting Tommy Triller dead—a motive more powerful than money or fame or competition. The righteousness," I said, "of a true believer."

CHAPTER FOURTEEN

K.O.

Siddartha West sat across from K.O. at the table in her suite, pouring coffee. It was not yet time for Hollywood glamour, so she wore Dockers and a man's dress shirt, and her make-up was applied for a trip to the supermarket, and not to a red carpet awards show. Her hair looked combed by her casual fingers.

She seemed on edge, like everyone else at the convention. The biggest VIP of the weekend had been snuffed out, and the other attendees were either terrified they'd be killed themselves, or that the police would pin Tommy Triller's murder on them.

"I imagine you're going crazy right now," Siddartha said. "A murder right here in your hotel. People frequently get killed in Hollywood." She sipped her coffee, making a face. "Unless it's a big star, it's just a short paragraph in the *L.A. Times*. But Triller was the biggest deal around here, with the biggest ego."

"You didn't like him?"

"How could anyone like that narcissistic shit? People take one look at that big, toothy smile and follow him anywhere—like the rats tagging after the Pied Piper of Hamelin." She lowered her hand slowly, whistling as she did so, and made the sound of a splash as the Piper's rats hit the river.

"Were you ever on one of his TV shows?"

"And not get paid? No way. He didn't pay celebrities—he thought he was a bigger star than any of us. And he always said I was a total nut for believing in reincarnation—announced it on *The View*, for God's sake, and that even took Whoopi Goldberg back a bit." She rolled her eyes as if nothing ever bothered Whoopi Goldberg. "He also told me in front of about twenty people at a Los Angeles benefit that I wasn't a very good actress. Well, fuck him! Where's *his* goddamn Oscar or his Golden Globe?"

"That was a lousy thing for him to say."

"Triller was the devil incarnate," she said, and then laughed. "Not that I'm religious. Everything he said was lousy unless he was on stage or on TV. These convention nuts love paying money to do one of his programs. Ninety-nine times out of a hundred, he's not at those programs himself, either."

"Hated him that much?" K.O. said.

"Hate? Don't try to hang his murder on me." She spread jam on an English muffin. "Besides, he'll come back, anyway—you know about reincarnation, don't you? I've written books on that. Triller will return—a bigger asshole than he is now."

"I thought we all came back as frogs."

"Nope. He'll be reincarnated as exactly the kind of person he attacks for being vulnerable right now. That's karma, kiddo."

"So you didn't shoot him?"

"I never even killed anyone in the movies—I've got a lifetime patent playing hookers with a heart of gold." She took a healthy bite of her muffin. "Do you think I'm a good actor?"

"I—gosh, I don't know. If I could guess, I'd say you were very good. I've never seen any of your movies."

"You're joking!"

"I'm too young."

Siddartha said, "If you saw one of my movies, you'd damn well remember it."

K.O. took a slug of his own coffee. "Did you work with anyone else on the list of top-level speakers this week?"

"All of them, one way or another. I've run into Hy Jinx a few times, we said hello, maybe chatted. We don't exactly run in the same circles."

"How about Tony Nardoianni?"

"Nope. I'm a big Dodger fan. Besides, he's gross."

"Gross? Why?"

"He chews tobacco!" Siddartha shuddered. "I'd never trust a guy who chews tobacco—and then spits."

"You don't chew?" K.O. teased.

Siddartha snorted. "I've had everything there is to drink, including absinthe. I've done everything I could smoke, swallow, sniff, inhale or inject—including LSD, which got me to the spiritual place I am now. But I draw the line at chewing tobacco. I even had an actor fired off one of my pictures; we had some love scenes together, but I wouldn't even *pretend* to kiss a guy who dipped snuff."

"Did Nardoianni get along okay with Tommy Triller?"

"Triller didn't pay attention to anyone unless he could manipulate them, or fuck them. I'd imagine Tony Nardoianni was jealous of him, like everyone else."

"Were you jealous of Triller, too, Ms. West?"

"I'm old enough to be your grandmother, but I wish you'd call me Sid. Look, I don't have anywhere near Triller's money, but I do own a rambling house on the beach in Malibu. I have three luxury cars, including a squeaky clean white Rolls convertible that used to belong to Dean Martin, and a brand new Mercedes I hardly ever take out of my five-car garage. In my entry hall, a big glass case displays the awards I've won—Oscar, Emmy, SAG Award, bunch of Golden Globes, the People's Choice. Triller screwed all the women who paid him a fortune to take his classes, but I've been to bed with half the major movie stars of my generation, and they were all pretty great. Am I jealous of Tommy Triller? In a pig's ass! If you're hunting the trigger guy, you're in the wrong hotel suite. But you just had coffee with one of yesterday's most famous women and heard her life story, so your day hasn't been wasted."

She pushed herself away from the table and stood up.

"Now scoot, K.O. If I don't go schmooze with all the despairing dimwits who want to learn how to make big money, I won't get paid—which means I have to slap on twenty coats of paint before I even walk out the door."

K.O. stood up, too.

"You don't need twenty coats."

Siddartha's face lit up from within. "What a terrific liar you are!" She hugged him, pressing her cheek against his. "Take care of yourself, K.O.," she said, "and love every minute you're alive."

"I promise—but I've got to ask you just one more question."

"Shoot."

K.O. beamed, too. "What's the name of that Oscar-winning movie of yours?"

Lorelei Singleton sat in a quiet corner of the hotel bar. It was only eleven a.m., so no one was drinking—yet. She had a notebook in which she'd been dutifully writing until some middle-aged woman had timidly approached her to ask how to save her marriage when her husband was more interested in playing golf, playing cards, or watching football. Dr. Lorelei informed her in no uncertain terms that she should call into the radio program next week and not bother her in person.

When K.O. appeared, she showed none of the interest of the previous evening; perhaps she'd found another willing companion. But when he asked to sit down with her for a few minutes, she reluctantly shrugged him into a chair.

"How do you feel about Tommy Triller's death, Dr. Lorelei?"

"You don't expect me to cry my eyes out, do you? There's just so much room in everybody's heart—or brain—for emotion. Loving—or hating, too. There's no room for anyone being sad when somebody they didn't like in the first place dies."

"You didn't like him?"

"He thought he was better than the rest of us, just because he made more money. He used people like they were Kleenex and then threw them away. He used *me!*"

"How?"

K.O. was startled as her cheeks and nose changed from pale alabaster to nearly clown-red—a fearsome way for someone to blush. "It's personal," she said. "Well, business-wise, too." She sniffed, took a deep breath. "We were talking about six months ago—possibly joining forces, working out some partnerships. He invited me to join him for a weekend at the Waldorf in New York, to talk about it."

Pillow talk, K.O. thought but did not say.

"After that, I never heard another word from him! I called more than a dozen times and always got one of his huge group of assistants. I texted him and got a form email back, like I was an ex-customer! I sent him snail mail and he never answered." She shook her head, more angry than sad. "He was a prick! A gold-plated, first-class prick!"

"That sounds like trouble."

Now Dr. Lorelei's blush turned chalky white. "Are you accusing me of murder? Because I'll sue your ass off for everything you've got!"

K.O. said, "I have about two grand in the bank—and an eleven-year-old car—so sue away. But I only said it sounded like trouble."

"I'm tired of feeling threatened all the time!"

"Who else threatened you?"

"Besides Tommy?" She gently rubbed both eyes with a thumb and forefinger. "Damn near everybody. Ben Mayo, for one; he thinks my radio show is stealing viewers from his TV show. Jonah Clary slammed me because I'm not nearly as Tea Party as he is, and Siddartha West because I'm *too* right-wing for her precious liberal bullshit. And that baseball guy—what's his name again?"

"Tony Nardoianni," K.O. supplied.

"Right. He wrote me and called me when he was managing a ball team and said some of his players were getting all fucked up listening to what I say and that I should—and this is a direct quote—shut the fuck up!"

"Wow," K.O. said, "you've covered just about everyone—except Hy Jinx."

"Jinx thinks I'm a racist."

"Are you? A racist?"

"No, not at all!" She shook her head vehemently. "But he puts me down because I don't usually talk to black people on the radio. My phone answerer screens them out."

"Why?"

"Have you ever tried talking to a black person? I can't under-stand half of what they're saying! Are they all from Ethiopia or something?"

K.O. felt his gut twist. "My boss's significant other is black, but she's not from Ethiopia. She's a homicide detective sergeant with the Cleveland police with a master's degree in law enforce-ment. You'll understand her when she questions you—and she will. But that's how far her college education went, because *she's* not a doctor, either."

"Fuck you, you little shit!" Lorelei exploded, so loud that even people walking by in the lobby heard her. "Get out of my face before I kill you."

K.O. chuckled as he rose from his chair. "Considering what happened last night, I wouldn't say that to the homicide detective."

He wandered out into the crowded lobby. There were many uniformed cops there, and a few elegantly dressed guys looking like hedge fund managers wearing boring ties, who must have been from the FBI. Everyone was shocked by the death of the man whose name appeared at the top of the bill. How many attendees knew Tommy Triller personally, K.O. wondered, or had walked barefoot over his hot coals to make themselves believe they were invincible?

He had another thought, too, courtesy of Lorelei. How many women had he spent a night or weekend with and pissed off by never talking to them again?

CHAPTER FIFTEEN

MILAN

F inally come to your senses, did you?" Dr. Ben asked.

He was sprawled across his suite's sofa, feet up. Caroline Mayo, in an easy chair, was a knockout in a white dress with blue piping matching her eyes. How Dr. Ben wound up with a beautiful woman like that, I'll never know. "I understand," he continued. "Yesterday we were tired, snapping at each other. Today our thinking is better."

I guess he hadn't heard that K.O. and I had been fired, or he wouldn't have let me get anywhere near him. He was still a jerk. Caroline looked as if she loathed conventions like this, but seemed anxious, too, twisting one strand of blond hair around her finger. After all, one of her husband's co-VIPs had been murdered.

"My thinking is about what happened here last night," I said, "and not much else. I'm wondering how friendly you are with the other speakers."

"We're competitors, not friends."

"Enemies?"

"You think everyone in the world is either a friend or an enemy?"

"It wasn't a comment—just a question."

"A dumb one. We're not friends, we're not enemies. We compete in the same business, but we do it in different ways."

"How about Dr. Lorelei?"

A dark cloud shadowed his face. "Pain-in-the-ass bitch! Total phony—and not even a doctor! Call her radio show and she'll crucify you. Psychologists should help people, not quote from the Bible to make them feel like shit."

"Has she crucified you?"

"She would have," he said, "if I wasn't smarter than her."

"You actually help the ones who come on your show?"

He smirked. "I never miss."

"How about Jonah Clary?"

A staccato laugh. "A joke governor, and now a joke speaker. I'll bet every morning he looks in the mirror and practices saying 'My fellow Americans' when he's not busy cleaning cow shit off his boots."

"You never had him as a guest on your show?"

"I'd rather watch a test pattern."

"Siddartha West?"

"Are you kidding me? She's a goofball weirdo."

"She mentioned she's been on your show."

Mayo flicked his hand at me as if I were a mosquito. "For laughs. She's a junkie, and admits it. LSD, mushrooms, weed. All that hippie crap went out thirty years ago. So did she."

"You dislike her?"

"If I only have people on my show that I *like*, I wouldn't have a show."

"Are your show ratings shaky?"

Caroline made a sound at the back of her throat as she uncrossed her legs and then crossed them the other way, nylon whispering against nylon. Mayo looked daggers at her for a heartbeat, then relaxed again. "TV ratings go up, they go down, and then up again. I'm not worried."

"So right now you're in a down cycle?"

He swung his feet off the sofa. "Where do you get all this shit?"

"Just guessing," I said, "but let's move on. Hy Jinx?"

"He's an actual murderer," Caroline volunteered, "but he's not in prison because he's a big rock star. If he never made another speech, he'd make millions doing rap."

"I make more money than he does!" Dr. Ben barked.

"And," I said, "you haven't murdered anyone."

His face paled, and he swallowed hard. "Exactly."

"How about Tony Nardoianni? Buddies with him?"

"Ballplayers move their lips while they read the sports scores every morning. He's at this convention because he's desperate to make a few bucks."

"How was he with Tommy Triller?"

"How would I know that?"

"How were *you* with Triller, then?"

He licked his lips and stared out across Public Square at a window washer dangling from the roof as he swung back and forth squeegeeing the windows of the office building facing the hotel—frightening to watch if one had a fear of heights, as I do. "Like I said—we were competitors."

Caroline leaned forward, looking into my eyes for the first time. "Triller was a bastard—negotiating with TV syndicators to put his TV show on instead of Ben's."

"That's a rumor, Caroline!" Mayo said sharply. "Don't spread rumors around."

"He was a prick!" Caroline Mayo's nostrils flared. "He was always a prick! Don't make him some saint or martyr just because he's dead."

Dr. Ben winked at me and jerked his chin towards his wife, one of those "can-you-believe-her" looks.

"Apparently Triller was unpopular among his peers," I said.

"None of us like each other. The self-help business is dog eat dog."

I thought of my tired old dog, Herbie, currently under the care of K.O.'s pretty girlfriend, Carli. Herbie wouldn't eat another dog if his life depended on it.

Dr. Ben was speaking of a completely different kind of dog.

I turned to Caroline. "Were you friendly with Tommy Triller, Mrs. Mayo?"

Her blue eyes widened, becoming more blue. "I know him through my husband, so I had little to do with him."

Only a few moments earlier she said Tommy Triller was a prick—something to think about, but I chose not to point out her contrasting statements. "Who do *you* think killed him?"

"How would I know?" she flared. "I've never known any murderers."

"You know a few, Caroline," Ben said. "I had them on my show. The woman who killed her mother . . . "

She put her hand to her throat. "I don't think it's one of the speakers at this con," she said to me. "They all have too much to lose."

"Could be. It wasn't robbery—nothing was stolen. You think it was random?"

She started to answer, but Dr. Ben interrupted her. "Why all the questions here?" he demanded. "You're not a cop."

"No," I said. "But I used to be. And being a cop is like riding a bicycle. Once you do it, you never forget how."

Dr. Ben stood up. "Well, I haven't forgotten how to tell somebody to fuck off! You're prying into personal affairs, and you have no right."

I stood up, too. Ben Mayo was almost as tall as me. I said, "Aren't you interested in who killed one of your fellow speakers?"

"I'm interested—but I don't want to be interrogated about it!"

"You call this an interrogation? Maybe you've been interrogated before."

"That's it!" he bellowed, our noses nearly touching. "Get out. Now!"

"Screaming in my face won't get you a damn thing," I said.

"Get out before I throw you out!"

"I suggest you not try that."

"Get out!" he sputtered, inadvertent saliva peppering my face. I hate that.

"Ask me nicely," I said.

"What?"

"Ask me politely to leave and I will. Otherwise you can wail all day long like a three-year-old, and I'll stay here and watch you do it."

"Ben," Caroline said, unwinding herself from her chair, "for Christ's sake, ask him nicely. You're acting like a jack-off!"

I learned something at that moment that I never knew before: when a bald man gets so furious that his face turns purple, the purple goes all the way up to the top of his head.

His words, spoken softly, barely made it through his clenched teeth. "Will. You. Please. Excuse. Us?"

I halfway relaxed. "Why, certainly, Dr. Ben—and thanks for your time." I turned to his wife. "A pleasure being with you, Mrs. Mayo—or may I call you Caroline?"

She didn't quite smile, but her blue eyes sparkled.

I imagined that as soon as I walked out of there, the Mayo couple would engage in a fight their neighbors could hear through the walls.

In the lobby, Swati Sathe was with the reservation clerk. Usually well put-together, she looked completely wrung out. I waited until she finished her conversation and then sidled up to her to say hello.

"I heard you were back here on a private job," she said.

"Is that okay?"

"Fine with me. Fesmire will be madder than hell—but right now he's too busy replacing Shamu the Whale with someone else just as important."

"Shamu the Whale?"

She shrugged. "That's what he calls the late, great star attraction—the one most of these people came here to see."

"Replacing him?"

She nodded. "He couldn't find anyone big enough to fill in at the last minute. Some conventioneers have asked for their money back—a disaster for Fesmire. He was on the phone all night. He called Warren Buffet, he called Derek Jeter, he even called every living ex-president and begged. No soap. So he's bringing in two people to make up for Triller and they'll give the big talk tomorrow night."

"Who?"

"A formerly married couple," Swati said, "who had a profitable business together until they broke up and went at each other's throats in divorce court. They're both from New York, and abhor each other—Bailey DeWitt and Jarvis Green."

"Never heard of them."

"They were invited originally, but turned down the chance because they didn't want to be anywhere near Tommy Triller— or near each other, either. Bailey is on early-morning network chat shows to talk about money, because she has a ton of it herself."

"And how about—what's his name again? Jarvis?"

"He invests—very well. Besides, he wrote one of those humongous books that everyone bought and read—*Men and Women from Alternate Universes*."

I said, "That's a ghastly title."

"It sold half a million copies, so it's not so ghastly."

"How long have they been divorced?"

"I'm not sure. Fesmire said they each had multiple affairs during the marriage, and because of their business, the divorce proceedings were as dirty as they get."

"Ouch."

"The real fun part? Neither Bailey nor Jarvis know the other one is coming."

"Now I want to see that Saturday night speech, too," I said.

An uncomfortable laugh. "You're not part of the convention anymore; they might not let you in."

"You can't pull some strings for me, and for K.O.?"

"I'm security for this hotel," Swati said, "and that's all. I have nothing to do with this convention. Anyway, Fesmire is mad at me, too."

"Why?"

"Because I hired you."

"I'm private security—not the Secret Service." I looked at my watch. "Will this divorced couple share a suite?"

"They each get a room, because we have no available suites left."

"Triller's suite is empty."

She shuddered. "Who'd want to stay in a room where a murder was committed after just two days? When this convention is over, I'll hire a shaman to burn some sage leaves and chase the bad juju out of there."

"Burning sage leaves? Is that an East Indian thing?"

"No, it came directly from Siddartha West." Swati frowned. "Maybe she killed Tommy Triller and hopes the shaman will destroy all the evidence."

"Burning sage leaves doesn't destroy DNA evidence," I said.

"Well—again, according to Fesmire—Jarvis and Bailey both *hated* Tommy Triller."

"They weren't here Thursday night, so I guess they aren't suspects—unless they hired somebody to ice him."

"They haven't done *anything* together since before their divorce."

"Well," I said, "keep them away from me. Not my job anymore, Swati."

Ten minutes later, Fesmire practically accosted me in the lobby, wanting to know the same thing.

"You're not supposed to be here! I told you to get out and stay out."

"We got hired by someone else—and here we are."

"Hired? By who?"

"Whom. I thought a speaker like you would at least know the rules of grammar."

"You can't be here!"

"This lobby is public space," I said. "You can't make us leave."

"I can have the police throw you out!"

"Be my guest," I said. "Detective Sergeant Blaine is heading this homicide investigation. Stick around and watch her throw me out personally."

He sputtered. Evidently he sputtered frequently. "You're not welcome at any convention events unless you pay to get in!"

"Maybe I'll be out of here more quickly," I said, "and clean up your problems if you give me a little help instead of being a relentless schmuck."

"That's rude."

I moved closer to him, forcing him to look up at me. Being tall helps—unless, of course, you were Tommy Triller. "You're a rude idiot! So either call a truce and be on my side—or get the hell out of my face."

He took at least half a minute to think it over, and I watched his expression as it changed from belligerent to fearful to thoughtful, as he realized I could either help him or make him look bad. At length he said, "What do you want from me?"

"The police investigation might take days. But you know the speakers well—the big shots—and they're the ones who interest me."

"Why?"

"They all had it in for Triller—and maybe one of them did something about it."

"They're assholes," Reeve Fesmire said, "not murderers."

"Siddartha West is an asshole? Tony Nardoianni is an asshole?"

"All of them are."

"Then why invite them to your convention?"

"All the attendees are paying *me* to see *them*. That doesn't mean I have to like them."

"You didn't like Triller either?"

Fesmire looked around to be certain no one overheard him. "I wrote him a check for a hundred grand—to show up and give the keynote talk tomorrow night." Scowling, "Not like he needed the money."

"You've invited Jarvis Green and Bailey DeWitt to take Triller's keynote speech place, haven't you? Are you paying them?"

He shrugged. "I had to, or they wouldn't have come. All the speakers are here to promote their businesses and their products. Jarvis and Bailey are afraid not to be here and be gossiped about."

"Did you tell each one that the other was coming, too?"

"God, no! They hate being in the same city together." Reeve's smile fell short. "The same universe."

"Isn't it asking for trouble to put two bitter exes together?"

Now his half-ass smile turned into one of those evil leers I remembered from wicked space aliens in old comic books. "I think," Fesmire said, "it's going to be fun."

CHAPTER SIXTEEN

K.O.

His back ached, his feet hurt, and he was dog-tired, as he had gotten very little sleep the night before. Driving home, his tie clawed away from his neck and the top two buttons of his dress shirt unengaged, K.O. sifted through the events of his day and decided that working to keep Tony Nardoianni clear and pristine was a waste of time. His name was hardly mentioned as one of the possible suspects in the Tommy Triller killing.

Then why was Victor Gaimari paying Milan good money to prove Tony's innocence—a man who was about as dangerous as SpongeBob SquarePants? A dork, certainly, but hardly a murderer. Yet, Triller had Major League Baseball ownership that might have put Nardoianni in a bad spot. As Tony's manager, Gaimari might be in a squeeze, too.

He guided his car into a parking space in front of the apartment he shared with Carli. The room at the Renaissance Hotel had been comfortable and clean—but this was home.

Anywhere was home to K.O. if Carli was there.

He didn't know why he was so in love with a young woman so different from him. Divergent backgrounds, contrasting levels of education, different families. Carli had two older brothers, both of whom lived more than a thousand miles from Cleveland, and parents who resided in Lake County, whereas K.O. was an only child, with a father he spoke to no more than once a year.

But Carli was his soul mate. Previously, whatever affection he felt for another human being lasted until the first argument, the first time sex became take it or leave it, the first time there were more important things in life. Carli, though, made him feel like a whole, complete man, his heart jumping into his throat every time he looked at her.

Inside the apartment, he knelt to pet his best cat friend, Rodney, who head-butted him with affection. K.O. had an affinity with animals, and when Rodney had entered his life, smoke-gray, slim, and loving, it grounded him after a long period of violence.

He picked Rodney up and buried his face in the animal's neck until both grew tired of it, then pulled off his jacket and tie, changed into a sweatshirt, and waited for Carli to get home from the public relations firm where she interned. For her, studying that particular art grew more difficult with each passing year, as people turned from newspapers and TV news to the more immediate social network connection, reporting every single thing that happened to every single person in the world. K.O. was into social media; Milan Jacovich, three decades older than he, rarely bothered with Facebook, and hadn't the foggiest idea of how to use Twitter—or why.

He was halfway through his first beer when he heard Carli's key in the lock.

"Hey," she said, surprised as he greeted her with a passionate kiss before the door was even closed.

"Missed you," he said. "How was your day?"

"Let me get my jacket off and I'll tell you." She hated being rushed, he knew. He wanted to keep kissing her—but she did things in their proper order. Taking off her jacket was one of them. She wore a dark blue blouse and gray knee-length skirt—and K.O. was profoundly affected by skirts. "I wouldn't say no to a beer," she said.

K.O. got her one from the refrigerator. "Here you go, babe," he said, recalling too late she didn't appreciate being called "babe." She slumped onto the sofa and put her legs up on the coffee table. "Long day."

"Me, too. It's good to be home."

"So," she said, "you're trying to catch a murderer?"

He shook his head. "Trying to keep one suspect's name respectable."

She upended the bottle and took a long pull. "That's a hell of a way to make a living."

"It's my business."

"Yes—but one of these days you might not come home."

"I would've been a cop if they'd let me," he said. "Then you'd *really* worry."

"Cops carry guns. You don't."

"Milan does."

"Why doesn't he let you?"

"He's not armed all the time," K.O. said. "Besides, if things go well, he'll buy me one himself when my probation is over."

Carli shook her head. "I wouldn't like you coming home with a loaded gun every night. But now, if someone pulls a gun on you, you'll be completely defenseless. That scares me."

"Not many homicidal maniacs running around the Renaissance Hotel."

She began scratching the label off the beer bottle. "*Somebody* had a gun there. You should find another profession."

"I like this profession."

"There are plenty of good careers, Kevin. You can learn whatever you want at Cuyahoga Community College, and make more money doing something else, like I do, and nobody's going to shoot you."

"You don't make any money at all, Carli. You're an intern."

"It's temporary." Carli sipped her beer. "Everything is temporary."

K.O. was stunned into silence. Finally he just said, "Wow. Temporary. Are you and I temporary, too?"

"We're cohabiting, Kevin, in case you haven't noticed."

"'Everything is temporary' sounds pretty temporary to me."

"Life is temporary. Either of us could get run over by a bus."

"Sure—or get carried off by a mountain lion and eaten."

"We've been together two years. Would I be living with you if I didn't love you?"

"I wonder if you love me as much as I love you."

Carli raised one eyebrow. "On a scale of one to ten?"

"That's a good way to measure it."

"Kevin, in every relationship, one person loves more than the other one—or in another way. That's how life works."

"You've lived a different life. Maybe you know more about love than I do."

"I live with you, I sleep with you, and I tell you nearly every day that I love you. What more do you want?"

"I don't know!" K.O. said. "I guess I'm insecure—about you, anyway. I'm not insecure about what I do, and I don't worry I'll be iced when I'm not expecting it. Right now I'm not trying to catch a killer; I'm protecting the reputation of an innocent man"

"Are you sure he's innocent?"

He shrugged. "In this day and age, the word *innocent* should be redefined. My guy is out of baseball—he's a public speaker. We were hired by his manager. Milan knows him a lot better than I do."

"Manager? What is he, like an agent for celebrities?"

K.O. reached down to stroke Rodney's neck. "Not—exactly."

Carli cocked one eyebrow. "Then what is he?"

"A stockbroker—or financial adviser."

"What's he got to do with baseball, then?"

His shoulders slumped and his sigh was loud and obvious. "Okay, then—he's also the Cleveland mob godfather."

Carli put down her bottle. "Holy crap," she said, shaking her head as if to get K.O.'s last comment to fall out. "You're working for murderers!"

"*I* was a murderer—in the army."

She shook her head vigorously. "That's not the kind of murder I'm talking about."

"Carli, the mob doesn't murder anymore. They have their rackets—and some aren't legal—but they haven't killed any innocent people for forty years. Those they did kill were also mob guys. They didn't kill dry cleaners or dog walkers or their next-door neighbors."

"A lot of next-door neighbors get killed!" she protested.

"Yes, but by crazy people with a cellar full of combat rifles who think their neighbors play music too loud—not by the mob. No gangster marched into Triller's bedroom and shot him in the head."

"Why would your new client give a damn about the baseball guy one way or the other?"

"He manages him. He wouldn't want people thinking Nardoianni actually killed some get-rich-quick superstar!" K.O. got up to fetch a second beer. "And because the baseball guy is Italian."

Carli stared at the dark television for a while. "I'm scared to death you're going to get killed."

"I only came close once, and that was in Iraq. Since we met, my only troubles have been four fistfights—and I won them all."

"You got hit in the face with a riding whip!"

K.O. kept his chin down to keep from grinning. "No scar, though."

"Maybe I have a scar from it," she said quietly, "where nobody can see it."

"Carli, I was an intern with Milan Security when you met me."

"I know—but I grew up watching re-runs of *Magnum, P.I.* and I thought it sounded romantic. Who knew I'd seriously fall for you—and worry whether you're going to come home in your own car or in a body bag?"

"I've been on nearly thirty cases since I started this job," K.O. said, "and twenty-six of them had nothing to do with violence or killing."

"It only takes one shot, Kevin."

"I move too fast; I'd make a lousy target."

"That makes me feel so much better!"

A soupçon of anger crept into her tone, and K.O. tried to calm it. "Honey, I love what I do. Being private, working with Milan, meeting all sorts of interesting people, learning new stuff every day, not having to put up with a lot of police rules that Milan ignores. And every day, he teaches me how not to be such an angry guy." He put his hand out and touched her cheek, but took it away quickly before she pulled her head back. He looked down at his shoes for a moment. "I figured you understood that from the get-go."

"I did. It bothers me. That's all." Frowning, she arose to go into the bedroom. He waited until he heard the shower running.

He turned on the TV—*Wheel of Fortune* time. He tried playing along, but wasn't very good at it, though he was even worse playing *Jeopardy!*, which came on next. He stroked Rodney lovingly, feeling the soft purr against his fingertips.

And he worried.

From the beginning, his feelings for Carli hadn't changed, but now he was uncertain whether hers had changed for him. If so, would he be forced to choose between the woman he loved or the career he loved?

He tried not to think about it.

Barefoot, she came out in a terrycloth robe, rubbing her short hair dry with another towel. She didn't look angry, exactly, but she wasn't looking at K.O., either.

"Shall I make dinner?" he said.

"I'm not hungry. I'll just snack on some fruit." She moved into the kitchen, removed a banana from the bunch of four on the counter, and peeled it.

Was this their first fight? Certainly not; no couple could ever stay together for two years and never argue. But, he wondered, was this a fight at all? Or was it something worse—trying to move an ocean liner past a huge iceberg they couldn't even see?

Not much was said until about nine-thirty; they'd watched several shows they didn't even like. Finally Carli said, "I think I'll turn in."

He watched her rise from her chair and make her way toward the bedroom. Then he said, "Do I sleep out here on the sofa tonight, or what?"

"You pay half the rent here, Kevin, so you're entitled to half the bed." She put her hand on the doorknob, then turned to him again. "*Your* half," she said, and disappeared into the bedroom.

K.O. stayed up until one a.m., unable to lose himself in any TV show. Finally he crawled into bed next to Carli. She lay on her side, facing away from him. She didn't move. Perhaps, he thought, she was sound asleep. At least he hoped so.

Gingerly he put his hand on her hip. She didn't move.

It didn't matter. The two of them stayed that way until the alarm jangled them both awake at six o'clock in the morning.

CHAPTER SEVENTEEN

MILAN

Saturday is a slow news day, so the Tommy Triller death was all over the *Plain Dealer* again. There's more about murder and crime on its pages every year than an entire section of mystery fiction at the public library. The newspaper frequently digs up the decades-old Sam Sheppard murder, the Danny Green automobile bombing, or the Kingsbury Run torso killings from the 1930s. I wondered how long they'd write about the death-by-gunshot of Tommy Triller.

It was shortly after seven in the morning. I sipped my first tea of the day and read one of the many columns on the subject while Tobe Blaine, dressed once again in her no-nonsense homicide detective clothes, made herself two cups of coffee. For much of my life I had been a coffee addict, but I recently switched to tea in the hope of getting a decent night's sleep once in a while.

"I thought you'd be reading the sports pages," Tobe said, coming from the kitchen with a steaming mug emblazoned "Dartmouth College." I have no idea why it's in my cupboard—I went to Kent State University—but Tobe likes it and uses it whenever she stays over.

Herbie was asleep at my feet, though he opened one eye to check her out as she emerged from the kitchen. "No sports news worth reading," I said. "Kent plays today and the Browns play tomorrow."

"Then you're looking for your own name in the Triller investigation."

"I didn't find mine—or yours, either."

"That's because I ducked reporters yesterday," she said. "They invaded McHargue's office for a quote instead."

"I read her quote—a polite way of saying 'mind your own business.'"

Tobe leaned against the back of the sofa, the butt of her Glock making a bump beneath her jacket. "You confuse me every day, Milan. That's why I keep you around."

I felt myself blushing. At my age, men don't often blush. "Did I confuse you this morning just after the alarm went off?"

"Sex isn't confusing," she said, primping her hair even though it didn't need it. "At least, not when you're doing it right."

"Am I doing it right?"

"You'll get your grade at the end of the semester."

"Let's discuss *your* grade, then," I said. "You poked around the hotel all day yesterday. Anyone you're calling a 'person of interest?'"

"I'm supposed to tell you, but you're not going to give me a scrap, huh?"

"I'm not looking for a killer, Tobe. I'm protecting a reputation."

"You'll have to clean up more than one, Milan. They all hated Triller—and sometimes for more than one reason. Now Triller's got a bullet between his eyes and one of his own CDs with his own name and picture on it shoved halfway down his throat, so they're all 'persons of interest.' Is this character whose reputation you're protecting a flannelmouth like the rest of the celebrities?"

I laughed. "Flannelmouth?"

"My father used to call people who wouldn't shut up flannelmouths."

"I'm going to have to write that down and use it."

"Before you write it down, answer my question. Or should I take a guess?"

"Can I stop you?"

Now she laughed, too. "Try to keep a straight face because I'll be watching you closely when I say—Tony Nardoianni?"

"Sonofabitch!" I unsuccessfully tried wiping the shock off my face. "What made you say that?"

"I've talked to most of the big-name speakers, and my people have talked to the others. I researched, too—my handy-dandy iPad—and discovered that Nardoianni, who had bad gambling problems while he worked in Major League Baseball, is managed as a public speaker—managed being the right word, I suppose—by Victor Gaimari of Cleveland. You and Victor have a history, so . . ."

"No wonder you earned your stripes," I said.

"Maybe—but everyone on the force knows about your connection to the local mob. When I started seeing you, McHargue called me in for a long chat." She lifted and then lowered her shoulders. "That was some chat, Milan."

"Amazing. You know everything."

"I know everything I want to know. Remember that, in case you do something bad that you want to keep secret." She walked back into the kitchen and poured herself a half cup more of coffee. Herbie trotted after her, tail wagging, and I heard her talk to him gently, followed by a crinkling of the bag holding his dry treats.

She came back out and sat next to me, dusting off her fingers. "Victor Gaimari is no old-time gangster like Al Capone or Lucky Luciano. These days, they're at least sixty-percent legit—and Gaimari's never been charged with anything more criminal than a parking ticket. It didn't take a genius to figure out who re-hired you after Fesmire canned your ass. Are you keeping Nardoianni's image pure and fresh, then? And is K.O. in on this Gaimari thing, too?"

Herbie came back, licking his chops as if he'd just eaten a porterhouse steak and not a dog treat, and settled down across Tobe's feet. I said, "K.O.'s into everything."

"The word is that both of you irritated everybody you've talked to. I knew K.O. was insulting, but I didn't think you were ever rude."

"Only with my clothes on," I said, squeezing her thigh above the knee.

She slapped my hand away. "No touching when I'm going to work." She swallowed the rest of her coffee and handed me the empty cup as she rose to leave. "Nothing against Gaimari, Milan."

She leaned down to scratch Herbie's neck. "But watch where you step today."

"I always watch where I step—especially after I've walked Herbie. I'll be downtown in half an hour. Shall we have lunch together?"

"No," Tobe said.

I parked across the street from the hotel. That open lot is only a few bucks cheaper than Renaissance's valet parking, but at least if I needed to get out of there in a hurry, I wouldn't have to wait fifteen minutes for somebody to look for my car.

Inside, there were fewer uniformed police officers than the day before, but still three times as many as usual. I looked around for Tobe but didn't see her. There was no answer in Tony Nardoianni's room. Fesmire was out of sight, either chewing out someone else's ass—he enjoyed that—or hiding someplace to avoid pressure. That was okay with me, naturally, as mutual dislike had begun within twenty seconds of our introduction and had never abated.

At the reservations desk, Bailey DeWitt was checking in—an attractive upper-middle-aged woman with bottle-blond platinum hair and a passionate green silk suit she obviously had worn on the plane, because the skirt was completely wrinkled. A few attendees wandering through the lobby seemed to recognize her from her appearances on early-morning news/talk shows, but most hadn't the vaguest idea who she was.

I was relieved I no longer worked for the Global Motivation Speakers Association; otherwise, I might have been ordered by Fesmire to tell the formerly married couple that they'd be sharing a podium later that evening.

My cell phone vibrated in my pocket. I stepped off to one side of the long corridor leading from the lobby to the parking garage.

"Where are you?" K.O. said. "I'm in the Avenue Food Court. Come down here and buy me a cuppa coffee, and I'll pass on some news you're not gonna like."

He was seated by a window when I got there. Over his shoulder, looking across the river, I could see the building I own, my office windows reflecting the autumn sun.

I sat down opposite K.O. "What'd you do this morning?" I said, nodding at the window. "Swim across?"

He pulled a smartphone from his pocket. At his age, everything he did was electronic. "I woke up early this morning," he said, "and put a call in to Jake Foote." Jake was a retired police officer in Lake County who'd arrested K.O. twelve years ago, then mentored and helped him when he got out of juvie and eventually came back home from the Middle East war.

"And how is Jake Foote?"

"He'll be touched that you inquired. I asked about our client."

"Victor Gaimari?"

He shook his head. "Everybody knows about Victor Gaimari. No, I asked him about Nardoianni."

"Jake Foote was a Lake County cop for thirty-five years," I said. "Nardoianni doesn't even know where Lake County *is*."

"Jake was, and is, a huge baseball fan, and he knows people you don't. He got in touch with a guy who used to play ball for Nardoianni in Denver. Not a big star or anything—just a utility infielder for about three-quarters of a season."

"Which season?"

"Tony's last one. I thought you were going to buy me coffee."

I fumbled in my pocket and put a five dollar bill on the table. "I'll buy it," I said, "but I'm damned if I'll run and get it for you."

He scooped up the bill and stood up. "Be right back."

"Bring the change!" I called after him.

I studied my own office building from this vantage point until K.O. returned with coffee. It was an old building, but the view from my second-floor office—and my paying it off so I didn't have to worry about a mortgage—made it very worthwhile.

K.O. took off the top of the cardboard coffee mug, and the steam rose into the air, then disappeared. "Nardoianni retired from baseball—but not really. He was eased out of his contract and out of the major leagues. Do you know how he got caught gambling?"

"Any time you do something outrageously dishonest," I said, "you get caught—one way or another."

K.O. checked his smartphone. "This came from top-level at the National League."

"So?"

"Want to know how the league found out?"

"Do I get three guesses?"

"No. The information came from one of the owners of another team."

"From the front office of the Pittsburgh Pirates?"

He nodded sagely. "Guess the minority owner, Milan."

"Son of a bitch!" I said, too loudly, as several people eating their breakfast at nearby tables turned and gave me dirty looks.

"I told you I had news you weren't going to like," K.O. said more quietly. "It was Triller who destroyed Nardoianni's baseball career—which is one hell of a good reason for Tony to show up at this convention."

"He's been out of baseball for almost a decade. Why wait so long?"

"Revenge is a dish best served cold."

"Where the hell did you read that? On the wall of a men's room?" I rubbed the back of my neck to soothe the tension.

"It zooms Nardoianni right up to Person of Interest Number One." K.O. slurped at his coffee.

I took a moment to get my thoughts together. "Will *you* tell Tobe about this?"

He almost blew the coffee out through his nose, choking off his laughter.

CHAPTER EIGHTEEN

K.O.

The small conference room on the second floor of the Renaissance Hotel was the same one in which Milan Security had first met Reeve Fesmire weeks earlier, but now it was reserved for the Cleveland Police Department, Homicide Division. Milan, Tobe and K.O. were sitting at one end of the table. No one had offered them snacks and coffee.

Tobe listened to K.O.'s report about Tony Nardoianni, and when he had finished, she said, "Not a bad motive, I admit—and I'll give Nardoianni a second look. But it doesn't make him my top suspect."

K.O. looked disappointed. "Why not?"

"The police searched the celebrity speakers' rooms for weapons and came up empty," Tobe said, "including Nardoianni. Nail files, scissors, tweezers, and everyone in this hotel owns more than one ballpoint pen—but Triller got a bullet in the head, and the gun that was used to shoot him is nowhere to be found."

"How about Kylee Graves?" K.O. asked.

"Who?" Tobe said.

"A young woman I met a few times—not a speaker. She came here to be close to Triller. They evidently had a one-night stand a while back. She kept trying to see him, talk to him, even phoning his room, but she didn't have any luck making contact with him. She believed he loved her—or at least he told her that."

"What's her name again?" Tobe said, flipping open her notebook.

"Kylee Graves. Beehive hairdo."

She found the name. "Yeah, here she is. Didn't I see you with her yesterday, K.O.?"

"Yeah—minutes before she asked me if I could ever love her." Sadly, "She's desperately looking for love—from just about anybody."

"She might have already left town," Tobe said.

"She's from Charlotte, where she and Triller had their one-nighter. Has anybody talked to the bodyguards who came here with Triller?"

"I think they just grunt," Milan said. "One of them thought seriously about ripping off my head just for wanting to talk with Triller."

"Think they'll rip off my head?" Tobe said.

"Wear your weapon outside your jacket," K.O. suggested, "and you won't have a worry in the world. Meantime, since Milan had a problem, maybe I should go talk to them, one at a time."

Tobe said, "K.O.—you can't float around interviewing suspects like you're a cop. You work for Victor Gaimari."

Milan asked carefully, "Tobe—are you mad because we're working for Victor?"

"I'm not mad. Work for him, cook him a dinner, iron his socks, scrub his back! I couldn't care less. But I'll do the talking to him. You stay out of my murder case."

"Nardoianni had baseball trouble with Triller in the past," Milan told her, "and one of those muscle boys might know something about that. You have to let us do our jobs."

"I'm not carrying," K.O. said. "And I'm not gonna make a citizen's arrest or anything. I just need a little slack, Tobe. Please?"

She shrugged. "It's not my ballgame."

"What happens if K.O. gets killed?" Milan said.

"My job is catching killers," Tobe said. "So that's different!"

When they emerged from the conference room, Tobe immediately spotted two of her detectives and herded them into a quiet corner to talk. Milan headed to Victor Gaimari's office to ask more questions, and K.O. went down to the lobby floor, thinking that anyone drinking too much at some benefit in the Grand Ballroom would have a hell of a time navigating those curving marble steps on the way home. Everyone in the lobby—mostly conference attendees who'd chosen not to show up for the unimportant talks being given this early in the day by obscure speakers—had gathered around what could most charitably be described as a screaming match near the reservations desk.

Jarvis Green, the recently arrived semi-celebrity who had been asked to be one of the speaker replacements at the Saturday night banquet, bellowed at the top of his voice to Reeve Fesmire, who was struck silent, looking less like the convention's organizer and more like an extra in a historically religious bible movie who'd forgotten to take off his wristwatch. Green was in his early sixties—smooth gray hair, a salon suntan, and wearing a sports jacket that probably cost more than most working people's weekly salary. Swati Sathe hovered close by, a clipboard and a thick file tucked under one arm, too wise to get involved in this conversation.

"You invited me here at the same time as Bailey DeWitt?" Jarvis roared. "You know goddamn well that miserable cunt and I are sworn enemies. How dare you? How fucking *dare* you?"

By the time Fesmire had pulled himself together enough to answer him, Jarvis Green came down on him again—hard. "And you're paying me *half* what you were paying Tommy Triller? On top of everything else, that's a fucking insult!"

Fesmire stammered, "I'm paying Bailey the other half."

"Jesus Christ! Jesus fucking Christ!"

Finally Swati approached. "Sir, I have to ask you to watch your language, please."

Green turned to look her up and down insultingly, finally zeroing in on her face. "Butt out of it!" he snapped. "Go back to some rice paddy where you belong!"

Swati's brown face paled, and her gasp was audible as she backed up uncertainly. But that was enough for K.O. He moved forward, placing himself between Swati and Jarvis Green. "You're done here, Sir. Calm down, go upstairs and unpack, and watch your language and your bigotry while you're in public."

Jarvis drew himself up to his full height—which was about the same as K.O.'s. "Who the fuck are you?"

"Someone who can twist your head around so hard that you'll be looking over your own shoulder for the rest of your life," K.O. said, with quiet menace. "Shall a bellman help with your luggage? Or would you prefer to discuss this further?"

Pale terror fought its way through Green's sunlamp tan. He turned away from K.O. and marched back up to the reservation desk.

A relieved Fesmire snarled to K.O., "You have no right talking to celebrity speakers like that!"

"To someone screaming 'cunt' in a hotel lobby full of middle-aged women, and telling an East Indian executive to go back to her rice paddy, I'll say whatever I goddamn please."

"You will cease and desist at once! You don't work for me anymore."

"You're right. I don't. That means I can twist your head around, too." K.O. leaned closer to Fesmire and said softly, "Don't fuck with me, Reeve. You won't like it."

Swati put her hand on his elbow. "Come on, Mr. O'Bannion— let's do a geographic," she said, pulling him away.

"What's a geographic?"

"Going someplace else besides where you are." She hustled him along the stretch of hallway heading to the restrooms and the escalator down to the garage. When they turned the corner, she said, "I appreciate your standing up for me. That might not be the most insulting thing anyone ever said to me, but it's in the top ten. Were you really going to turn his head around?"

"No. That would've killed him."

"Have you ever killed anyone?"

He hesitated, then nodded. "I never asked their names when I was in Iraq."

That made Swati take another step backwards. "I'm glad you're here anyway," she said finally. "We've never had a murder in this hotel, and the general manager is crawling down my throat about it. And *he* gets chewed out by the corporate big shots. Damn! It's downright dangerous being a hotel's head of security."

"Don't worry about this job, Swati," K.O. assured her. "There's always room for one more private eye."

"You're right—and I wouldn't irritate people as much as you.

As far as I'm concerned, you do whatever you want to until this killing is solved and our hotel gets off the front page. That includes getting in Reeve Fesmire's way if you have to."

"I wonder how Detective Sergeant Tobe Blaine will feel about it."

"That's your problem, I'm afraid."

"Actually," K.O. said, "it's Milan Jacovich's problem."

Hy Jinx wandered the lobby, wearing a mid-calf-length black leather trench coat that flapped around his legs when he walked. When K.O. hailed him, Hy said, "Damn! Glad to see you! I didn't think anyone was ever gonna talk to me. This place is like a country club for old white guys."

"Killing some time?"

Jinx held up a hand. "Don't even *say* killing around me today, or they're gonna throw me in a cage and toss away the key."

"Where you headed?"

Jinx shrugged. "Bored. I walked around the square out there the other night. Don't feel like doing it again."

"Seen the Avenue shopping mall?"

"Where's that?"

K.O. pointed to the stairway at one end of the lobby, where this morning a female police officer stood guard. "Down the stairs and turn right. Want to take a walk?"

It took them less than a minute to reach the second level of the sprawling shopping mall without having to go outside. Hy seemed most interested in looking over the balcony at the fountain, which sprayed different-colored water in the air in time with whatever music was playing.

K.O. said, "Are you sticking around for the main event tonight?"

"I got to. The po-po told me I couldn't leave town."

"Did they tell everyone at the convention the same thing?"

"Hard to tell two thousand people they gotta hang out in Cleveland and pay for another two-three days at the hotel. I think us celebrity folks have to stay here until they let us leave." He shook out the sides of his coat. "I better not run into that shitkicker governor."

"Jonah Clary? You and he have a problem?"

"Lemme explain something to you. There are a few words white folks aren't supposed to say. Him and me were talking to a group of people yesterday and he used the n-word—three times. And then he looked right in my face and said, 'No offense meant.' That motherfucker! There's *lots* of offense meant—and lots taken."

"I don't blame you. What did you say to him?'

Jinx grinned. "I called him a redneck ant-fuckin' hillbilly, and I walked away—'cause if I stayed there, I woulda bought him a one-way ticket to hell!"

"I hope you don't run into him again."

"That's why I'm takin' walks," Jinx said, "'causethere ain't much to do in Cleveland otherwise. Unless you got tickets for tomorrow's Browns game?"

"They're playing in Cincinnati," K.O. said. "Sorry."

"No biggie. I got no bet down on that game, anyway."

"You gamble?"

"I been known to lay a wager on occasion." Jinx turned and looked over his shoulder at a particularly attractive black woman going the other way, and made a quiet "Mmmm" sound in the back of his throat. K.O. didn't think she was much older than fifteen, though, so he said nothing about it.

"You bet on football?" he asked.

"Yeah—basketball, too."

"Ever bet on a baseball game?"

"Thirty teams play 162 games a year each? Who the hell could bet on that?"

K.O. said, "Tony Nardoianni was a baseball manager."

"I never even heard of him until yesterday—and he never heard of me, either."

"Did you know Tommy Triller was a minority owner of the Pittsburgh Pirates?"

Jinx whined, "I don't even know who's the vice president of the United States."

"You weren't pissed off at Triller, then?"

"I didn't have no reasons to . . . " Hy Jinx stopped walking, and turned furious eyes on K.O., his voice high and screeching. "You accusing me of killing Triller because I'm black? Or because when I was younger, I used to carry a gun?"

"Nobody accused you of anything. I just asked a question."

"Whaddya askin' questions for, anyway?"

"Because it's my job."

"Fuck you an' your job, motherfucker! I thought you was my friend!" He poked K.O. in the chest with a hard finger.

"Don't poke me, Hack. I don't like it."

"I'll do more than poke, you honky-ass motherfucker!" he said loudly so that everyone within twenty feet of him could hear it.

"Hack," he said quietly, "don't make yourself look bad."

Hy Jinx considered that, grinding his teeth, his eyes wide and brimming with rage. Eventually he spun on his heel and stomped back the way he he had come, open trench coat flying behind him like a cape, leaving K.O. embarrassed and feeling stupid. He hadn't meant to insult the guy, but he'd done so, anyway. He was now certain Jinx would never speak to him again.

Jinx blasted through the crowd of shoppers that parted for him like the Red Sea, heading for the hotel entrance. While everyone shot him the stink eye, few in the shopping crowd recognized him for who he was.

To hell with him, K.O. thought. He had the absolute worst trigger-quick temper—and his music sucked, anyway.

He found an empty table in the Food Court and sat down, his hands trembling. After a few moments of people-watching— Tower City was one of the best people-watching spots in all of Cleveland—K.O. saw Kylee Graves wander around the edge of the fountain, twisting a tissue in her hands. When she noticed him, she came right over.

"You're still here," he said, standing up and pulling out another chair for her. "I thought you'd have checked out by now."

Kylee shook her head. Her hair was longer, loose and more relaxed. She was also wearing slacks and a sweater, having ignored her small-town print dresses. "I wanted to," she said, "but the police told me I shouldn't leave town. I don't know who else they're keeping from leaving. Did you tell them I had a more— personal relationship with Tommy? It had to be you, because I never mentioned it to anyone else."

K.O. said, "You want a coffee?"

"I'm too upset to eat or drink anything." She folded her arms across her chest as though she were cold. "Tommy was no saint. I mean, he dumped me! He never even said he was going to, he just did! I hate him."

"Enough to kill him?"

Kylee's shoulders slumped. "I don't even know how to shoot a gun. Everyone in Charlotte owns one except me." She shivered, hugging herself. "I'm almost glad he's dead."

"Did you say that to the police?"

She looked stricken. "Not—in those words, exactly."

K.O. massaged his forehead. "No wonder you're a person of interest. Stay out of the police's way, okay? Don't hide—but don't put yourself out there where they can get to you. Don't answer their questions; tell them you need an attorney present."

She looked lost. "I don't have an attorney. I've never had one— not even in Charlotte. I never needed one." Her eyes got watery— she was moments away from crying. "Oh my God, what am I gonna *do?*"

A few minutes later, as K.O. was walking back to the hotel alone, he liberated his cell phone from his pocket and dialed Milan Jacovich's number.

"I'm in a meeting," Milan said. "What's up?"

"Milan," he said. "What's the phone number for your lawyer?"

CHAPTER NINETEEN

MILAN

W hat do you need a lawyer for?" I said into my cell phone as I sat across the desk from Victor Gaimari in his lavish offices in Terminal Tower.

"That nut job Kylee Graves," K.O. said. "She's just about destroyed herself with the cops about the Triller killing. She'll need a Cleveland lawyer to protect her."

"Did it ever cross your mind that she's guilty?"

"She's a weirdo, but I don't think she killed anyone—and now the police are looking at her, hard."

"Our job is Tony, not some chick you picked up in the lobby."

"I didn't pick up—"

"I'm sitting with the client right now," I said, looking at Victor, "and we can't take time away from him because of somebody else's problem. Kylee Whatsername is *not* our business."

"But if she didn't do it—"

"Find out who did. It'll help her and it'll help Tony Nardoianni."

"What if Nardoianni's really the killer?"

"Then," I said, "we're screwed."

As I returned my cell phone to my pocket, Victor Gaimari leaned forward, both elbows on his desk. "Do you need a lawyer, Milan?"

"I have one. K.O. is still young—he worries about everyone, even people he doesn't know. But he's pretty sure Tony didn't kill anybody."

Victor frowned, which was rare for him. Except for the now-gone mustache, he looked exactly the way he did a quarter-century ago when we first met. "I dislike people talking out of turn. That could get dangerous."

"Is that why you hired us, Victor? Because people might talk?"

He sighed and leaned back in his chair. "I assume what I say won't leave this room?"

"Not unless you confess to murder."

The frown turned into a look of annoyance, and he leveled one perfectly manicured index finger at me. "I've never killed anyone, and I never ordered a killing, either. My—family doesn't work that way."

"Then you have nothing to worry about," I said.

He swiveled his chair to stare out his eleventh-floor window at the expanse of Lake Erie a few blocks north. It was a gray-water, gray-sky autumn day to which Cleveland had grown accustomed. "All right, then," he said, and turned back around. "Triller blew the whistle on Tony's gambling and got him kicked out of baseball, right?"

"That was a decade ago."

Victor nodded. "Do you know that when Tony started giving talks around the country—when I took over his career—Triller was going to go public with it? Give the story to all the TV news departments and the major newspapers, and totally destroy whatever vocation Tony had left?"

"Why would he? Tony was no threat to him to become America's most popular success guru. Why would Triller want to hurt him further?"

"Publicity."

"Triller got more publicity than anyone except Donald Trump."

"Yes and no. He got publicity because he was a superstar in this particular venue, but, frankly, most people who don't go to these speaker conventions or spend their lives in front of cable TV trying to learn how to get rich don't know Tommy Triller from the man in the moon. Telling the world what a bum Tony is, how he cheated on Major League Baseball, would have made more people aware of Triller and probably got them in line to spend their money on him. As I said: publicity."

"His hundred million dollars a year wasn't enough?"

Victor raised an eyebrow at me. "To the rich, there's no such thing as 'enough.'"

"Why didn't Triller go balls-to-the-wall with this particularly embarrassing news?"

"Because," Victor Gaimari said, "I sat him down and—had a little talk with him."

I wondered if Victor had invited several "family members" to that conversation—all carrying Louisville Sluggers. I said, "Did he know you were Nardoianni's manager?"

"Sure. That's how I got the appointment with him in the first place."

"But he didn't know who else you were."

"He knew I was a financial planner."

"He was no dummy, Victor. Didn't he know . . . "

"About my Cleveland business? Not until I told him."

"You *told* him?"

"Personally, Milan. Not over the phone."

I sat back in my own chair. "That must have been some little talk!"

"I didn't threaten Triller in any way. I didn't have to. I never threaten, as you know." Victor hiked up one shoulder. "It was a short meeting. I got what I wanted—and it didn't cost Triller a nickel."

"So you hired us to make sure none of this stuff got out about *you*."

"Yes."

"You could have hired one of your friends to do it."

He cocked his head, almost like a sparrow listening for the whirring wings of a hawk. "You're my friend, Milan."

"Are we friends?"

Victor took too long of a contemplative pause. Finally: "Yes." He cleared his throat. "Sort of."

I returned to the hotel and found my way upstairs to a small suite Tommy Triller had reserved, and knocked gently on the door. It was opened by one of the three huge men who'd arrived here as assistants or bodyguards to Triller. Now that he was gone, they were lounging around, bored, watching a college football game on TV.

The door opener, wearing one of those sleeveless T-shirts showing off biceps as thick as an obese man's thighs, seemed annoyed and sullen at the interruption, but I think he was secretly excited to have *anyone* show up at their room. Even me.

"Are you a cop?" he asked.

"Security," I said—not exactly a lie. "Mind if I come in?"

I wondered, now that his boss was dead, whether he even had a job anymore. "Suit yourself," he shrugged, standing aside. The other two men unwound themselves from the sofa, skirting around the coffee table containing bowls of chips, popcorn, and several beer bottles. One of them, the one who'd almost thrown me out physically the day they arrived—the one I'd secretly christened Godzilla—walked toward me. His muscles arrived ten seconds sooner than the rest of him.

"I remember you," he growled. "Mr. Triller didn't like you much."

The third guy, the Incredible Hulk—I even imagined his skin looked green—said, "Triller didn't like anybody."

"I thought he was a kind, caring, helpful kind of guy."

"If you cough up seven grand or so every couple of weeks and put it in an outstretched hand, anybody's going to seem kind and helpful," the Door Man said, running a hand over his shaved head. "But Triller—if you didn't give him money or buy his books, well . . . "

The Hulk said, "He gave advice to anybody who paid him. If you didn't pay him, he wouldn't piss on you if you were on fire." He shook his huge head. "You can get advice from your next door neighbor, your barber—your *mother*, for chrisakes!"

"He didn't give you guys advice, too?" I asked.

Door Man said, "He paid us to work for him—bodyguards, luggage haulers, limo drivers, packers and unpackers—and one of us had to cook his breakfast and lunch when he wasn't on the road. He wouldn't give us advice unless we paid back our salaries."

"Will you still get salaries now that he's gone?"

The Hulk said, "We have year-to-year contracts with the—whaddya call it again?"

"The Triller Foundation," Godzilla said. "One of three different—uh—foundations he owned. But you think they'll honor our
contracts now? By the time we took them to court and paid our
lawyers, there'd be no money left, anyway."

"So this is Saturday, gentlemen," I said, "and Mr. Triller died on
Thursday night. Why are you still here?"

Hulk said, "Because the cops told us not to leave town until
they said so."

"Do you know the people coming here to replace him tonight?
Jarvis Green and Bailey DeWitt?"

"Never had the pleasure," Door Man said.

The Hulk added, "They've never come to one of these conventions or meetings if Triller was there, too. From what I hear, they
hated his guts."

"Where'd you hear that from?"

"The man himself. Being godalmighty rich, he made lots of
enemies."

"So anyone at this con could've hated him enough to do something about it."

"Makes sense to me."

"Hey," I said, "as long as I'm here anyway, would it be okay if I
snagged a beer and got off my feet for a while?"

Godzilla became suspicious. "I thought cops weren't supposed
to drink on duty."

"It's okay—I'm in civilian clothes."

The Hulk dug a beer out of the refrigerator and tossed it to me.
It wasn't my favorite brand of beer—Stroh's—but beggars can't be
choosers. "Now that you're at loose ends, what kind of jobs will
you look for?"

Door Man said "The same thing as before, hopefully with some
gorgeous Hollywood chick who makes a gazillion bucks a picture
and spends it like there's no tomorrow."

"Right," Hulk laughed.

Godzilla didn't chuckle with the other two. He was obviously
out of sorts by how his life had rapidly changed. Instead, he
snarled, "There's one part of this job with Triller I sure hated and
will never do again."

"What's that?"

"Pimping."

"Pimping?"

Godzilla patiently said, "Everyplace we'd go, Triller would pick out some chick in the audience or group—he didn't give a damn if they were married, single, or over eighteen. Then he'd make one of us go find her, get her name, and invite her to a private—*meeting* with him."

Door Man said, "None of us were sure, but I bet he had the drinks doped so they probably didn't even know whether he was fucking them or not. He did drugs himself. I couldn't count the different bottles he carried around with him all the time."

"You cops already collected all his drugs from the bathroom in there," Godzilla said. "I bet you already found the roofies."

"Rohypnol?" I said.

"Date-rape drug—what they call Easy-Lay. But my name's on some of the labels. The other guys, too. He had his personal doctor write prescriptions for all three of us so his name wouldn't be on any of them. We had to run out to get them refilled for him."

"Triller was covering his ass. If anything bad went down," I said, "you guys would swing—because it was your prescription."

Rubbing his fisted knuckles with the other hand, Godzilla's rage simmered. "It doesn't sound as if you liked Triller any better than he liked you," I pointed out.

Godzilla took a few steps closer to me and inhaled deeply. I waited for the blast of fire. Instead he said, "Are you accusing us of killing him?"

The Hulk added, "Accusing all three of us?"

"No, just trying to understand the playing field. Did Triller get along with Tony Nardoianni? They were both in the baseball business."

The Door Man said, "None of us were around back then. How would we know?"

Godzilla said, "Yeah—but I've heard stuff."

"What stuff?"

"Nardoianni bet on baseball, and Triller was the one who blew the whistle on him. Everybody kept it hush-hush so's not to make the game look bad." Godzilla lowered his voice to a half-whisper. "A few years ago, when Nardoianni got into this speech racket,

Triller threatened that if the two ever wound up at the same event or convention, he'd make the baseball gambling thing public."

"Why would he do that?" I asked.

"Ego," Godzilla said. "I've worked for movie stars and politicians. Ego is part of their DNA. But nobody had an ego as big as Triller's."

"Why did Nardoianni show up here? He was taking a risk."

"A risk? Maybe." Godzilla moved to the coffee table and grabbed a huge handful of potato chips and began shoveling them into his mouth, then drinking half a bottle of beer to clear his throat. "Or maybe he came here to shut Triller up once and for all."

I didn't hang around much longer. Now I had a much stronger reason to suspect the man I was being paid to save from humiliation. Maybe Victor Gaimari wasn't as innocent as he proclaimed.

As the elevator brought me down from the twelfth floor, I thought again of Triller's muscle-bound dogsbodies—Hulk, Door Man, and Godzilla—and realized I had no clue as to what their real names were.

CHAPTER TWENTY

K.O.

ailey DeWitt was at the lobby windows, looking out on Public Square. K.O. had never seen her as an irregular regular on one of the network morning talk shows. Better known than her former author-husband, Bailey was gawked at by some conventioneers, though nobody approached her for a conversation or an autograph. She wasn't all that comfortable with people she didn't know.

At the moment, she didn't look happy. "I almost turned around and walked out again," she told K.O. after he'd introduced himself to her as "Security."

"Why?"

"My ex-husband and I are incapable of saying hello to the other without going for the jugular. It was not an amicable divorce."

"I don't know that much about it," K.O. said, "but this convention needs you—or they wouldn't have asked you to come on such short notice."

"If I just went home now, without selling a single one of my books or signing up anyone to be members of my programs, I'd get zilch. So here I am." Bailey rubbed her forehead. "Is Jarvis on the same floor as me? I break my ass making sure I never run into him. Nobody told me we'd share the podium tonight. That was a shitty thing for Fesmire to do—but then he's famous for doing shitty things."

"Like what, Ms. DeWitt?"

"Like screwing me over to make money. Conventioneers paid to get in to hear Tommy Triller say something fatuous and stupid—like he always did. When he got killed, Fesmire went into a panic that attendees would demand a refund—which comes right out of his tender pink ass. So he called both Jarvis and me to pick up the slack, hoping against hope he wouldn't wind up with a half-empty convention and an empty pocket, too. He didn't give a damn Jarvis and I absolutely despise each other."

"Jarvis wouldn't knock on your door in the middle of the night, would he?"

Bailey sneered. "He's more likely to come knocking on *your* door. Jarvis is the Queen Bee. You didn't know that? I was already on television and bringing in lots of business, and he needed to ride on my coattails. It took me only about three months to figure out he liked twinks more than he liked me. How the hell did I know I'd be sharing a marriage bed with a chicken hawk? One of *many* reasons we're not married anymore."

"Thanks for telling me," K.O. said.

"And then there are those incredibly crappy books he writes about the differences between men and women. If you don't realize women are different than men, just by looking at them, his books won't help you because I don't think *he* knows the difference, either." A big, weary sigh. "I'll have to see him tonight, damn it. But I warned Fesmire that I'd be the last talker—the big closer—or I'd walk out of here in a shot!" Her smile was wry. "When you're willing to fly halfway across the country to save somebody's ass, it gives you a certain amount of clout."

Clout, K.O. thought. Making money, manipulating others, gathering power like senators on Capitol Hill—that's what kept the self-help actualization movement pressing inexorably forward, like a shark. The formerly married Bailey and Jarvis were both as Machiavellian and devious as all the other convention speakers. They held themselves out as unselfish advisors to the masses, but needed to be coddled and kowtowed-to before they'd even nod to a stranger.

Maybe Carli was on to something, after all. K.O. was certain he wouldn't be shot to death doing the jobs that private investigation seemed to toss his way, but so many truly bizarre weirdos crossed his path on a day-to-day basis, they might just drive him past the outer edges of sanity.

And of course the biggest scoundrel of them all was Tommy Triller, whose monumental ego, stupendous bank accounts, and the bullshit that came with it had earned him a bullet in the forehead.

Walking upstairs to the mezzanine floor, K.O. saw the one VIP speaker he'd somehow missed. Dr. Ben Mayo had practically pinned Reeve Fesmire against the side of a pillar and was poking him in the chest, his voice rising to a roar.

"Bad enough," he said, "you brought me here to give my talk, not telling me you were giving that arrogant *cunt* the closing spot! But now that Triller's dead—and you won't see me weeping and wailing—you're putting that faggot and his bitch wife on in Triller's place and leaving me in the fucking *dust!*"

"Calm down, Ben," Fesmire was saying, wincing at each chest poke and making soothing gestures with his hands like a symphony conductor urging his orchestra to play more softly. "If they hadn't come at the last minute, half the people here would have demanded a refund and gone home. Then you'd have made no money at all. And Ben—lower your voice. Everyone's looking at you."

Everyone in the immediate vicinity was indeed watching, mostly with displeasure, two grown men in what seemed from a distance like a gay marital spat. Dr. Ben was fortunate that most convention-goers were at one or another of the events currently going on, thereby missing his ghastly public tantrum.

Caroline Mayo stood ten feet away from the two men, pretending she wasn't paying attention to them. She looked hot, though—K.O. considered her one of those MILFs from the Internet—wearing butt-hugging gray slacks and a long-sleeved shirt of emerald green silk that reflected in her blue eyes and made them seem greenish, too.

K.O. approached her. "Excuse me, Mrs. Mayo, I'm K.O. O'Bannion—security. Are you all right?"

She was momentarily surprised, but too disconcerted by what was happening with her husband just a few feet away that she didn't think to ask K.O. for official I.D. She said, "No, I'm not all right. But there's not a damn thing I can do about it. He—does what he does." She forced a humorless chuckle. "When you get to be a celebrity, the rules for everybody else don't apply to you."

"He *is* loud, isn't he?"

"All the big shots are loud. That's how they get to be big shots in the first place." She turned away from K.O. for a moment to observe her husband. "Compared to usual, he's being pretty polite today."

"Maybe Dr. Ben is upset at what happened to Mr. Triller."

Caroline didn't answer—but her lips almost disappeared, and K.O. saw the muscles in her jaw jump.

"I suppose you met Tommy Triller."

"Oh, yes," Caroline Mayo almost whispered. "Yes, I've met him."

"Did he have enemies you knew about?"

"Everybody has enemies." Caroline stood rigid. "That's the way life works."

"Do you know of any problems between Mr. Triller and, say, Tony Nardoianni."

"Who?"

"He's one of the speakers today," K.O. said. "He used to be a baseball manager. He tried to convince your husband to book him on his show."

"Everyone who won twenty bucks on a lottery scratch-off ticket wants to be on *The Doctor Ben Show*, but he only accepts celebrities—or ordinary people all fucked up in some situation that the tabloids will love. Sex is a big reality TV topic, followed by drug abuse, impossibly difficult children, and married couples being torn apart by their in-laws. So this baseball guy—whatever his last name is—was probably as mad at Tommy Triller as the rest of the people who didn't get on."

K.O. said, "Does Dr. Ben have bodyguards like Tommy Triller did?"

"Several in Los Angeles, but here—just one," she said. "Ben hired him when we were in Columbus earlier in the week. He played football for Ohio State before he flunked out of college. He won't go back to L.A. with us. He's just temporary."

"Isn't there another woman in your party, too?"

"Oh, that's Claire Crane—one of the producers of Ben's TV show."

"One of the producers? There are more?"

What she did with one short breath might or might not have been a come-on. "I lost count. In old TV days, they'd have one producer per show. Now—I don't know what half the producers *do*. Maybe call Claire. She's been with the show since the beginning."

"She came with you from California, but you hired the bodyguard in Columbus?"

Caroline nodded. "I'm not even sure of his last name, but Ben calls him Paddy."

"Paddy as in Patrick?"

"He's got muscles, that's all I know. We rented a limo in Columbus and he drove us here Thursday. I suppose he'll take us to the airport and then drive the limo back to where we got it."

Dr. Ben had apparently finished with Reeve Fesmire, who was now sneaking quietly away, and he almost charged over to his wife.

"Get packed!" he ordered Caroline. "We're out of here!"

His wife looked frightened. "We can't leave, Ben—the police won't let us. Besides, you have a talk to give tonight. If you don't, nobody will buy your books and CDs and courses."

"I don't need the goddamn money!" Ben thundered. "I make more money in a week than Fesmire does in a decade! Fuck him!" He turned and looked at K.O., his lower jaw pushed forward like a football coach's. "Are you bothering my wife?"

"I'm O'Bannion, Dr. Ben. Security."

"Take a hike, O'Bannion. We're going—and we don't need any more security."

"Didn't the Cleveland police say you couldn't leave town?"

Mayo's eyes turned furious, like two armed rocket launchers. "I do what I goddamn please, *when* I goddamn please."

"The police won't look at that the same way."

"Then they can kiss my ass."

"They won't let you get on a plane if they told you not to leave. As for them kissing your ass—bad idea. They're tough cops—even when a big shot like you disobeys an order."

Ben's eyes narrowed into slits. "I don't like that expression, 'big shot.'"

"Excuse me, then," K.O. said. "I'm looking forward to your talk tonight so you can solve all my problems in one hour—just like you do on your television show."

"You little shit, you think you're so smart. Don't come to my talk because I don't want you there—I don't want to look at your goddamn face!"

Caroline moved quietly to her husband's side. "Come on, Ben, let's go."

"You're not much of a psychologist," K.O. said, "making wise pronouncements when you haven't got a clue what you're talking about."

"I resent that!"

"You don't know what resentment is!" Something inside K.O. had burned for a few days now—maybe it was Carli nagging him to quit the business, and maybe something else, but whatever was simmering suddenly boiled over. "When you were fifteen, did they lock you up because your next-door neighbors cooked a dog alive in their backyard Weber kettle and it upset you? Did you have to fight every goddamn day to keep from getting gang-raped? Did a best friend ever die in your arms while you were sitting in a burning truck—or the top half of him, anyway, because the rest of him was several feet away? Don't give me your warmed-over bullshit, because, as big as you are, I can take you. I've been doing it every day of my life."

K.O. turned to Caroline. "Don't leave Cleveland without an okay from the police," he said. Leaving the Mayos with a shocked look on their faces, K.O. stormed off feeling marginally better for letting loose on that self-righteous prick.

Waiting for the elevator in the lobby, K.O. saw out of the corner of his eye Dr. and Mrs. Mayo arguing as they headed for the stairway and the entrance to Tower City, probably for lunch. That gave him another idea.

Claire Crane answered K.O.'s knock. In her mid-thirties, with dirty-blond hair, an elongated jaw, and carrying a stack of papers in her hand, she looked frazzled and frumpy. The dark circles beneath her eyes, K.O. thought, were permanent, and she moved as if she might have a backache.

"Dr. Ben isn't here," she explained wearily.

"I was hoping to speak to you."

"Me?" She brushed a hank of hair from her brownish eyes. "Why?"

"Security," K.O. said. "Can I sit down?"

"Sitting down?" she said dreamily. "For me, that's a fantasy."

"I'll only stay a few minutes." He held out a chair at the desk in her room, and she melted into it. He sat on the edge of the bed. "How long have you worked for Mayo?"

"Since his show went on the air. Eleven years ago? Who keeps count?"

"Easy to work with?"

She laughed without amusement. "Do I look like I have an easy job?"

"Long hours, huh?"

"Long *weeks*!" Putting both elbows on her thighs, she let her chin drop to her chest. "It's a good thing we don't tape shows in the summer, or I'd never get laid again."

"So you were in Columbus this week?"

She nodded. "He gave a speech at a big-deal chamber of commerce event down there, which worked out nicely because we were due in Cleveland two days later."

"You drove up?"

She nodded. "Rented a limo and hired a driver—less hassle and a lot cheaper than first class airline tickets for three."

"Where did your boss hire the driver? I understand his name is Paddy?"

"Not sure. He introduced himself as Patrick Owens."

"Tell me about him," K.O. urged.

"Like a third-string football player at Ohio State," Claire said, "before he dropped out of college—or they expelled him. I'm not sure which."

"He didn't mention it?"

"He didn't mention anything. He keeps to himself. What are you writing in that notebook?"

"His full name," K.O. said, scribbling quickly. "The police like to know who they're talking to."

"They already talked to him," Claire said. "They talked to me, too."

K.O. attempted a smile. "Did they ask if you killed Tommy Triller?"

"Sure they did—but I've never even held a gun in my life, much less fired one."

"What about Paddy? Has he ever fired a gun?"

"How would I know? I met him three days ago, and I doubt he's ever heard of Tommy Triller." She pushed more hair out of her eyes. "He'd barely heard of Dr. Ben!"

"Where is he now?"

"He doesn't check in with me," she snapped. "I'm on the phone twelve hours a day, setting up guests for the shows we'll tape a week from now. We're supposed to fly out of Cleveland tomorrow, but we don't know if we can because of your local cops. In Columbus, I never stuck my nose out the door of the hotel, just like here. Neither did either of the Mayos. I've been doing this backbreaking job for a decade, and I'm sick of it. Now I'm in the middle of a murder investigation?" She rolled her eyes toward the ceiling. "Give me a fucking break, okay?"

K.O. did give her a break—he left. Something buzzed in his head, though. He went downstairs, looking for a man he hadn't noticed before—Paddy Owens.

CHAPTER TWENTY-ONE

MILAN

The Food Court crowd in The Avenue had thinned out after the lunch crush, leaving coffee-drinkers, loafers, and homeless people not wanting to be bothered while they simply hung out in chairs—and Tobe Blaine and me. We'd hardly spoken since Tobe had taken over the Triller investigation. Now, sitting by the window and scrutinizing the boat traffic on the Cuyahoga River, I could see that she appeared exhausted. Jumpy, she bestowed hard, inquiring looks on everyone who came anywhere near her and then relaxed momentarily until the next stranger wandered by. She picked at a salad she'd bought from a nearby vendor, and I sipped a cup of tea.

"Tobe," I said, "you're running yourself into the ground."

"My four detectives only have to interview two thousand people who were in or around the hotel Friday night. Just try keeping all of them from leaving town!" She speared a piece of green pepper. "This is a bad dream—it's worse that I'm awake!"

"The other guest speakers hated Triller, but most convention attendees loved the hell out of him, lining up to spend money on his crap in the vendors' room. So maybe you should zero in on the speakers."

She nodded. "I'd still love to know what you're doing here, Milan, and what Gaimari wants from you. Did Nardoianni pull the trigger and Gaimari wants you to save his ass?"

"I'm not working for a killer, if that's what worries you."

"As far as you know." She pushed her salad away. "I have to get back to work."

"Wait until your blood pressure drops a little bit."

"I can imagine McHargue's blood pressure when she thinks about you putzing around in a homicide case."

"Not putzing around. If I found out anything, you'd be the first one to know."

She looked serious. "Don't get in our way, Milan, or she'll hang your license on her wall and throw darts at it."

"What I was hired to do," I said, "is wrapped up anyway—or I hope it is."

"Then you won't be back here tomorrow?"

"No guarantee. I'll stick around until my employer tells me I'm no longer needed."

"Or until I arrest you for hampering an investigation."

"Then I want to talk to my lawyer."

"I've already talked to your lawyer! We had dinner at his home about six weeks ago, remember? His wife couldn't cook worth a damn." She stood up and gathered her food dishes on a tray. "I'll be here through all the speeches tonight," she said.

"Me, too. Let's get together afterwards for a cocktail someplace."

"A cocktail?" Tobe said. "In the past two nights I've had three and a half hours sleep. I've been on my feet since seven this morning, and I've got eight hours left before I can close my eyes. And you want us to have a cocktail?" She started walking away, toward the fountain. "Get real, lover boy."

Lover boy. Holy crap!

She'd called me "lover boy" about a year ago, in front of a suburban deputy sheriff when I was on a case and she, with only Cleveland authority, was getting in *my* way. It bothered me more than she thought it would. She'd used the expression a few times since—whenever I'm close to pissing her off.

I finished my tea, watching her stride away. One wouldn't know by looking at her that she's a cop—I saw a youngish middle-aged woman with self-confidence to spare.

I considered going back up to the hotel, but the approaching figure of K.O. O'Bannion changed my mind. I stood up and waved until he saw me and headed over.

"Late lunch?" I said.

"No." He slid into the chair Tobe had recently vacated, leaned back, and stretched his legs out under the table. "You got your little recorder with you?"

I took it out of my shirt pocket and showed it to him. Then he said, "Kick it on, and I'll tell you all about my morning."

He filled ten minutes of recording space explaining conversations with Bailey DeWitt, Jarvis Green, the Mayo family, Hy Jinx, Claire Crane, and even Swati Sathe.

When finished, he said, "Claire told me about the Columbus bodyguard Mayo hired. His name is Patrick Owens—Mayo calls him Paddy. I'll try and find this guy and talk to him. Claire said he played football for the Buckeyes until they kicked him out of school."

"Kicked him out for what?"

"I'll ask him when I see him."

"Wait," I said. "I saw him when the Mayos were arriving—and he wouldn't let me near them. Football player going to seed pretty fast, was my take. He's approximately the size of a full-grown rhino."

"Okay, then—I'll ask nicely."

I mulled this over. "Let me have this one. He's about your age—and twice your size. Young guys swing first and ask questions later. I'm probably too old for him to hit."

"Probably," K.O. said, "is the operative word. In the meantime—why are we trying to make Tony look like St. Francis of Assisi?"

"Because," I said, "we're getting paid to do so. All we need is to collect nice things other people say about him so the police . . . "

"So *Tobe* . . . "

" . . . so *the police* don't look at him as Suspect Number One." I leaned forward and lowered my voice. "I don't work for Tobe."

"What happens if we find out Tony did kill Triller?"

"We turn him over to the police."

"Won't that get Gaimari mad at us?"

"Probably," I said. "So we return the money he's paying us."

K.O. laughed. "Then I'm going to bust my ass to prove someone else pulled that trigger—because I'd hate to work this job for nothing."

"Good enough. Meantime, I'll try to find this Paddy character."

"It might take ten minutes just to walk around him. Don't let him scare you."

"Not to worry. Only my age scares me, K.O.," I said, hauling myself from my seat. "Everything else that's bad is just a pain in the ass."

I went up one level to get back into the hotel. When younger, I always took the stairs. Today I chose the escalator. Maybe what I told K.O. was right—my age does scare me. Even the steep stairway to my own apartment leaves me out of breath sometimes.

Swati Sathe was at her desk behind a small mountain of papers, talking on the phone. Behind her on a file cabinet was a framed picture of her with a man I assumed was her husband, both holding glasses of champagne at Giovanni's, one of Cleveland's most elegant restaurants. She waved at me to sit down until she finished the conversation.

Finally she hung up, rubbing her forehead. "Life was simpler in India."

"Having your celebrity guest of honor blown away isn't just another day."

"I know. More than half the convention attendees want to go home—but Reeve Fesmire won't give them a refund. Besides, when they make a three-day hotel reservation with us in advance, they have to pay for three days whether they stay or go. I guess they'll hang around at least until tomorrow." Swati waved at the stack of paper. "It'll take me until Thanksgiving to get through all this paperwork." She frowned. "Are you here to give me more grief?"

"Just a question. I'm looking for someone who came with the Ben Mayo party, Patrick Owens. I was hoping you'd tell me what room he's in."

Swati made an angry sound. "I suppose you want this information ASAP?"

"It'd help."

"The Mayos are in a large suite, and they rented two more

rooms on the fifth floor across the hall from each other—all under the Ben Mayo name."

"Darn," I said. "I was hoping this would be easy."

"Dream on," she said, moving away.

On the elevator, I found myself face-to-face with Reeve Fesmire.

There are many people in this world that I don't like. As far as I knew, Reeve Fesmire had committed no crime. However, he's a greedy, money-grubbing, arrogant, unpleasant creep, and when I saw him, the skin prickled on the backs of my hands.

"I thought I threw you out of here two days ago," he snapped. "Why are you and your juvenile delinquent still hanging around?"

"You're not nearly big enough to throw me out," I said. "In fact I have another job and I can go anyplace I choose. And if K.O. O'Bannion hears you call him a juvenile delinquent, he'll probably remove one of your kidneys with his knuckles." I punched the floor button marked "5."

"Where do you think you're going on the fifth floor?"

"I'm thinking about jumping out a window—but from any higher than five, I'd hurt myself."

He came closer to me than I wanted, and stuck his finger in my face. "Fuck up this convention for me any further, and I'll sue your ass off."

I slapped his hand away—hard. "You'll have a reason to sue me—for breaking off your finger and making you eat it."

Stunned, he backed against the wall of the elevator and stayed there, white lines encircling his lips, until I got off.

It was a hefty walk getting from the elevator to Rooms 524 and 525, far away from the deluxe suites. I stood in the hallway between them. Behind which door was Patrick Owens?

I'd seen Claire Crane, clutching a clipboard and an iPad, coming up the winding staircase with Ben and Caroline Mayo, but I hadn't known her name then, nor who she was. When she opened her door, I saw that her makeup had faded, and her hair needed a good combing-out and a shampoo. A lank of it kept falling into her eyes.

I introduced myself as security—both K.O. and I were becoming adept at that particular falsehood—and asked if I could have a few minutes of her time.

"I already talked to the police," she said, "and a different security guy this morning. I don't know how else I can help you."

"Just a few minutes?"

She sighed. Her room was smaller than the bedroom in my own apartment in Cleveland Heights at the top of Cedar Hill. "I'm stressed. I've never been anywhere near a murder before, and I'm sick of talking about it."

"We're all sick of it—but we want to figure out who did it."

Put-upon, she leaned back on her elbows, half-sitting and half-lying on the bed. "Yeah, yeah, I know. Did I kill Tommy Triller? I wish I had an alibi—like some gorgeous hunk was in here banging my brains out when it happened. Triller was an arrogant shit, but if that's the only reason for a murder, everyone else would be dead, too."

"Including your boss?"

"Dr. Ben? He might be the world champion arrogant shit."

"Why do you stay, then?"

"Where else," Claire said, "could I make a hundred seventy-five K a year?"

"Wow."

She nodded. "When you get a TV producing job like this, you're lucky to last for two seasons. Yet here I am, a decade later. I could retire for the rest of my life without getting off my ass. But doing this show, meeting different people every week, year after year—it can be exciting."

"Really?"

"For that kind of paycheck, you put up with Ben's crap." She took a deep breath. "And Caroline's."

"Caroline is a problem?"

"The Queen of Flakes. She expects to be treated like a goddess—and she doesn't *do* anything except show up, sit in the audience, smile, and wave. She thinks she's the white Oprah." Her rogue hank of hair descended over her eyes again. "After eleven years, I still have to call her *Mrs. Mayo.* Do you believe that?"

"If you say so."

"Back in L.A., there are three other producers on the show, and six associate producers. On the road, it's just me. I make sure they're comfortable, treated right, make their flights on time, and

I still have to call all over the country trying to book guests for the next month."

"Have most of the other big-name speakers this week been on your show?"

"No. Dr. Ben thinks they're all jerks. Of course, Triller refused to come on our show because he had his own, but the rest—well, they'd *kill* to be on." Then she gasped, frowned, straightening up. "Damn, that wasn't a good thing to say. I don't mean that they'd kill—"

"I know what you mean."

"Thanks. Well, let's see—all Jonah Clary wanted was to tell everybody on TV why he should be president. Dr. Ben thought he was a half-wit—and so did the rest of us. Siddartha West has been on once—but Dr. Ben wasn't nice to her. She's a hippie from fifty years ago—all that reincarnation stuff. She's a great actress, but Ben doesn't like that, either. She's kind of old, which doesn't interest people who watch our show. She's a nice person, though. She actually did Tarot cards with me in her dressing room."

I was amused. "Did she tell you anything you might want to share?"

"Share? Are you out of your mind?" She laughed. "We missed some names here—Hy Jinx and Tony Nardoianni."

"Ah," Claire said. "Jinx would never get on our show. Ben hates hip hop music—and frankly he doesn't like the people who sing it, if you know what I mean."

"I've seen black people on the show."

"I know," she said, "but there's a quota."

"In the twenty-first century?"

"About twelve percent of the American population is black—so that's approximately the percentage of black people we invite to our shows. And Ben's very particular about them. They have to talk like white people do, and they have to be well-dressed—no loud, gaudy clothes."

"Did you happen to meet Tobe Blaine of the Cleveland P.D., Claire?"

"Sure. She left me her business card. Oh!" She straightened up. "I see what you're getting at. No, she looks and talks fine. She could get on our show."

"She wouldn't go on Ben's show at gunpoint," I said. "How about Tony Nardoianni?"

"Nope. Ben doesn't like baseball. He's from Nebraska; all he understands is football. Besides, he thinks Nardoianni is a dummy."

"Is Nardoianni mad at Ben because of that?"

"I don't think so," Claire said. "He's an easy-going guy. I *do* like baseball, and I always liked him when he was a manager."

If Nardoianni wasn't mad at Dr. Ben for not inviting him onto his show, he probably wasn't mad at Tommy Triller, either—at least not mad enough to shoot him. I tried another tack. "I'm looking for Patrick Owens."

She pushed herself up off the bed, nodding. "Oh, yeah—the Mount of Olives."

I laughed. "The Mount of Olives?"

"He's as big as a mountain, and twice as quiet."

"You've only known him a few days?"

"Since Monday."

"He's friendly?"

"Hardly. He speaks when spoken to, he does his job. And he's—hmm. I don't know how to say this. He doesn't ogle after women like most guys do. He hasn't looked at me that way—or even at Caroline." She walked to the window and gazed southward at the steel mills belching fire and smoke—not an inspiring view for a Cleveland visitor. "Every guy *looks* at Caroline. You probably do, too."

"I'm committed," I confessed, "not blind."

"The other thing is, Owens doesn't look at guys that way, either." She turned around and looked at me. "Maybe it's my own nuttiness," Claire said, "but I haven't been in a relationship for more than two years, so I notice things like that."

"Where did you find him?" I asked.

"Dr. Ben made me phone a friend of a friend of his in Columbus before we left L.A., and the friend found this guy—Paddy, Ben calls him."

"What friend?"

"You got me, Mr. Security. I didn't memorize his name."

I stood up. "Is Owens's room across the hall?"

"Yes," Claire said. "I haven't been in it—and I have no desire to, either."

It was a few steps to the door. Tiny room. "I'll take care of it, Claire."

She moved to the door. "A dirty job," she said, "but somebody's got to do it."

I walked across the hall and knocked on the door. It was almost jerked open by Patrick Owens, and he did indeed look like a small mountain—broad and over-muscular, with a butch cut that didn't hide his unfortunate hair loss. That he was more than thirty years my junior made the nascent baldness that much more painful.

"*What?*" Defensive, almost angry—and I'd done nothing wrong. Not yet, anyway.

I stretched the "security" label again, and he reluctantly let me in.

"I hardly know who Dr. Ben *is*," Owens said, too close to me because there wasn't much room to stand. His beefy arms were defensively folded across his chest. "A friend told me to drive the Mayos up from Columbus and bodyguard them while they're here. I needed the money, so . . . " He jutted his chin out at me, a bulldog with an underbite. "I didn't kill nobody, okay? I already told the cops."

"Not accusing you," I said. "Didn't you know who Tommy Triller was, either?"

He shook his head. "Never saw him on TV or read about him in the paper. I watch sports—and porno."

And this was a guy who went to Ohio State. I said, "Who's this Columbus friend?"

Owens took enough time before answering. I thought he was considering a lie. "An OSU alumni, I think."

How could anyone who attended The Ohio State University not know the difference between alumnus, *individual*, and alumni, *plural?* I said, "He knew Dr. Ben?"

"You got me."

"Does he know Tony Nardoianni, too?"

"He wasn't into baseball. Just football."

"He played football, too?"

Owens shrugged his shoulders. "He's older." He uncrossed his arms and let them hang at his sides, fingers curled up into almost-fists. It bothered me not at all, as there was virtually no room for a fight.

I said, "Can you tell me his name, Mr. Owens?"

"You're no cop," he barked, moving his shoulders as if to strengthen them, "so I don't have to tell you shit."

"True enough. But if I suggest the cop running this investigation should talk to you, you *will* have to tell her shit. So tell me instead. Life will be a lot easier."

He considered this for at least half a minute before he said, "George."

"George? We should talk to everyone in Columbus named George?"

Chagrined, as if he'd failed in trying to get away with something, he finally said "Lufton. George Lufton."

I scribbled the name in my notebook. "How well do you know George Lufton?"

"Some."

"Know him very well?"

"Some." This time he snarled it.

"Well," I said, "I've asked enough questions. Thanks for your time."

I turned, putting my hand on the doorknob.

Patrick Owens said to me, "You come back here and bother me again, I'm gonna rip your fuckin' head off. You dig?"

"I dig," I said, "because you're much younger than me. But I guarantee that before you rip my fuckin' head off, I'll leave you with something you'll remember for the rest of your life. Do *you* dig?"

Down in the lobby, there were few conventioneers, as most had repaired to their rooms to get ready for dinner and the dreary, boring speakers to top off the entire weekend. I wondered how many would stay awake long enough to get through this endless evening of carefully massaged horse puckey.

I'm not supposed to call Tobe while she's on duty, but I did have a few important little gems for her. I tapped in her number on my cell phone. She answered after one ring.

"What's going on, Milan?" she said. No hello, no nothing.

"Do you know any detective-grade police officers in Columbus?" I asked.

"Yes. Why?"

"If you do, can you run a few names by him?"

"Him is a her. What names?"

"Patrick Owens, Dr. Ben's driver and bodyguard he hired in Columbus."

"I already talked to him. Why?"

"He played football for Ohio State but was dropped from the team and eventually kicked out of school. We should know why. The other name is George Lufton."

"Mm-hmm," she said. I could tell she was writing the name down. "Who's that?"

"Ben Mayo's producer called Lufton to supply someone like Owens."

"Do we know anything about this Lufton?"

"Not yet," I said. "Do you have time for a quick bite with me?"

"Late lunch? Sure, but I can't face another meal in the Food Court. There are pretty good restaurants right down the street, on Euclid. If you could run out and get me a decent burger and some chips, I'll be your best friend."

"You're already my best friend," I said.

"Okay, friend with benefits—except not tonight or any time until this Triller murder case is on the books."

I sighed. "What kind of burger interests you right now," I said, "and where do I find you to deliver it?"

"A burger that's not just chopped beef fried up and smothered in cheese—especially fast-food cheese. Bring it to that little conference room in forty-five minutes and we can spend some time together. Or are you hot on a lead?"

"Not hot—just warm," I said, "hoping to get hot after you make your phone call to your fellow cop in Columbus."

"Just keep the burger warm," Tobe said, "and the rest of it will take care of itself."

CHAPTER TWENTY-TWO

K.O.

Five o'clock. The beginning of transition time, changing your clothes, your activities, even your lifestyle from busy afternoon to a different kind of busy evening.

For three days, K.O. had been joined at the hip to the Global Motivational Speakers Association convention, and the phony, pious hard-sell that came with it. The removal of the corpse of Tommy Triller had occurred early in the morning before most people had arisen. There were a few, though, who lined up sorrowfully on the street level as what was left of their idol was trundled out in a zipped-up body bag and into an ambulance. A few wept openly. Their key to riches and salvation was gone forever.

There were still some who'd likely traveled halfway across the country for nothing more interesting than getting hammered in the lobby bar late in the afternoon. K.O. looked at them with uninterested contempt, hating once more having to stay at the hotel until eleven o'clock, when everyone but the drunkards had gone to bed. He was anxious to get back to his own home.

To Carli.

She'd probably be asleep by the time K.O. arrived, unless a late-night talk show was featuring a celebrity guest she wanted to see. But slipping under the covers and falling asleep with his arm around her and his face buried in her fresh-smelling hair was almost as good as making love. Almost.

K.O.'s close look inside the lounge revealed Reverend Jesse Paulin, sitting alone at a table for four, drawing irritated glances from those drinkers who wanted those seats. In front of him was a bottle of Perrier, a glass, and an open bible.

Milan and Ed Stahl had butted heads with him, K.O. knew, and found that his anger against Tommy Triller had been real and frightening. K.O. figured another conversation with the good reverend couldn't hurt.

K.O. stopped in front of Paulin's table, leaning on the back of one of the chairs. "Afternoon, Reverend," he said. "Catching up on a little privacy, I see."

Paulin nodded almost pleasantly. "I don't seek privacy, young man, when I try to spread the words of Our Savior, Jesus Christ. I want to tell the whole wide world."

"This became a strange convention, didn't it—considering Tommy Triller's death?"

Paulin closed his bible. "Not strange. God decides who lives and who dies."

"God decided someone should shoot Triller in the head?"

"Don't you realize, son, that everything that happens—*everything*—is God's will?"

"Like taking another person's life?"

"God wrote the words on the tablets: Thou shalt not kill. But sometimes," Paulin said, "he makes exceptions."

"I had no idea," K.O. said, "those ten commandments had any exceptions. That's why they're *commandments* and not suggestions. So whoever squeezed the trigger did so because God told them to?"

"You don't study God's words, do you?"

K.O. recalled times in juvenile detention when he had nothing else to read. "I read the Bible from cover to cover."

"Read it again."

"Too busy making a living."

"What's your business?"

"Security," K.O. said. "Right this minute, security for this convention."

"You're doing a rotten job," Paulin said, "if someone was murdered right here in this hotel."

"I can't be everywhere. I didn't realize Tommy Triller was in danger of losing his life."

"Of course he was in danger! He was a liar, a manipulator, a fake!" Paulin shook his head sadly. "Taking money from people— lots of money—to make them walk over burning coals barefoot. Sticking his face on television every chance he got. A womanizer. A man so full of himself that he couldn't see anyone else. A cheat! A devil child who *hated* God!"

K.O. let that simmer for a while. Then he said, "Where is your church, Reverend?"

"Independence, Missouri—for the past twenty-three years."

"Nice church?"

"It's a beautiful church. Bought up forty-seven acres of land and had it designed and built to my specifications. It's a house of God."

"God owns the mortgage on the house?"

Jesse Paulin's face turned frightening and ugly. "You think you're funny, do you? Have you accepted Jesus Christ as your personal savior?"

"Did Tommy Triller accept Jesus Christ as *his* personal savior?"

"I'm not surprised Triller is dead because he didn't—and it wouldn't surprise me if something happened to you, too." Paulin pointed at the ceiling—or what he believed was beyond the ceiling. "It's God's will."

"So you don't feel anger toward the person who killed Tommy Triller?"

"God's will," Paulin repeated as casually as if asked what time it was. Opening his Bible, he flicked K.O. away with his fingers, as if shooing a fly. "I will no longer talk with you. Come back to me when you accept Jesus Christ into your miserable life."

K.O. left the cocktail lounge. For one brief, shining moment he elevated Revered Paulin to the top of his suspect list—until he realized that just about everyone he or Milan had spoken to so far was under suspicion.

The main ballroom was now empty except for hotel staff cleaning up, running vacuums and straightening chairs for the big closing ceremonies later that evening. K.O. eventually wound up in the Resources Room, and was surprised at the number of people. The longest line of would-be buyers clutching credit cards in their hot little hands was in front of the Tommy Triller table—

actually a double table, twice as wide as most other vendor stations. Two pretty young women, wearing fist-sized Tommy Triller
buttons on their chests, looked hassled and overworked—not
Triller "regulars," but local models hired for the weekend to sell
whatever books, CDs, and even high-priced firewalking programs
the idolaters of Triller had come to buy.

There was another model behind the Dr. Ben table, but she
wasn't working nearly as hard. K.O. strolled over.

"Hey there," he said. "Looks like they're keeping you busy in
here."

"Not really," she said. "But if Dr. Ben got killed, I'd be going
crazy ringing up sales." She tossed her hair out of her face—and
K.O. knew flirting when he saw it, but chose to ignore it.

"You know Dr. Ben pretty well?" he said.

"Not at all. I never met him."

"Oh? Who hired you?"

"That woman TV producer, Claire Something-or-Other. She
called the model agency I work for, and they picked me for the
weekend. I've talked to her a few times, but I've never been anywhere near Dr. Ben. I don't watch his TV show, anyway."

"Do you watch Tommy Triller's TV specials?"

"Nope. I've seen him on, like, the *Ellen* show and stuff—but I'm
not into that silliness, either."

"Triller told people how to become wealthy, didn't he?"

"I have a good career," she said, "but I wouldn't call myself
wealthy. There are more things in life than getting rich, you
know." She snickered. "Claire told me Dr. Ben hated Triller's guts
anyway."

"Many people did," K.O. said, "one of them mad enough to kill
him."

A shudder vibrated her shoulders. "That makes it scary working
here."

"Did this Claire person call your agency this week?"

"Oh, no—at least six weeks ago—and it's a good thing. Half
the women working this room are with the same modeling
agency. And even one of the men." She nodded over at a prepos-
terously handsome young model looking very bored behind Tony
Nardoianni's small sales table.

K.O. checked out the rest of the vendor stations. Some were manned by the speakers themselves, the ones who spoke on Thursday afternoon or Friday morning. Of the prestigious VIPs, only two were selling their own merchandise: Siddartha West and Jonah Clary. Siddartha was more involved with signing autographs than peddling her many books and her merchandise, like Tarot cards and pamphlets that were spiritual but not in the least religious. At least she seemed happy. Clary, however, looked downtrodden despite his shiny silver cowboy shirt with sparkles and the giant Stetson hat that looked strange inside a busy Midwestern hotel.

K.O. approached him pleasantly. "Afternoon. How's it going?"

The bored, sad Clary suddenly switched gears and became friendly as all get-out. "Doin' great, there, my friend. There's usually a pretty girl here selling my stuff, but I had to let her go out for an early dinner, so . . . " He stopped and frowned at K.O., his face changing from garrulous angel to hungry wolf. "Wait up, there! I know you."

"We've met."

"Uh-huh, that's right. Tell me again why I don't like you."

"I'm security. We got off on the wrong foot."

It took Clary nearly a half minute to recall. "Yeah, right. I remember now. I don't like people who aren't in step with me. You're rude. You don't even have the respect to call me 'Governor.'"

"You're not a governor anymore—and you were never a governor of my state."

Wrinkling his nose in what he hoped looked like anger, Clary held his thumb and forefinger a half inch apart. "I came this close to being president."

"Close only counts in horseshoes and hand grenades," K.O. said. "I'll step away and not bother you again—if you'll answer a few questions."

Clary surveyed the room. "If anybody comes up to buy something from me, you're outta here. Understand?"

"No problem. Wondering how well you know some of the other speakers. Siddartha West, for instance."

"Don't know her well at all, and I don't like the best part of her."

"Why?"

"She's a Hollywood broad—and all those Hollywood women are whores. Also, she's a goddamn libtard."

"Libtard?"

"Who the hell you hanging out with, boy? Retarded liberal. Libtard."

"You hate her because of her politics?"

"I don't hate her—I just don't like her. How 'bout you, boy? You a libtard, too?"

"I never ran for president," K.O. said, "so my politics are none of your business. How about you and Tony Nardoianni? Friends or foes?"

"Neither. He came to my office one time when he was in town, and we posed for a picture or two. We're both famous for different reasons, and publicity-wise, a pic together didn't hurt either of us. That's about it."

"He never talked to you about Tommy Triller?"

"He didn't talk about anything except one of the legal assistants in my office who has gigantic titties. He was there for about ten minutes, and then he was gone. I never saw him again until we both showed up here."

"You didn't like Tommy Triller."

"No. That's no crime." He moved out from behind the sales table and stood over K.O., who was at least four inches shorter. "Are you accusing me of murder?"

"I'm just asking questions."

"Ask 'em someplace else. Damn, boy! You think I can't even count to ten, but I'm dumb enough to come all the way to Cleveland to shoot Tommy Triller?" Jonah Clary gave the brim of his Stetson a slight tug. "If I'd wanted Triller dead, I'd have hired somebody—and they woulda killed him someplace else when I was clear across the country."

K.O. rolled that over in his mind as he wandered around the vendors' room looking at things without really seeing them. Clary had been known politically for his ridiculous sound bytes, but he'd sounded correct about the twelfth-floor killing. He wouldn't have waited until they were both in Cleveland at the same time to kill Tommy Triller—he would have hired an anonymous hit man to blow Triller away someplace else.

He had found out as much as he was going to about Clary, and virtually nothing about Tony Nardoianni, which Milan Security was getting paid for.

On the other side of the room from Jonah Clary's table, Siddartha West was busily signing autographs for those who remembered her great film performances. She saw him, beamed, and waved him over.

"Hey, cutie," she said, "sit and talk to me for a while. I'm signing too damn many autographs and not selling enough books." She waved at the stack in front of her. There were seven different books on display, each with a different cover photograph of her, from some of her earliest beginnings, when she was a hot young movie star, and then as she aged. She seemed to have written a book every two or three years. The last two were vintage, though, showing her as a sublimely talented sexpot.

"I'll talk," he said, "but I don't make enough money to buy books. I can find you in the library, can't I?"

When she laughed, the years disappeared and she looked like her thirty-year-old photographs. "My books, movies, stuff written about me. Everything in the library except my list of ex-lovers." She sighed. "Unless somebody wrote about *them*, too."

"That would be something to read."

"I got around, kiddo. Most women in the movies do—you live an exciting, bizarre life and everybody in the world sees you swap spit with every other actor in town, and then it gets to be something you just *do*. Either that—or become a nun." Then she laughed again. "I played a nun in one of my movies, but I'm not sure anyone really believed that. Is there anything I *haven't* done?"

"Commit murder?"

"Not even on film. I got killed myself a few times—" She stopped smiling and frowned. "Are we talking about movies—or Tommy Triller?"

K.O. said, "I'd go to the wall thinking you're innocent. But one never knows."

"Well, he sure as hell wasn't one of my lovers. I'd never go to bed with a phony asshole like him. He's said bad things about me, I know—things about my particular brand of spirituality. But everybody and their uncle has put me down for that, so Tommy Triller wasn't exactly my number-one enemy."

A woman in her sixties approached the table for her autograph on the back of the program schedule. Siddartha was pleasant and kind with her for almost five minutes, even though she didn't buy a book.

"Tony Nardoianni," K.O. said when the customer left, "might have bumped heads with Triller while he was still in baseball. Were you aware of that?"

"Honey," she said, "if it wasn't a movie, and if it didn't have anything to do with Tarot cards or reincarnation, I'm totally unaware of it. Don't waste your time worrying about the baseball manager. I'll tell you who had a real hate-on for Tommy Triller, and she's right here in this hotel. Dr. Lorelei Singleton."

"Really?

"She hates everything—gays, lesbians, pit bulls, scientists, abortion, abortion doctors, higher education, Democrats—and anyone who ever fucked her and then never called her again, and that encompasses a hell of a lot of people." Siddartha drummed her fingers on one of her books. "But we *are* talking about Tommy Triller, aren't we?"

CHAPTER TWENTY-THREE

MILAN

Carrying Tobe's lunch, I found her in the small conference room on the mezzanine floor—on the phone, making rapid notes as she spoke. She smiled and nodded when I came in, but kept talking. I took the food from the bag and set it up in front of her—a pesto burger, potato chips, three pickle slices, and a bottle of Snapple iced tea.

"So Lufton has no record?" she said into her phone. "Interesting. He tiptoes quietly, then." Pause. "I have nothing solid on Owens, either. At least not yet. Okay, Meg, thanks. I owe you one." Pause. "Yeah, let's figure out a time to slam down a couple of beers. See you."

She hung up.

"Who's Meg?" I said.

"Margaret Pinckney, detective second grade, Columbus Police Department."

"How do you know her?"

Tobe took a deep breath. "A few years back, a police officer was shot down in cold blood in Youngstown. Every cop in Ohio who could get away showed up, in uniform—including me when I was serving in Cincinnati. Meg and I met at the funeral, hung out together for two days, and kind of kept in touch ever since. FYI, it's hard to find a good restaurant in Youngstown."

"Does she have anything on Patrick Owens?"

"Nothing more than we already found out. But George Lufton—that's another story."

"Are you making everyone at this convention stay in town?"

"Two thousand people? No. But I'll keep the celebrities until I get to the end of this road. Tough shit on them. They're rich—they can afford changing their flights."

"There'd be security records if any of them flew here carrying a weapon, right?"

She nodded. "We checked with TSA, first thing. Everybody arrived unarmed. I haven't yet figured out who left this hotel any time before the killing, and who didn't. I will, though." She unwrapped her burger. "What's this?"

"A pesto burger." She raised both eyebrows. "You said you wanted something a little different."

"We'll see." She took a bite, chewed thoughtfully. "It's good. Different, but good. Where'd you get it?"

"A little joint about half a block away, right on Euclid—the Flaming Ice Cube."

She put down the burger. "You've got to be kidding."

"Why?"

"I've eaten there a few times for lunch—strictly vegan. No meat, cheese, eggs, dairy, no honey." She tilted her head to study her sandwich. "I don't know what this burger is made out of."

"I didn't know the place was vegan. It was close by, you said you wanted a different kind of burger—how would I know the difference?"

She took another bite. "It tastes just like a hamburger. I like it."

"Enjoy your dinner," I said, "and tell me about George Lufton while you eat."

She pulled her notepad in front of her with her free hand. "Lufton is Columbus's idea of a temporary employee agency when it comes to hiring tough guys to do the kind of work most people don't want to do."

"Hit men?"

"I don't know. Lufton covers his tracks well. He hires people to collect debts, and then takes a slice off the top."

"That sounds like a collection agency," I said. "I'd rather clean toilets than call people and make them miserable for money they owe somebody else."

"According to Meg, Lufton's people don't use the phone," Tobe said. "They bang on your door at three in the morning, they approach you when you're getting in your car, or if you're really in serious debt, they confront you on a lonely street where nobody's around to hear the punches landing. And most of them look like Patrick Owens."

"Lufton's never been arrested?"

"He's not a corporation, he's just a guy. Everything he does is strictly cash, so there's no paper trail."

"How did he find Patrick Owens?"

"A football player for one of the most powerful athletic programs in college sports gets kicked off the team and bounced out of the university. No pro career, no degree, hard-pressed to find any kind of job, and built like a Mack truck? It wasn't hard for George Lufton to find him and recruit him."

"I wonder," I said, "how Dr. Ben happened to know Lufton, then?"

Tobe popped too many potato chips into her mouth and signaled for me to wait while she washed it all down with a slug of Snapple. Then she said, "One simple phone call to the right person would have turned Mayo on to Lufton."

"Mayo hired Owens to kill Triller? Or was it in Owens's head to knock on Triller's door in the middle of the night and shoot him?"

"I don't know much about Owens and I have no proof he's done anything wrong. Right now he's a person of interest—and I'll chat with him again." She reached for her sandwich. "Just as soon as I finish eating my plant-grown hamburger."

What was I supposed to do with my time, now? Nobody really suspected Tony Nardoianni of anything—at least not this weekend— and therefore my Victor Gaimari assignment was pretty much a washout. It was my responsibility, though, to tell him so.

Victor's office has always been on the eleventh floor of the Terminal Tower, but it was fairly late on a Saturday afternoon and I knew he wasn't there. I stepped out of the hotel's side door on Public Square into relatively fresh air, filled my lungs with it, and called his home number on my cell.

"You have news, Milan?" he asked.

"Yes and no," I told him. "Can I drop by your house?"

"When?"

"Now."

He was silent for a moment. Then he said, "I have an eight o'clock dinner engagement—but if you get out here right away, I'll make time for you."

"Forty minutes, tops," I said.

I hung up, then crossed the street to the open-air parking lot. After getting in the car, I dialed K.O.

"You're leaving me alone?" he said when I told him I was heading to Gaimari's.

"Talk to people. There's not much left to find out—but as long as we're getting paid, maybe we discover something interesting. When the program starts at seven-thirty, sneak in and listen. If Reeve Fesmire gives you any crap, get Tobe to lean on him. I'll get back as soon as I can."

"How do I keep from falling asleep standing up?"

"Pull out a nose hair. That'll keep you awake."

Victor Gaimari's home in the eastern suburb of Orange was impressive. I'd been invited there to parties back when we were remotely friendly. To his beautiful Tudor mini-mansion with a sculpted lawn, Victor had added a wrought-iron fence completely surrounding the three acres of property, closed off at the curb— and a sign warning that the fence was electrified. I announced myself over a sound system mounted on one of the columns. The additions, new since I was last here more than a decade ago, must have cost upwards of one hundred thousand bucks.

But now Victor was The Godfather, and the protection didn't seem excessive. Two dark-suited men stood at the house's front door, bulges beneath their jackets. When I got out of my car, one asked my name, and the other opened the front door for me.

A middle-aged housekeeper greeted me inside and bade me go upstairs to "Don Victor's" suite. I'd never been above the ground floor before. There were only two doors on the second level, one of them a double, and I realized Victor had ordered a complete remodel when his uncle, Don Giancarlo, died, naming him the only heir and permanent replacement.

I entered Victor's suite—an elegant sitting room, a walk-in

closet with its doors open, a bedroom with an enormous custom bed placed so Victor could look east at the rising sun each morning, and a bathroom larger than most in neighborhood rec centers. The shower was big enough for six, there was a raised marble tub, and enough storage cabinets to supply one entire floor of a hotel.

Victor wore the pants to an inky-black suit, a white shirt that looked like it might have been ironed minutes earlier, and slippers on his feet. He carried an old-fashioned glass of what I guessed was scotch. The suit jacket and a necktie the color of ancient polished silverware were hung neatly over a valet stand.

"Milan," he said, approaching me with a handshake, "good to see you. Want something to drink?"

"No thanks, Victor. I know you have plans, but I wanted to report to you in person. I hope I'm not hanging you up."

His smile was almost halfway. "Don't worry about it. She'll wait."

She'll wait. Whoever she was. That's Victor Gaimari for you.

I said, "I have no proof of anything—but we've talked to a hell of a lot of people, and I have no reason to believe Tony Nardoianni did anything wrong. He seems decent, has a good sense of humor, isn't demanding as far as VIPs go, and everyone seems to like him. Except maybe Siddartha West, who'd never kiss anybody who chews tobacco."

"Amusing," Victor said, "but you could have told me that on the phone."

"Maybe in another fifty years or so, I'll be convinced that my telephone—or *your* telephone—isn't tapped."

"I assure you, it's not tapped—at least it wasn't at nine o'clock this morning. But I don't only want you cementing Tony's good-guy reputation. I want you to find the killer and get the pressure off him."

"Private investigators," I said, "can't solve capital murder cases under the noses of the local cops."

"Don't give me that crap. You've solved more murders than Sherlock Holmes."

"Not even close. Besides, Holmes was a genius."

"He was also fictional—and a cocaine addict, too, but that's beside the point. I want you hanging in there until there's a solid arrest—and it better not be Tony."

"Victor, why are you so passionate about Tony? I know you take the money he owes you out of his hide every time he makes a buck or two—but busting your ass to make sure he's proved innocent is a long reach."

Victor snagged his silver tie and slipped it under his starched collar. "The Italians have gotten a lousy rap in this country for more than a century—especially from the movies. We're all fat, stupid, money-grubbing, greaseball gangsters. I grew up hearing that, even though nobody dared say it to my uncle."

He tied a perfect Windsor knot in his tie, but he was as agitated as I'd ever seen him. "The Italian mob, as you probably call it, didn't go around killing innocent people on the street. They killed off each other for power and prominence in their own families. I know what my uncle did wasn't always kosher, but he refused to deal in illegal drugs or prostitution. He was a very moral business-man. I'm a businessman, too. And Tony was a baseball manager who gambled when he wasn't supposed to. I don't want to see his name—or mine—dragged through the mud just because it ends in a vowel."

"Why didn't you hire an Italian private eye?"

"It'd make me look like I'm conniving to change the investiga-tion results."

"Victor," I said, "you thought I always blamed Italians for some-thing illegal that happened. Nearly every conversation we've ever had wound up being about Italians. We talk about baseball, you bring up Joe DiMaggio. Politically, you're all agog that New York state has had many years of Italian governors named Cuomo, and you were involved with some Italian Clevelanders in office who went to jail for fraud and bribery. That's just your—your thing."

"It's an Irish thing for Irishmen, a Jewish thing for Jews, a black thing for blacks. It's how the world works." He put on his suit jacket, straightened it, brushed invisible lint off the collar, and wandered over to a full-length mirror mounted on the wall. "So I'll pay you until whoever wasted Tommy Triller is caught. Unless you just walk away." He turned and glowered at me. "If you do, Milan, I won't forget that."

"If I find Tony Nardoianni is guilty, you know I'll inform the police."

"To save your P.I. license?"

"No, Victor—to preserve my integrity."

As I was heading back down the driveway to the gate, I passed another car going toward the house. The driver was stunning, probably no more than thirty, and dressed expensively to match her car—a new Mercedes Benz. Victor's date for the evening.

I marveled at my strange and ever-changing relationship with a man who's now Cleveland's boss of bosses. Victor rarely surprised me, but he still caught me off-balance too often—and I prefer having both feet squarely on the ground.

CHAPTER TWENTY-FOUR

K.O.

The lobby was crowding up again. The attendees looked as though they'd just wolfed down a huge dinner at one of the many restaurants in and around Public Square. Now they champed at the bit, waiting for the big Saturday evening program, which would feature lengthy and ultimately boring yadda yaddas from Dr. Ben Mayo, Dr. Lorelei Singleton, Jarvis Green, and Bailey DeWitt, all not-so-cleverly disguised versions of the same speech: *How to Get Rich Quick.*

Green and DeWitt added an extra speaker to the Saturday night wrap-up, so former governor Jonah Clary, originally scheduled to open the program, had been bumped down to speaking at lunchtime on Saturday. After being voted out of his governorship and embarrassed during the presidential primaries the year before, he now had something else about which to sulk.

Probably the only person who didn't give a damn about the schedule was Siddartha West. K.O. could tell she loved selling her books, but he guessed the truth was that she'd prefer everyone buy DVDs of some of her best film roles and adore her all over again, as they had during the seventies and eighties.

She was also the only one on the VIP list that K.O. liked.

Siddartha had given him quite a heads-up, too—one he should at least explore. So before the program started, he got into the elevator and rode up to the suite of Dr. Lorelei Singleton.

When she opened her door to his knock, her welcoming greeting was memorable.

"What the fuck do *you* want?" she demanded. She had donned the dress he figured she was going to wear when she spoke later, but was in her stocking feet—no shoes. In her hand was a glass of clear liquid and ice. K.O. could smell the gin.

"K.O. O'Bannion. Security. Remember me?"

"How could I forget you?" It was a curled-lip snarl. "The only man I ever met who was too busy to spend time with me."

"I was working." At least that was a small part of the truth. "I have a few minutes to spend with you now."

"Sure," she said. "Drop me like I'm a sack of garbage Thursday—and Saturday you've got a few minutes to come scratching around for a little head. Is that it?"

That caught K.O. back on his heels. He hoped words wouldn't stick in his throat. "I'm still working, Dr. Lorelei."

"You mean I can't throw you out even if I want to?"

"You can," he assured her, "but then you'll have to talk to a police officer."

"I did that already," she said. "Yesterday morning."

He nodded. "You won't like them showing up again with more questions. They get snarky when they have to come back."

Lorelei let her head fall back, sighing, "Oh, shit," stepping aside so K.O. could enter.

"May I sit down?"

"No," she snapped. "Ask your questions and leave."

"Whatever you say. You came here Thursday. From—?"

"Los Angeles. I live in Los Angeles."

"Direct flight?"

"No. I had to change planes in Dallas. What's the point?"

K.O. ignored that. "Did a limo pick you up at the airport or did you rent a car?"

"I reserved a car from Enterprise before I left home."

"Did you stop anywhere between the airport and here?"

Eye-roll—teen-aged girl style. "They don't let you carry liquids on the plane anymore. I stopped at a drugstore on the way here and bought shampoo and some mouthwash."

"Was that all?"

"No, goddammit!" Dangerous explosion—K.O. had to take a step backward. "I bought condoms, too. How dare you ask . . . ?"

"Where was the drugstore? Downtown?"

"No. On some street on the West Side. It was on the way. I don't see why you're—"

"And then you came right to the hotel?"

"Yes."

"After you checked in, did you leave the hotel for any reason? Dinner at some restaurant? A drink in a bar a bit more quiet than the one off the lobby? Or just take a walk?"

Lorelei was having difficulty keeping her temper. "I checked in, thanks to you. I made a few phone calls. I scoped out the shopping center right next door—what do they call it again?"

"Tower City."

"Right. I came back and ordered dinner from room service. Then I did go to the lobby bar, had a nightcap, talked to some people I knew and some people I didn't know, and wound up in bed at eleven o'clock. You want to know what kind of toothpaste I brush my teeth with, or what color my nightgown was?"

"Who did you call on the phone Thursday?"

"I can't remember."

"The hotel has records of your calls."

"I used my cell phone, asshole."

"You didn't call anyone who also stayed in this hotel?"

Lorelei took a ragged breath before answering. "Like I say, I can't remember."

"You didn't call Tommy Triller?"

She didn't reply, but walked over to the dining table to rummage in her purse for a small container of aspirin. She shook three of them out into her hand and popped them between her lips, swallowing them without water. Then she removed something else and held it concealed in one fist. "What if I did? We knew each other a long time—even talked about going into partnership a few years back. So, sure, I called him—on the hotel phone—and we chatted for a while. We also talked briefly, face to face, just before the opening ceremonies. That hardly makes me a murderer, does it?"

K.O. said, "He promised you a partnership and didn't come through with it—and he had sex with you in New York one weekend, and then never called you again. That *does* make you a suspect."

"You miserable, insulting little prick!" Dr. Lorelei suddenly detonated—and before K.O. thought to step back out of the way, she squirted him directly in the face with the aerosol mace she'd hidden.

K.O. gasped, his hands immediately going to his eyes, and stumbled away in fiery pain, but Lorelei came after him, swinging punches at wherever she could hit him. "You son of a bitch! How dare you come in here and say terrible things to me? You had no interest in me on Thursday. Now you come back here and call me a murderer!" Her bashing landed on both his ears as well as his hands, and there were a few uppercuts to his ribs and stomach. She even tossed a few low blows, but even half-blinded, K.O. knew enough to turn his body away so her knuckles landed on his hips and thighs instead of where they'd been aimed.

"Get out!" she screamed, tears streaming down her cheeks along with glistening streaks of mascara. "I'll tell the police you tried to rape me!" She opened the door and shoved K.O., hard, clear across the hallway toward the elevator.

K.O. could hear her wailing and screaming and swearing— and at one point she hurled something against the door that shattered.

He managed to fish a handkerchief out of his pocket to mop his own tears of pain from his eyes while he listened to her lonely tantrum. Finally, when he could see a little, he pressed the DOWN button on the elevator with a hand shaking in anger. In his short life, he'd been punched at least a hundred times, if not more. He'd often been shot at in the Middle East during the two wars many Americans refuse to admit *are* wars, and he'd been sitting in a military truck when it ran over a land mine and blew apart, taking his best friend with it. But getting squirted in the eyes with mace was a first.

When the elevator arrived, another couple was already inside. They looked at him and then, sadly, at each other, thinking that he'd been crying over some love tragedy.

"Allergies," he told them.

On the mezzanine level, he hurried to the men's room, collected wads of cloth towels, and soaked them in cold water to wash some of the spray from his eyes.

He stood in front of the mirror behind the basin as he dried his face, and when his eyes focused again, Jarvis Green was standing at the adjoining sink, studying him.

"Are you all right, young man?"

"Pretty much. Thanks for asking."

"I saw you come in here. You were actually crying. Something awful must have happened to get you to cry at a crowded convention like this."

"Not crying."

"I don't want you angry with me, too. I realize you and I got off badly when we first met," Jarvis said. "Tension rubs people's tempers raw sometimes."

"Don't worry about it."

"After all that, it really bothers me that you're still upset."

"Not upset—just taking care of things."

Jarvis moved a few steps closer. "Nice-looking young man like you shouldn't have to go into a men's room to cry."

K.O. tried not to sigh. "I'm having an eye problem, that's all."

"I hope it's not serious. If you don't take care of your eyes, you'll wind up with some serious vision problems."

"I'll have to remember that."

"Good. But don't let it keep you from coming to the program tonight to listen to my talk. I'm the second-to-last speaker tonight." He moved two more steps closer. "I'm sure there are things I have to say that will—touch you."

"I'm not attending this convention. I'm security. I get paid to be here."

"Well, good for you, then." A pat on the shoulders—and then a slight squeeze. "In that case, you won't have to listen to that miserable bitch who's speaking after me. She's my ex-wife, in case you didn't know." Jarvis rolled his eyes. "Wives—phew!" He didn't move his hand. "Allow me to buy you a drink afterwards, then— around ten-thirty or so." Another gentle squeeze. "I can order any- thing from room service—anything you ask for. I think we need to get to know each other better."

"Nice gesture, Mr. Green, but I don't think that's a good idea."

"Why?"

"I think you know why."

The unctuous smile transformed into a suspicious face. "I have no idea what you're getting at."

"Of course you do. You're—hitting on me, Mr. Green."

Now suspicion turned to rage. "Hitting on you? Don't flatter yourself, you little bastard! You have the wrong cookie!"

"Maybe so."

"There's no maybe about it!" Jarvis Green filled his chest with air, then released it in a rush to carry his howl. "I can report you for this. Report you to the police if I have to—they're all over this hotel, you know."

Threatened with a police report twice within ten minutes by two different people furious with him because he didn't want to have sex with them! For a brief moment K.O. wished he'd stayed in the army. Finally he said, "You're not going to the police about anything, because word will get out and you'd be the one ridiculed and laughed at. Not me."

"You sound homophobic!"

"Either way, I wouldn't discuss it here in the men's room if I were you." He nodded down the row at the closed-door toilet stalls. "You never know who might be sitting in there listening to you."

Though his hands were still damp, K.O. left Jarvis Green fuming in front of the sink, and headed back to the main lobby. He was looking for Tobe Blaine, as he had information to report, but didn't see her anywhere.

Passing by the cocktail lounge, now packed with those wanting a few relaxing drinks before filing into the main ballroom to listen to the final speeches, he couldn't help noticing a beautiful middle-aged blonde sitting alone at the far end of the bar, crouching over a Long Island iced tea the way poverty-stricken people sometimes did to protect their food from everyone else, as if someone might try to steal it. Wearing a dark blue silk dress without an inch to spare, with large sunglasses over her eyes, Caroline Mayo was turned toward the wall, ignoring the man who sat next to her.

But sunglasses? At six-thirty on a mid-October Cleveland evening, inside a bar? If Caroline thought she had disguised herself, she had no idea how much attention she invited, despite her stay-away attitude. That she was in the studio audience virtually every time Dr. Ben taped a show, and was always introduced as she waved to millions of viewers at home didn't help her, either.

K.O. moved behind her and said softly, "Good evening, Mrs. Mayo."

She didn't even look at him. "Not interested," she said.

"I'm O'Bannion. Security. We've met."

She turned her head far enough to look at him. What he could see of her face was tense and strained, and the incipient wrinkles on her forehead were not covered over by TV makeup. "What's your problem? Someone make you cry?"

"Yes, ma'am," K.O. said, with no intention of explaining, "but we worked it out. Is everything all right?"

"Peachy keen," she said, turning back around to study the wall next to her.

K.O. looked at his wristwatch. "I imagine you have a seat reserved right in the first row for your husband's speech."

"I'm not going to any goddamn program!" she said, with poison in her voice. "I listen to enough of his shit every day without sitting through more." She took a big gulp of her Long Island iced tea. "And the police won't even let us leave town. We're stuck here for Christ knows how long." She shook her head sadly, though no one but K.O. noticed. "At least back in Los Angeles he goes to the office every day. Here, he never leaves the hotel." She made motions with her fingers as though a duck were quacking incessantly. "He never shuts up—not for a minute!"

K.O. said, "Can I order you a coffee?"

Now she swiveled around on her stool to look him straight in the eye through her dark-tinted glasses. "I'm on my third Long Island iced tea—and I don't have plans of stopping any time soon. Why would I want coffee?"

"Enjoy your evening then, Mrs. Mayo," K.O. said. "But if you need help—about anything—the hotel operator will put you in touch with Security. Okay?"

She shrugged, then swiveled around again with her back to K.O. and the rest of the room, and sighed wearily. "Whatever," Caroline Mayo said.

K.O. went back out into the lobby, and up to the mezzanine, where he found a quiet spot and called Milan on his cell phone.

"Where are you?" he said.

Milan sounded distracted. "Ask somebody where the First Aid room is, K.O.—and get your ass here, pronto."

CHAPTER TWENTY-FIVE

MILAN

When K.O. walked into the First Aid room, Tobe was sitting on the edge of a medical table, being tended to by the hotel's full-time nurse, whose name tag announced she was Lauren Brooke. She was applying an ice pack to Tobe's face. I stood against the opposite wall, trying to stay out of their way, but my concerned look would have made anyone worry.

K.O. stared at Tobe, stunned. "What the hell happened to you?"

The left side of Tobe's face was swollen to nearly twice its normal size, as was half of her mouth. Her left eye was practically shut. She said, "No bullet holes, no saber cuts. Don't worry. I'll live." It was hard for her to talk through the swelling.

"You have a concussion, Tobe," I said, not for the first time. "I've had enough concussions, so I know what I'm talking about."

"Are we scoring concussions? Okay, Milan—you win."

"Will anybody fill me in on the details," K.O. said, "or should I just assume Tobe walked into a door?"

"Don't try to talk, Detective," Nurse Lauren said.

"If I don't talk, I'll fall asleep—and you warned me not to do that." She brushed the nurse's ice pack away from her face. "Give that to me, I'll hold it there myself. You have other things to do."

"But—"

"No buts, Nurse. Homicide cops don't take sick days. Find someone else to mother while I talk business with my two buddies here."

The nurse considered arguing, but wisely changed her mind. Nobody ever says no to Detective Sergeant Tobe Blaine—not even me. "I'll be in the security office if you need me," she said. "Keep that ice on there, or you'll be sorry."

"I'm already sorry."

"Cops!" Lauren Brooke shook her head, mumbling as she left the room.

Awkward silence between the three of us for a moment. Then K.O. said, "How many guesses do I get?"

Tobe started to answer him but I cut her off. "The nurse was right, Tobe. You shouldn't be talking."

"I talked to *you*," she said. "Told you all about it."

"Fine—and that's enough talking for a while. I'll tell K.O. the long story, and you can correct me if I get anything wrong."

"Oh, boy," Tobe muttered, "here come the Brothers Grimm. Once upon a time . . . " She leaned back on the table, the ice pack on her cheek, while I told K.O. what had happened.

After hearing of my meeting with the surly Paddy Owens and his connection with the elusive George Lufton, Tobe immediately called her cop friend in Columbus, Meg Pinckney, and asked her for any background she had on both men. I'd thought Owens was banned from playing football and then, a few weeks later, expelled from The Ohio State University because of something like gambling—which had cost Tony Nardoianni his baseball career—or even of shaving points during a game. I'd missed it by a mile.

Patrick Owens had apparently had sex with an unconscious coed at a post-game victory party—and several of his teammates videotaped him doing it. The woman's parents wanted Owens arrested for rape, but the powers at OSU were more worried about the school's reputation than that of a young woman who'd imbibed too much vodka. They covered up the incident instead, before it hit the national newspapers, and expelled Owens as punishment.

So there he was, floating free in Columbus with no team, no school, no job, no friends, and very few prospects. When George Lufton contacted him, he fairly lunged at the opportunity to make money.

Lufton's main profession was usury—loaning cash and charging staggeringly high interest. His side business was collecting unpaid debts for other people and skimming twenty percent off the top. Columbus bookies looked to Lufton as their BFF, and Lufton—an Ohio State alumnus vitally interested in Big Ten football—was happy to have a big, muscular guy like Patrick Owens to intimidate people into emptying their wallets and bank accounts to avoid a severe beating.

Although Lufton was infamous around Columbus, he'd never been arrested or convicted of anything. Besides his money-making chicanery, he was also skillful at covering his own ass so no case could be made against him.

To what extent Dr. Ben Mayo was involved with Lufton was a mystery.

Obviously, Tobe wanted to talk to Paddy Owens even more, so she found her way up to his hotel room.

She began by asking him some of the same questions I'd fired at him, which put him on edge. When she got around to talking about George Lufton, he really didn't want to discuss it anymore. "I haven't done anything wrong," he said. He swore that he hardly knew who Dr. Ben was, he'd never even heard of Tommy Triller, and she had no right to question him.

"You haven't done anything wrong, huh?" Tobe said. "I guess you've forgotten getting kicked off the football team and out of OSU altogether because of the rape."

He became agitated. "It was consensual!"

"The woman was unconscious—at least according to four different videos your good buddies took at that party—but the sex was consensual? What a major load of crap!"

That's when Patrick Owens completely lost it. His dream was to have been starring in the National Football League by this time— big money, sexy cheerleaders, a certain amount of fame, and *not* playing a low-level tough guy, punching scrawny businessmen who'd made lousy bets in the first place. Now, permanently stained with the rape accusation and being questioned about an actual murder had put him right over the edge. Screaming, "Leave me the fuck *alone*," he took one powerful swing at Tobe. It caught her unprepared, almost took her head off, and left her out cold on the floor of his hotel room.

When she finally fought her way back to consciousness fifteen minutes later, her head and face throbbing and her neck as stiff as she could ever remember, Patrick Owens was gone. So was his suitcase. When she had staggered to the telephone and checked with the valet, she had learned he'd ransomed the limousine and gone roaring off.

"And that's the last anyone heard of him," I told K.O.

"Don't be too sure." Tobe's words were slightly mangled through the pain and the swelling, and both of us leaned forward to better understand her as she removed the ice bag from her face. "I alerted the Highway Patrol, and Meg Pinckney will be all over tracking him down in Columbus. They'll get him." She touched her own cheek lightly, with just her fingertips, and her right eye—the one that wasn't nearly swollen shut—narrowed in pain. "Then," she said, *"I've* got him."

"In the meantime," I said, "you're coming home with me."

"I'm on duty."

"Not tonight, you're not."

"Milan . . . "

"Don't argue with me, Tobe. Not this time. The police will make sure none of the VIPs sneak out of town, and K.O. will hang around to listen to the speeches and tell us all about them in the morning."

K.O. made a muffled sound I could have sworn sounded like, "Shit!"

"Don't boss me around, goddammit," Tobe warned. "I'm a law officer."

"What will you do? Shoot me? Stop whimpering, or I'll call Flo McHargue, and she'll *order* you to go home."

Her tone grew desperate, as she knew what McHargue would do. "Give me a break, Milan."

"Tobe, you need painkillers and to get off your feet. No more discussion."

"I'd rather go back to my own place by myself."

"And what's going to keep you from falling asleep while driving?"

"You can stay with me."

"No—we're staying at my place."

"I don't want to stay at your place!" she said, her tone was as close to a whine as I've ever heard from her.

"Nope." I moved toward her and took her free hand—the one not holding the ice pack. "You need someone to take care of you. Besides, I haven't been home all day, and poor Herbie can't keep his legs crossed until morning. He needs a potty walk, and you need someone to watch over you."

She didn't look the least bit happy about staying at my place. Gently, I hope, I helped her down from the table.

Once we got into my car, it was barely a fifteen-minute drive from Public Square to the triangular Cedar-Fairmount district where I lived. I kept glancing over at Tobe to make sure she didn't fall asleep while I drove. At one point, I saw her eyes close and her head drop forward, and I leaned over and squeezed her hand. She opened her eyes wide and shook her head slightly.

"Are you my nanny?" she said, annoyed.

"Something like that. Stay awake."

"The good news is that you've never bored me to sleep."

"That's why I'm staying with you—to keep you awake for the next few hours."

"And what's going to keep *you* awake?"

"Looking at you," I said.

I took her elbow as we climbed the stairs to my apartment, but she shook me off. Not to be shunned, I slipped my arm around her waist, feeling her weight, hoping she wouldn't fall backward. Evidently, it wasn't that easy to get rid of my hug, so she relaxed against it until we got inside and she collapsed wearily onto the sofa. Herbie seemed delighted to see her, wriggling his butt and putting his head on her knee.

She said, "This day's been a toughie."

"Not your first concussion. There was last year in Ashtabula, if you recall."

"Don't remind me!"

"I won't. Herbie has to take a walk anyway. Need anything?"

"To be back at the hotel with my detective squad."

"Tomorrow," I said. "Now stay awake for the ten minutes I'll be out."

"And what if I don't?"

"Then you'll be at the Cleveland Clinic before you can say Jack Robinson."

"Jack Robinson was the first black ballplayer. Why would I say his name for no reason?"

"Because you're a cop," I said, "and not much of a baseball fan, either. He was known as *Jackie* Robinson." I took down Herbie's leash and clicked it to his collar. He was so enthusiastic to get outside that he started bouncing.

The walk didn't take long—Herbie was more anxious than I'd expected. Back upstairs, he immediately lay down on Tobe's feet and moaned his contentment.

"He likes you," I said.

"Unmarried living-alone homicide detectives don't have dogs at home," she said.

"That could change—"

"Don't start with me, Milan!"

"Just saying." I rearranged the pillows on the sofa against her back. "Want something to drink?"

She nodded. "I'll get it."

"Let the upstairs butler do it," I said. "That's what I pay him for."

When I returned from the kitchen with a chilled bottle of distilled water, she took it from me and said, "When did you get so tough—telling me what to do?"

"This is my home."

She put her hand gently against her swollen face and winced. "I see. You're only tough at home."

"I've always been tough. You just didn't notice."

"Are you kidding? You give in all the time."

"I give in," I said, "when you're being a cop—even if I disagree with you. I don't give in other times. We compromise on occasion, but plenty of times I just say *no*."

"I don't remember your ever saying no."

"That's because I say it gently."

"You didn't bitch about it last year, when I got a concussion in a chicken barn."

"By the time I saw you, you were on your feet, holding the bad guy on a leash, and anxious as hell to get all of them to the lock-up. I had no idea you were concussed until later that evening, or I'd have hustled you off to the nearest hospital."

"You're not mean enough, Milan."

I sat down next to her and took her hand. "What do you think I've been doing for the last thirty years? Some people would tell you I'm mean as shit—the ones still living, anyway. If I weren't tough, I'd take a job selling ties at Dillard's. This is what I *do*. I don't have to follow cop rules, and I don't have to shine my shoes, either."

Tobe closed her eyes and rotated her head on her neck, her groan almost too soft to hear. "I know you've got more guts than brains—I've seen you operate."

I laughed. "Was that a compliment or an insult?"

"If I've stuck with you for all this time, it's no insult."

"I'm relieved. You're too sick to punch out."

"I'm not sick!" Tobe growled. "Slowed down, that's all. Besides, you should be at the hotel listening to those dreary lectures—in case one of the speakers is also a murderer."

"K.O.'s there, and probably taking notes."

"K.O. just wants to be home with his girlfriend."

"Screw him, then," I said. "Now I'm home with mine." I looked at my watch. "I've kept you awake for three hours. I guess it'd be okay if you went to sleep."

"Here on the sofa?"

"Of course not," I said. "In bed."

"With you?"

I helped her stand up. "It's a big bed, if you recall."

As we moved into the bedroom, Herbie at our heels, she said, "I hope you aren't expecting some sort of festivities, are you? I'm in no shape."

"Festivities?" I got one of my comfortable old sports shirts from the closet and handed it to her. "Festivities weren't exactly on my mind."

"Thank God for small favors."

"Cuddling, however, is another story altogether. Cuddling," I said, "is just as important as—festivities."

Sometime during the night, Herbie found his way onto the bed and snoozed until morning, lying across our legs.

Tobe's cell phone rang just after seven a.m.—and Herbie and cuddling and festivities were completely forgotten.

CHAPTER TWENTY-SIX

K.O.

K.O. had once again planted himself at the rear of the Grand Ballroom so he could watch people come in. Most of them had shown up to hear Tommy Triller speak, to shake his hand, and to give him a whopping check so they could visit one of his weekend seminars and head back home, thinking they were one snooze away from becoming rich as Croesus. Now that Triller was gone, the faces of the faithful ranged from annoyed to angry to sorrowful. They'd paid in advance for their stay at the hotel, and as much as they wanted to go home early, they couldn't wangle a refund—so they were stuck at the Renaissance for the weekend, like it or not.

Some of the attendees nodded to K.O. as they filed through the doors, although most ignored him, which suited him just fine. He didn't want to be here any more than they did. He was glad to see Siddartha West coming through the back door along with every-one else, rather than through the VIP entrance behind the stage. She'd given her talk that morning, but like the other big-name speakers, she'd been ordered by the local police not to leave town.

"Hey, cutie," she said, "you really have to listen to all this gob-bledygook tonight? Poor kid. Why don't you come sit with me, and we can giggle at the crap these schmucks put out?" She nudged him playfully with her elbow. "We can even hold hands."

"I'd like that," K.O. answered, "but I'm still on duty."

"Rats!" she grinned. "I haven't held hands with someone young enough to be my grandson in weeks."

"You're something else, Ms. West."

"Sid," she corrected him. "Use my nickname. We're best buds now. Have a good evening."

"You, too—Sid."

He watched her walk away, stopping to talk to everyone who wanted one brief moment with her, even signing autographs. Best buds, he thought—with an Oscar winner, too! Something he could brag about to his children one day—if he ever had any.

The next familiar face was a furious Reverend Jesse Paulin. He'd given his talk at ten o'clock the previous morning on the theme that if you tithed money to the Lord, you'd make it back tenfold. Nearly two thousand were attending the convention, but only sixty of them showed up to listen to Paulin—humiliating for a "celebrity" to give a talk in a too-big room with hundreds of empty chairs. His talk was interrupted several times by shouts of "Hallelujah!" and people standing and waving their arms in the air, supposedly so God could see them. He had not been compensated for his speech, the hotel room he'd been assigned was small and uncomfortable, with barely any sort of view, and his sales table in the vendors' area, crammed with books, religious pamphlets, pictures, trinkets, and gewgaws that one could buy in any Christian store anywhere, looked almost untouched.

K.O.'s thoughts went to Tobe, and his own revenge. He not only knew how to hurt, but *where* to hurt as well. Rip out another man's eyeball and much of the fight goes out of him.

He shifted from one foot to another. He'd been standing too much in the last three days, and hoped tomorrow, Sunday, would be the end of the GMSA gig. But unless someone came up with enough evidence to arrest a suspected killer, this case could drag on for weeks.

Kylee Graves entered the ballroom tentatively, hunched over so no one would notice her or try to mug her. She'd probably shampooed that day, and her beehive hairdo had been put together sloppily—crooked, with more hair on the right side of her head than the left. Her dress, like the others she'd worn this weekend, was thirty years out of style, and K.O. imagined she was one of those women with the days of the week embroidered on their panties but always wearing the wrong day.

Thinking she might be prettier if she dressed more currently, he found himself looking at her too long. Their eyes met; two red spots appeared on her cheeks as if she'd just been slapped forehand and backhand. She quickly looked away, and hurried down the center aisle to find a seat somewhere in the middle of the crowd.

K.O. had tried explaining Kylee to Tobe Blaine. He was certain she couldn't possibly have shot Tommy Triller in the forehead, afterward jamming his own CD into his mouth as he lay dead on the bed. This was no ordinary murder, K.O. thought. This was pure brutal revenge.

Unless Kaylee was the best actress in the world, that simply wasn't her style.

Swati S. Sathe came in tentatively, too, so exhausted and worn-out looking that K.O. almost didn't recognize her. She carried her thick files of reservations and her usual clipboard low and heavy, like an old-time salesman lugging around his cases of samples.

"It's all over in the morning," K.O. assured her.

"Probably not," she said. "Every big shot has already called his or her lawyer about being kept here—and they'll all invade Cleveland Monday morning to give this hotel more trouble—to say nothing of the police department and the courts."

"The cops checked with TSA. As far as they know, no speakers got on a plane to come here carrying a weapon of any sort, even in their suitcase." He turned away from the crowd to look at her. "How many of these orators left the hotel on Thursday?"

"I have no idea," Swati snapped. "I don't care if they all walk into the middle of Public Square, strip down, and do the Hokey-Pokey naked—as long as they behave themselves on company property."

K.O. said, "Hy Jinx was about a block away, eating dinner Thursday night—with me. I have no idea whether he bought a gun from some low-level street thug." He scratched his head. "He already killed somebody—when he was a street punk himself."

"Doesn't that make him the Number One suspect?"

"They're all suspects—that's why they're being kept here until they're cleared."

"It'll cost them more money. Extra nights in our hotel. Changing their plane reservations. Missing work."

"They can afford it," K.O. said. "Besides, a human being was killed. Most people can't just walk away from that."

"They're trying," Swati said. "Reverend—what's his name again?" She flipped through papers on her clipboard. "Paulin. Jesse Paulin. He told me, he told Mr. Fesmire, and he told several of the Cleveland police detectives that he was a man of God—and that men of God don't have to follow the same rules as everybody else."

"What happened?"

"I laughed in his face. Fesmire begged him not to make a fuss. And the police said that if he even stuck his nose out the door, they'd slam him into a jail cell." She shook her head. "Just one more spoiled brat. I don't care if I see him again or not. We have his credit card on file, so he can stay here until his card maxes out."

Up on stage, Reeve Fesmire made an entrance from the wings to a smattering of applause. His feelings seemed hurt; all the other speakers had received a more robust welcome.

"Thank you all," he said, "for staying with us these past few days. We're shocked and stunned at this awful tragedy, and I'm sure each of us suffers in his or her own way. But we must be proud of ourselves, too. Tommy Triller always said 'Never give up.' And he's looking down on us all, proud that we didn't give up, we didn't quit and go slinking home. We stayed here to make ourselves better—the way he would have made us better."

The applause was slightly more enthusiastic at that one. Slightly.

"So as not to disappoint you too much," Fesmire went on, "at the last minute, we were able to corral not one but *two* top speakers in the country. Jarvis Green wrote one of the best-selling books of all time, *Men and Women From Alternate Universes.* I'll bet you've all read that one, right?"

Maybe thirty people applauded.

"Great! Well, if you haven't, or you want a copy for a friend, they're on sale in the vendors' room until the convention officially closes. And trust me, you'll want to get the book as soon as you hear Jarvis talk.

"Then," Fesmire said, "making the final speech tonight is the wonderful daytime TV star whose business acumen has made her a multi-multi-multi-million-dollar celebrity, Bailey DeWitt."

More clapping.

At last, Fesmire finished, eliciting an audible sigh of relief from the crowd. As the CEO of a giant organization that made him a lot of money each year, Reeve Fesmire envisioned himself as a great speaker, too, blissfully unaware that he was unattractive, had a haplessly high, squeaky voice, and that almost everything he said was boring.

The first actual speaker of the evening—the beginning of the final Big Deal of the convention—was Dr. Lorelei Singleton. The stage manager ran out before she was introduced and put an eight-inch step for her to stand on behind the podium so everyone could see her. There was more applause for her, from the many people who listened to her radio show religiously—no pun intended—five times each week.

"Before I begin my talk," she said solemnly, "I'll ask you to bow your heads and take a moment for Tommy Triller. He's with the Lord now, and he'll hear your silent prayers." She clasped her hands together on the edge of the podium and appeared to be looking down at her feet, as did most of those in the large throng, beseeching God to take good care of Triller. Interesting—because Triller had put Dr. Lorelei in the same category as fuck-and-forget Kylee Graves.

Speaking of Kylee Graves, she had her face in her hands, and several other women wept quietly, too, which made K.O. wonder if they were also one-night stands who had believed themselves to be Tommy Triller's number-one lady.

The female convention attendees outnumbered the males two to one—and most seemed less interested in Dr. Lorelei than in some of the other speakers. K.O. was probably in agreement with them on that.

Next in line was Dr. Ben Mayo, and when he appeared from

the wings, it was obvious that, with Triller gone, he was the most popular speaker of the weekend. He strolled out to cheers from everyone, waving as he always did on his TV show.

Unlike Dr. Lorelei, Mayo made no reference to Tommy Triller or to the surprisingly tragic turn of events. As completely unreligious as he was, K.O. would have had the killing at the beginning of his talk. Not that he'd ever be asked to give a speech anywhere, as he knew that whatever he said aloud was either sarcastic or angry—or both.

He'd never actually seen a Dr. Ben show all the way through, so K.O. didn't recognize most of the folksy clichés he heard that evening, although one of them—"I don't have a dog in this fight"— truly angered an animal lover like him. The listeners, however, chuckled when they should.

Most of the Mayo speech was a re-run of his hundreds of television programs, urging those present to take control of their own lives—the general talk every other speaker had given throughout the weekend. When his twenty minutes were up, Dr. Ben said good night and thank you, leaving through the wings the way he'd entered.

Reeve Fesmire was back to introduce the first of his two replacement headliners, mentioning again the best-selling book that would be sold in the Resource Center until tomorrow at noon as he brought out Jarvis Green.

Green had evidently decided upon a bright blue ascot instead of a tie. Whether the ascot was a turn-off, or if nobody really knew who the hell he was, his reception was muted.

His lecture had very little to do with getting rich. He spoke mostly about people trying to understand the opposite gender, which apparently was not what most of the conventioneers had come to learn. Many wriggled and changed positions in their chairs.

Finally finished, Jarvis slinked off into the wings as Fesmire came out once again to introduce his final speaker.

"You've seen her on television dozens of times," he said, trying to infuse the audience with the same kind of excitement he was obviously faking. "You know she's one of the most successful business entrepreneurs in America today. And most exciting, she is co-anchoring this last convention evening with her famous husband, Jarvis Green. So put your hands together to welcome the wonderful, dynamic Bailey DeWitt."

More applause than for Green, but when Bailey came out, her expression was dark and fierce as thunder, and her stink eye at Reeve Fesmire could have peeled the skin off a rhinoceros. The clapping died out quickly.

She tried venturing a smile a few times during the next twenty minutes, but was unsuccessful, so enraged was she over Fesmire's unthinkable introduction of her as "co-anchoring with her husband."

When she got to the end of her talk, she said, "I'm glad I was invited to come here at the last minute, and to meet and talk with some of you. I'll be around tomorrow until about noon. You can find me in the lobby somewhere, or in the vendors' room, and take a few minutes to chat with me personally. I hope some little glimmer of what I've said tonight helps you take that next step toward becoming successful and wealthy.

"But I have to say something else right now." Her deep inhalation made her appear to grow taller. "First of all, I'm extremely uncomfortable replacing Tommy Triller so soon after his demise. It's a tragedy, of course, and I wish it hadn't happened, but I heartily disagree with most of what Tommy Triller has been telling you all these years—and I think walking barefoot over hot coals is the dumbest thing imaginable."

The shock throughout the gathering was palpable, and she took a moment waiting for it to subside. Then: "I also want to correct something Reeve Fesmire said. He told you I was co-anchoring this evening with my husband, Jarvis Green. Well, Jarvis Green is my *former* husband, and neither of us would be here if we'd known the other would attend, too. So we've both been totally *screwed* by Reeve Fesmire. Perhaps before you come to another of these conventions, you should give a second thought as to whether Reeve has screwed you, too. Good night, and good luck."

She marched off the stage. The crowd seemed confused, and when Fesmire didn't appear again, they began wandering out of the Grand Ballroom, shocked and puzzled. Many headed for the bar, but most repaired to their own hotel rooms. Kylee Graves, her face buried in a handkerchief, rushed past K.O. without looking at him.

One of the last to leave because some attendees had made a point of stopping to talk to her, Siddartha West threw an arm around K.O.'s shoulder near the exit doors. "Wow!" she said. "I hope you had as good a laugh as I did. This craziness is over tomorrow at noon. Stop by my vendor's table in the morning and I'll autograph one of my books—as a personal gift to you." She backed off a few steps and looked at him. "I'll bet with a little effort you can turn out a lot like me."

"Minus the Oscar, though," K.O. said.

"You never know," she said, hugging him like a favorite aunt would, then floating out into the mezzanine lobby.

Becoming friends with Siddartha West was making K.O. feel as if the entire weekend had been worthwhile.

He looked at his watch. Ten-fifteen. Time to go home. He wanted to call Milan to find out how Tobe was holding up, but afraid he'd wake her or disturb her in some way, he decided to wait until morning.

Before leaving, he ducked into the men's room just outside the ballroom, and was surprised to discover Reeve Fesmire standing at one of the sinks. One quick look told K.O. his musings had been right on the money—as Fesmire was busy with towels soaked in cold water, pressing them over his face, his head titled way back, trying to stop the bleeding that was splashing all over his suit and shirt. K.O. wanted to ask whether it was Jarvis Green or Bailey DeWitt who'd given him a bloody nose, but he chose discretion instead. He peed, washed his hands, and said, "See you tomorrow, Mr. Fesmire," as he left the men's room without looking at Reeve again.

At seven o'clock the next morning, his phone rang. He wasn't asleep, but wasn't quite awake yet, either—simply enjoying the feel of Carli's body next to him and her head tucked into his neck.

"It's Milan."

"Hey," K.O. said, trying to sound awake. "How's Tobe doing?"

"Recovering," Milan said. "Try to get to the hotel by about nine-thirty if you can. You're on your own today. I won't be there."

"Really? Why?"

"After Tobe gave them a call last night, the State Highway Patrol nailed Patrick Owens while he was barreling down I-77—speeding, as it turned out. Now they've got him in custody in Columbus, and I'm driving Tobe down to have a nice, friendly, little talk with him."

CHAPTER TWENTY-SEVEN

MILAN

I t was seven-ish on a Sunday morning. The sunrise comes later and later in autumn, and I hate waking up in the dark. I look forward to June, when the sky gets bright at six a.m. I was up, though, wearing my tacky, old, yellow-and-green bathrobe and drinking a cup of tea after making coffee for Tobe when she finally opened her eyes. I'd deliberately kept her awake for hours the night before, worried that one should not sleep directly after a concussion, but eventually I let her quietly enter the Land of Nod, curled up into a ball, taking up more than half of my bed. When I finally crawled in beside her, I had to nearly hang off the edge of the mattress for fear of waking her.

This was her second concussion within a year, reminding me of the old days, the Muhammad Ali days, when I really cared about professional boxing, and those fighters who were knocked out too many times were called "punch-drunks," who could barely count to ten. Now the concussions happen on a regular basis in the National Football League, which doesn't seem to be doing a damn thing about them. Personally, I've had more concussions than I can count, so many that my doctor told me to slow down and avoid the rough stuff, or I'd wind up rocking my golden years away on a porch, dribbling Cream of Wheat onto my pajamas and staring into nothingness as my life ebbed away.

I carried my tea mug to the doorway of my bedroom to check on Tobe. I love to watch her any time—she's beautiful in a classic way, like an aristocratic African princess—but to me, she looks especially remarkable when she's asleep. The professional, aggressive "cop look" falls away, and her expression is relaxed, her hair loose around her shoulders, rather than up in the no-nonsense bun she wears to work most days, and her sleep shirt—one of my oldest—flipped up at the collar, framing her coffee-with-cream face.

I knew Victor would want me back at the hotel, looking out for Tony Nardoianni—but for me, Tobe Blaine was a hundred times more important. Without discussing it, we both kept the "L" word unspoken, but I knew how much I loved her, and hoped she loved me back, too.

She was my soul mate.

I went back out into the living room and sat where I usually do, in a big overstuffed chair tucked into a bay with windows overlooking the Cedar-Fairmount Triangle, the supermarket whose name had changed several times over the last twenty years from Russo's to Giant Eagle and now to Dave's, and the Mad Greek restaurant, which specialized not only in Greek food, but in East Indian cuisine as well. I watched the light traffic navigating Cedar Hill until I heard Tobe's cell phone jangle.

I returned to the bedroom. She was wide awake, speaking quietly into her phone. The swelling on her face had grown smaller, but squinty eyes let me know she had a headache. She finished her conversation quickly, then clicked off and swung her shapely legs out of bed.

"Get dressed, Milan," she said. "Call and let K.O. know he's alone at the hotel today because you have to drive me to Columbus. Their P.D. has my favorite guy in custody."

On our way, we had to stop at her place so she could change clothes, get rid of the make-up she'd worn all day Saturday and replace it, and then pick up a uniformed detective sergeant to ride downstate with us. His name was Lloyd Swanson, who mostly rode his desk now that he'd aged and grown way too chunky. I remember him vaguely from when I was a Cleveland police officer more than a quarter century ago—he wasn't a sergeant then, but a wet-behind-the-ears rookie just like me.

Being official, he wore blue and a visible badge, and carried a weapon at his hip, while I could do neither. He might help her out with the arrest, if necessary, but I insisted on driving. After the attack, I didn't want her buzzing around central Ohio by herself.

I had no idea whether he'd been prepped on my relationship with Tobe, nor did I care, because when Tobe explained to him what had happened the day before, Swanson's throaty growl mimicked Clint Eastwood's. "I give a murder suspect the benefit of the doubt whenever I can," he said from the back seat, "but if somebody goes out of their way to hurt another cop, his ass is *mine!*"

Tobe said over her shoulder, "It was a sucker punch, Lloyd."

I thought but didn't remind her how lucky she was, and that a sucker punch from a man built like Patrick Owens could have decapitated her.

Why would he hit a police officer in the first place? Why run back to Columbus? Was he guilty of murder? I wasn't sure, but I did know he wasn't the sharpest knife in the drawer, which made me even more angry. It was a good thing I couldn't bring a weapon with me.

I could have. I can carry concealed anyplace in Ohio. But if there were serious trouble once we got to Columbus police headquarters, there were plenty of armed badge-wearers running around, plus Lloyd Swanson and Tobe, on official duty. If I shot Owens instead, even if it were deserved, I'd be in a pickle of my own.

We'd been driving for ninety minutes and were approaching Mansfield, proud of its Malabar Farms, owned by the family of the late novelist Louis Bromfield, where Bogart and Bacall were married and spent their honeymoon, and the legendary prison featured in *The Shawshank Redemption* film. I said to Tobe, "How are you doing? Want to stop for a bit?"

She gave it some thought. "Sure, let's stop—unless you have an empty coffee can in the car."

"Not this time," I said.

We pulled off at an exit with several gas stations and fast-food restaurants, including one I had visited many years earlier, investigating a so-called suicide. Tobe disappeared into the restroom, and Swanson got a small coffee with lots of cream while we waited.

Finally, he said, "You get around nowadays, huh, Milan? I even read about you in the paper sometimes."

"Comes with the job," I said.

"You and Blaine. You two are a—thing, right?"

"We're a thing, yes."

He nodded and slurped his coffee. "As I remember from the old days, she's not your usual type."

I waited about fifteen seconds, then I said, "What *is* my type?"

He brushed his fingertips against one side of his face—a gesture once used insultingly to describe a person of color. "Well—you know."

"I suggest you don't go there, Swanson."

His smile was all nasty amusement. "Really? What are you gonna do about it?"

"Wait until you're not wearing your badge and gun. Don't push it."

"I always have my badge and my gun. Those are rules, in case you don't remember anymore." He shrugged and turned half away. "I'm not pushing. Just saying."

I walked to the other side of the shop and studied the various brands of potato chips on display as though I were trying to make a decision about buying a new car, trying to shake my need to bloody Swanson's nose. I stayed there until Tobe tapped me on the shoulder.

"Can't decide between the classic and the rippled chips?" she asked.

"Just catching up on my reading, Tobe. Ready to go?"

"Let's roll," she said, waving at Swanson to follow us out.

Back on the road, I asked her how Patrick Owens had wound up at the city police department headquarters.

"Last night," she said, "I called Detective Meg Pinckney in Columbus and told her to keep a BOLO for Owens. She notified the highway patrol, who nailed him up by Polaris before he got into downtown. They figured assaulting a Cleveland cop was more serious than driving ninety miles an hour on the freeway."

"So Meg has him now?"

"Right under her thumb," Tobe said.

The main police HQ was close to both I-71, which brought us there, and I-70, on which, if we turned right and stayed straight for three days, would take us to Sacramento, California. I'd never been to Sacramento and had no desire to visit there, though I wondered whether the capitol building was as elegant as ours in Columbus.

Detective Meg Pinckney was ten years younger than Tobe, approximately six feet tall, and her sculpted features recalled a Gauguin painting of a Tahitian maiden. She wore her long hair straight and in a ponytail. Tobe and Meg shook hands.

Meg checked out Tobe's swollen face. "Girlfriend, you look like the end of a wasted life."

"'Fraid so."

She shook her head. "I should've kicked him in the stones this morning, then. Who'd know the difference?"

"Everybody would," I said, "when he started singing soprano."

That got me a look from Meg. "Tobe said you were funny sometimes."

"Sometimes," Tobe said.

Detective Pinckney beckoned us to follow her—first Tobe, then me, with Lloyd Swanson bringing up the rear. Swanson's body language telegraphed that he didn't like Pinckney any better than he liked Tobe.

I had no right to say anything, under the circumstances, but it amazed me that Lloyd Swanson had worked as a Cleveland cop for thirty-five years and somehow had built up a dislike—if not something worse than that—for Americans of color. Or maybe it was just black *women*.

In the interrogation room, Patrick Owens was already seated, wearing baggy prison orange shirt and pants and plastic orange slippers. His wrists were cuffed in front of him, and had been attached to the immovable table. He would need an acrobatic stretch just to scratch his nose.

He looked scared, but I knew this was not his first experience in Columbus law enforcement custody; the earlier OSU rape incident had him modeling orange for a few days as well. But when he saw Tobe, he looked worried, obviously wondering whether she would beat the crap out of him for revenge while he was hand-cuffed.

"We meet again," Tobe said easily, sitting across the table from him. "Are you having a pleasant Sunday morning?"

Owens gulped—loudly.

"Before we get started, I have to compliment you, Paddy O. Pretty good punch, there. A sucker punch, but you hit pretty hard."

"I'm sorry, Officer. Really." He barely got the words out—and we hadn't even started yet.

"I'm sorry, too—sorry I didn't see it coming, or I would've shot off your johnson. And by the way, it's 'detective sergeant,' not 'officer,' you dickwad."

Owens's eyes opened wide.

"I'm still pissed at what you did," Tobe said, "but I'm here for a different reason, Paddy O, which might wind up with you in a state prison for the rest of your life. So you damn well better talk to me like we're old kindergarten buddies, or they'll lock you up and plumb forget where they put that key."

"But I didn't do nothin'!" His voice was already up so high that only dogs could hear him.

"You were being questioned about a murder that took place in your hotel," Tobe said, "and instead of being helpful, you knocked a law officer unconscious and ran."

"I was scared!"

"Nowhere near how scared you're going to be—and OSU won't lift a finger to help you again. So let's give this a go, shall we? When you can't sucker punch anyone."

He actually groaned and wouldn't look at anyone except Tobe.

"You were hired as Dr. Ben's chauffeur and bodyguard for the weekend." Owens nodded his head up and down like a ventrilo-quist's dummy.

"*Say it*, goddamn it! Is that right?"

"Yes, ma'am."

Say *ma'am*, I thought, to someone you nearly killed? I'd make a note of that.

"How did you get hired?"

"Through, um, George Lufton."

"Who's he?"

Meg said, "I know all about that bastard. He's a loan shark, mainly—and God help you if you don't pay off on time."

"Is that right, Paddy O?" Tobe said. "You were a leg-buster for this Lufton guy?"

"I was a—collector," Owens stammered.

"So when did you get hired as chauffeur for the Mayos?"

"Umm—on Monday."

"And where'd you get the limousine?"

"It's George's limo."

"You got it Thursday morning?"

"Yes ma'am, I got it at George's place."

"When you picked up the Mayos in Columbus on Thursday to drive them to Cleveland, did you have a weapon with you?"

"Nuh-uh!" he said, shaking his head hard. "I don't own any kind of a gun. I'm no gun person. People carrying guns get hurt."

"So Ben Mayo didn't send you out on the street in Cleveland on Thursday to buy one from some sidewalk punk?"

He shook his head again. "I never left the hotel once we checked in. I wouldn't know where to buy a gun."

"You can buy one in Columbus, though, can't you?" Meg said.

Owens shook his head. "Never owned a gun."

She looked over at Tobe and nodded; she'd already checked that.

"All right, then," Tobe said, "let's go over *exactly* what you did Thursday—and I mean exactly. What time you picked up the car, what time did you get to the Mayos, what happened on the way north. Did you stop to pee? Did you eat potato chips while you were driving? Was the glass partition up or down? Did you get to look up Mrs. Mayo's skirt in the rearview mirror? Did you scratch your balls? Fart? I want every fucking minute of your time on Thursday accounted for."

Owens gulped. "Uh—could I get a drink of water?"

"I don't know. Do they let prisoners die of thirst in Columbus?"

"Where do you think you are?" Meg Pinckney snapped. "Applebee's?" She looked meaningfully at Lloyd Swanson.

"I'll get him something to drink," Swanson said, annoyed, "and piss in the bottle before I give it to him." He stomped out.

Pinckney said, "First, let's see how good you can talk with a dry mouth. Detective Sergeant Blaine asked you a question, shit-burger."

Paddy O licked his lips as Tobe took out her police notebook. "I—picked up the limo at George's house."

"What time?"

He shrugged the best he could, considering he was chained to the table. "Maybe ten o'clock. Then I took it to a car wash, like George told me."

Tobe nodded. "You have to make a limo as clean as a whistle." Then she looked at me. "Where'd that expression come from, Milan? Why are whistles always clean?"

"Don't ask me," I said, "I only got a master's degree."

"Well," Owens said, "that's what I did—and he gave me a hundred bucks spending money for while I was in Cleveland."

"You didn't register at the Renaissance Hotel when you arrived, did you?" Tobe said. "Mayo had your room and Claire Crane's under his name."

"No," he said, "I was busy keeping people away from Dr. Ben. In the hotel, I wasn't the chauffeur anymore, I was the bodyguard—and nobody got near Dr. Ben unless he said it was okay."

I remembered K.O. telling me he'd gone chest-to-chest in the hotel lobby with this guy while the Mayos were registering.

Tobe said, "You and Claire didn't go up to the Mayo suite?"

"Not then. There was too many guys carrying luggage."

Swanson returned with a small paper cup full of water. I didn't ask where he'd gotten it.

"At least Paddy's screwed for something—assaulting a police officer," Tobe said, caressing the swollen side of her face. "Running from the scene of a crime, too. Did you really think we'd let you get away with that? You're under arrest, Mr. Owens, for attacking a police officer and for leaving the scene of a murder without permission." Tobe turned to Pinckney again. "I want him in Cleveland, Meg. Can you get him back into civilian clothes and out of that cute little orange ensemble? It doesn't go with his eyes." She turned to Swanson. "You can help him tie his shoes, Sergeant Swanson."

Pinckney called another officer to unhook Owens from the

table, and then he and Swanson marched him upstairs to where he'd left his clothes.

"May I ask you something?" I said to Pinckney.

"Shoot."

"Is George Lufton so protected that you can't even get him down here to talk?"

"Nobody's caught Lufton doing anything worse than jay-walking," she said. "We know he's loaning poor people money at nearly criminal interest rates, and he has guys like Owens do the dirty work. He also has a successful limousine service, and as far as I know, that's legit, except some of his limo drivers are also his punch-out guys. But we've never nailed them, either. Lufton practically owns several of the biggest, best lawyers in Ohio—so my hands are tied." She turned to Tobe. "We only nailed Owens for driving at ninety-five miles per hour and kept him in custody because of your phone call, Tobe. If we do get him back here, we can process that—but I don't think he'll go to state prison for speeding. His felony was in your jurisdiction, not mine. And as far as your celebrity murder is concerned . . ." She sighed heavily.

"You know about Tommy Triller?" I asked.

"Everybody knows *about* Tommy Triller. I watched him once on one of his paid-program TV shows. It took me less than that long, boring hour to figure out he was the king of the bullshitter's bullshit. He didn't deserve getting killed, but I can't be all torn up about it."

About fifteen minutes later, Swanson and the other Columbus cop brought Owens downstairs, dressed in his own clothes, and Tobe and I marched him out to my car. Before we got in, Swanson cuffed Owens's hands together in front of him.

"Sergeant Swanson," Tobe said, "the protocol is to cuff his hands behind his back. What's the deal here?"

"It's a three-hour drive," Swanson said. "He'll be too uncomfortable with his hands cuffed behind his back all day. That's cruel and unusual punishment."

"This is an arrest, Sergeant, not a Sunday drive in the sunshine. Besides, I'm goddamn uncomfortable right now, too—thanks to him. Re-cuff his hands behind him." Swanson didn't move, and all of a sudden there was a stare-down between two law enforcement professionals. Finally Tobe said, "That's an order."

Swanson waited another moment, then rolled his eyes toward the sky. "Whee!" he said, and sulkily did what he was told.

We proceeded northward in awkward silence. After an hour, when we were about halfway to Cleveland, Owens said, "Can we stop somewhere? I gotta go to the john, or I'll piss all over the back seat of your car."

We wound up at the same place we'd stopped on the way down earlier. Swanson said to Tobe, "I'm no babysitter—and if you think I'm gonna go in there and hold his dick for him, you might as well can me right here and now."

"I'm seriously considering that, Swanson," Tobe snarled, with a savagery shocking even Swanson. "Get out of my face before I do something we'll both be sorry for."

Swanson's face grew as red as if he'd spent an entire day at the beach, and he started to say something to her, but changed his mind and retreated. She waited until he stalked angrily away to the other side of the store—where he probably read the same potato chip bags I'd read that morning. Then she turned to me. "Milan?"

"I'll go in with him, Tobe. But uncuff him first—if you get my drift."

Her angry face relaxed. "Well—under the circumstances . . . "

She took Paddy Owens's elbow and steered him to the door of the men's room, where she removed the cuffs. Nearly everyone in the shop saw that, and immediately decided whatever they had to buy could be purchased elsewhere. Their rush to the doors was a stampede.

"Paddy," she said, "there's no way you're getting out of that men's room except through this door. I'll be waiting—and my weapon will be in my hand, not in my holster. Are we clear?"

We walked into the john together, and he headed directly to one of the urinals and unzipped. I looked around, as I always do when I'm in a strange place for the first time with a guy who might try to escape from the law. Two of everything, it seemed— urinals, toilet stalls, sinks, liquid soap dispensers, and both an electric hand dryer and a roll of paper towels. There was a high window above the sinks, October sun streaming through, but getting oneself through it would be a tight squeeze. Not impossible, though.

He finished, got himself together, and said, "Don't you have to piss, too?"

"No, but it's nice of you to ask."

He walked to one of the basins. "Gotta wash my hands. Gotta be sanitary."

"I'm proud of you," I monotoned.

"I didn't do nothin', you know?"

"You assaulted a police officer."

"Police officer, huh? Big fucking deal," he mumbled, turning the water on. Then, before getting wet, he squirted some of the liquid soap onto his hands. A *lot* of liquid soap. He could have bathed a Saint Bernard with that much soap.

Then he spun around quickly and threw two handfuls of it into my face.

My eyes burning, I put my hands up to wipe the soap away, so when he swung a punch at me, it hit my left wrist rather than my face. It was hard enough to send me backwards across the room and down on my ass. Ever sat down hard on the tile floor of a public men's room? I don't recommend it.

By the time I got my eyes open, Owens kicked me in the head, then turned quickly and hoisted himself up to stand on the sink, trying to open the window through which he hoped to escape. I scrambled to my feet and tackled him around his knees. He tumbled down off the sink, landing practically on top of me. Big man, hard to handle.

We wrestled around for about ten seconds until he got me into a tight headlock and squeezed. Things I could see from that angle—like my feet—were beginning to fade away into darkness. I couldn't have that. Bent over at the waist as I was, it was easy for me to punch *him* hard, for a change.

In his testicles.

That got his attention.

He let go, screaming and clutching his crotch, and I straightened up, grabbed him by the back of the neck, and slammed him into the door of one of the stalls, face first.

Several times. The fourth time, I heard the bones in his nose crunch.

Tobe blasted through the door, weapon in hand, but stopped as Owens sank slowly to the floor, his face bloody and his nose flattened between his cheekbones.

"I can't leave you two boys alone for one minute!" Tobe scolded. We lifted the half-conscious Owens to his feet. I twisted his hands behind his back as she cuffed him again.

I started pushing him toward the door, and we emerged into the relatively empty store. Only the two employees and Lloyd Swanson were left.

When Owens saw Swanson, he tried moving toward him, bellowing, "Police brutality!"

Tobe and I grinned at each other. Then I said, "You won't be breathing through your nose anytime soon until you have a plastic surgeon fix your face, and then you'll be cute as a button again. But quit bellowing about police brutality, Paddy—I'm not a policeman, and I can do whatever I want to you, because I'm just a brute."

We threw him into the back of my car, with Swanson watching over him and pressing paper towels against his face so my car seat wouldn't be ruined. In the meantime, I went back into the john, ran some cold water, and tried flushing the liquid soap out of my eyes and cooling off my head where he'd kicked me.

We got Patrick Owens back to the city jail in downtown Cleveland at about four o'clock in the afternoon.

CHAPTER TWENTY-EIGHT

K.O.

K.O. didn't have much to occupy himself with while waiting for Milan and Tobe to return from Columbus. His only job—and several civilian-clad cops hung around doing the same thing and looking equally stultified—was to make sure none of the celebrity speakers sneaked out of town. All the conventioneers and mostly unknown presenters had already left—some of whom were happy, though considerably lighter in their wallets from buying all the merchandise the speakers and their temp workers had peddled in the Resource Room.

Reverend Jesse Paulin was furious, of course. He wanted desperately to leave town. But K.O. knew he was secretly pleased he was considered one of the VIPs ordered to stay in Cleveland until further notice.

Milan had called K.O. from the car while heading north, telling him quickly about the events of the Columbus trip, including the men's room incident. K.O. was impressed as hell that Milan was able to easily handle a guy as big and young as Patrick Owens.

"Now," Milan told him over the phone, "we've got Paddy on a second assault charge, this time on me. Besides, he's jumped clear to Number One as a person of interest. He's sitting in the back seat right now, so he can hear everything I say. Can't you, Paddy?" There was an indistinct mumble as an answer. Milan cleared his throat. "And how was *your* morning, K.O.?"

K.O.'s morning had been just dandy, thank you very much. He and Carli wound up throwing all the blankets and top sheet onto the floor during their acrobatic lovemaking, as they often did when they first woke up. Now he felt somewhat better about her disapproval of his sometimes dangerous job. It still bothered her that he'd been maced, but one would never know it early that morning when she was straddling him, head thrown back, eyes closed, moaning loudly as she savored every bit of her vibrant orgasm.

Make-up sex? Probably, K.O. thought. Any long-term relationship had its ups and downs, its fighting and fussing. One couldn't really live with another person, no matter how much love was involved, without sometimes *disagreeing*. But that was new to K.O. Never had he experienced a long relationship. Since he had no idea *how* to fight with Carli, he often simply clammed up, gritted his teeth, kept his head down, and hoped the moment would pass.

Two uniformed police officers were stationed at each hotel doorway to make sure none of the big shots tried leaving with their luggage. Two more prowled Tower City, checking for the same thing, and two homicide detectives lurked around in plain clothes, taking notes and discreetly snapping photographs on their smartphones. The speakers were not under "house arrest," so they could go wherever they pleased until the cops released them, but they couldn't take their luggage with them. It was silly, when K.O. thought about it. Where could these famous VIPs run *to* without being instantly recognized?

K.O.'s duties were more or less unexplained, other than to "keep a lookout," so at the moment he was in the main lobby with one eye on the elevator and another out the window at Public Square. Sunday mornings were quiet at that usually bustling location, so he could easily spot someone walking around outside who shouldn't have been.

He was surprised, though, when Victor Gaimari came up the winding staircase, glancing around until he saw K.O. sitting in an easy chair near the window, and walked over and sat down opposite him.

"Good morning, Mr. O'Bannion," Victor said. No crisp formal suit this time—it was Sunday, after all—but he was dressed in two-hundred-dollar slacks and a six-hundred-dollar purple sweater. K.O. thought the few times he'd seen Victor that the man dressed so expensively because he wanted to impress everyone with his wealth and stylish tastes. Now he figured Victor always dressed that way because he owned no jeans or Dockers or anything else he might have bought with a thirty-percent discount card from Kohl's. "May I buy you a drink?"

"Thanks, Mr. Gaimari, but I'm on duty. For *you.*"

"True. Have you seen Tony?"

"No. He's probably in his room, chowing on room service. Or maybe he went for a swim—if he brought a bathing suit."

Victor laughed. "He wouldn't be caught dead in a bathing suit. I wish the police would tell him he's free to leave and go back home to Denver."

"He's not a Denver native, is he? He sure doesn't sound like it."

"Born and raised just south of Greenwich Village in New York. A solidly Italian neighborhood. His father was a Brooklyn Dodgers fan, and stuck with them when they moved to Los Angeles, so Tony has always been into baseball. Couldn't ever get with the Dodgers, or with either of the New York teams. He coached in Milwaukee and Atlanta before he managed the Colorado Rockies."

K.O. digested that. Then: "Was Tony ever violent?"

"If you watch baseball enough, you'll know that every major league manager has several explosions every year going nose-to-nose-with an umpire. Same with Tony Nardoianni. There were times he'd be furious enough to rip first base up out of its moorings and kick it clear across the infield. Let's face it, he *is* Italian. But I don't think he's ever hurt anybody."

"He didn't bring a gun. The police already checked the airlines—and they searched his room. He didn't have one with him."

"So?"

"I'm wondering," K.O. said, "if you gave him one when he arrived in town."

Victor's eyes narrowed. "I don't distribute guns to visitors, just in case they want to kill someone. You have a strange idea of who I am."

"I know who you are. I work for you, remember?"

"*You* remember, then, that I never carry a weapon. Never have, never will—nor have I had anyone killed. My—business has changed over the years, and my family hasn't operated with the fear of violence since the 1950s. Before I was born."

"I didn't mean to offend you," K.O. told him.

"You did—but I won't have you 'taken for a ride,' so don't worry." Victor checked out the ceiling in the lobby for a moment. "Do you do anything in your spare time besides watch gangster movies?"

"Yes, sir. Sitting around wishing I *were* one."

Victor smiled quietly. "Be careful what you wish for, son." He unfolded himself from his chair, looking at his flashy gold watch—a different watch from the one he'd worn when K.O. last saw him in the lobby. "I'm going up to see Tony. Come along, if you want, to make sure he hasn't gunned down the room service guy or strangled the chambermaid."

"You'll probably do a better job watching him than I would." K.O. stood up, too. "You've got my cell phone number, Mr. Gaimari, so I'll be around if you need me."

"Thank you—Mr. O'Bannion."

Victor moved off, gliding across the carpet. Most people don't glide. K.O. watched him head for the elevator, thinking Victor was the most confident person he'd ever met.

He returned to the vendors' room, in which most of the tables and stacks of merchandise were all but torn down, the hired workers and models packing books and trinkets away in boxes to be shipped back where they'd come from. The only VIP speaker in there was Jonah Clary, standing with arms folded while a pretty young woman, no longer dressed in her model glam but in Dockers and a sweatshirt, was shoveling some of Clary's two ghost-written books and an entire stack of "Clary for President" buttons and photos into a series of cardboard cartons, already addressed with a "Clary for President" office in his home city.

Clary sported a buckskin-fringed Eisenhower jacket that stopped at the waist over a checkered Wrangler cowboy shirt—

with too-tight blue jeans that allowed his unfettered gut to spill over his belt, his ten-gallon Stetson, and a pair of extravagant cowboy boots no one would dream of wearing anywhere near a cow. K.O. noticed that Clary's wallet was in the right-hand hip pocket of his jeans, and a silver flask poked out from the top of his left, and when he got close enough to the ex-governor's breath, he realized that flask was not completely full.

Clary growled, "*Again*? Nobody else to hang around with and spoil their day?"

"Sure, but you're my favorite, Governor. Packing up, I see. Or, actually, the lady is doing all the packing."

Clary chose to ignore that. "We have to be out of the vendors' room by tonight—but damn it, I can't go home until you cops tell me I can."

"I'm not a cop, remember? But the TSA won't let you on the plane anyway. You're on the Cleveland No-Fly list."

He puffed and wheezed, "I was almost president of the United States! So *get out of my goddamn face!*" Clary bellowed so loudly that the woman filling his shipping boxes looked up, frightened.

K.O. smiled at her. "He's just joking—because he loves me."

Nearly a whisper now: "I'd show you how much I love you if I was wearing my Colt six-shooters."

"Didn't bring them with you?"

"How the hell could I get on a plane carrying two guns around my waist?"

"Are they loaded?"

"Why would I carry unarmed weapons?"

"I don't know," K.O. said. "To shoot people?"

Clary gritted his teeth. "I never shot people, you little prick!"

"Really? *I* did. They shot back, too."

"Who?"

"I couldn't speak Farsi, so we were never properly introduced."

The ex-governor brightened considerably. "Ah. A veteran. Well, damn, boy, let me just shake the hand of a veteran. I thank you for your service."

K.O. shook Clary's hand with little enthusiasm. "You really carry those Colts around in your home state? Twin holsters?"

"Sometimes. But I didn't bring them with me. Not much to shoot in Cleveland."

K.O. shrugged. "How about Tommy Triller?"

Clary gulped loudly before he answered. "That—that was just a doggone shame."

"You hated Triller. Could've been you who shot him."

Jonah Clary stood up tall as he could and puffed his chest out, looming over the much smaller K.O. "I'm sick and tired of all your goddamn hinting! If I had my Colts, I'd stick one right up your ass."

K.O. snickered, and it came out nasty. "You'd have to get pretty close to do that—and if you tried, I'd take your Colt away from you and make you eat it."

Strolling briskly out through the narrow hallway between the vendors' room and the huge space used for big, important meetings, K.O. found himself wishing and hoping Jonah Clary *was* the bad guy.

In the main lobby, he saw Swati S. Sathe getting off the elevator, dressed in a topcoat over a slacks suit. She saw him, and waited for him to reach her.

"Going home already?" K.O. said. "Had enough?"

"More than enough, thank you. I was supposed to have Saturday and Sunday off—but I didn't expect a murder in my hotel, so—here I am." She smiled almost sadly. "Despite all this Triller business, I've enjoyed meeting you, K.O., and your boss, too. You did a terrific job, and the hotel really appreciates it."

"It's a nice hotel, Swati. Maybe if I'm looking for a romantic weekend, I might bring my lady here for a good time." He shuddered slightly. "Just don't book me on the twelfth floor, okay?"

She checked out the lobby quickly. "FYI, Reeve Fesmire is still here—the police won't let him leave town, either, and he's about one whisper away from a complete meltdown. I'd stay clear of him, if I were you."

K.O. nodded. "Milan can take care of him. I've insulted enough people this weekend."

"Where is Milan, anyway? I haven't seen him all day."

"Took a trip to Columbus with Detective Sergeant Blaine—to see all the leaves turning colors."

She chuckled. "You're not the first man to lie to me—but I don't give a damn where they went today, or why. I'm going to make a big pot of Indian tea, cuddle up with my husband under a blanket, and watch television or something." Swati shook his hand. "Good luck, K.O. I hope you find the guy you're looking for."

"Or the gal," K.O. said.

CHAPTER TWENTY-NINE

MILAN

After Tobe booked Patrick Owens and tucked him into his own private cell, I dropped her off at the hotel and drove home to feed Herbie and take him for a walk. I had lived without a dog, or pet of any kind, for my entire life—and now I sometimes forget that we have obligations to our four-footed family members that affect our schedules every day.

When I returned to the hotel, I found K.O. almost immediately—seated close to the beautiful marble fountain in the center of the main lobby. Little did I know that from then on, he would always refer to it as "The Michelangelo Fountain." Not that Michelangelo had anything to do with it.

"Anything interesting happen when I was gone?" I said.

"Not as interesting as what happened with you. Have you been crying?"

"If I threw liquid soap from a men's room into your eyes, you'd cry, too," I said.

"We've both shed tears at this convention."

I blinked my eyes again a few times; they still smarted. "Find anything out?"

"Mr. Gaimari spent his money well on us. Tony Nardoianni is almost saintly, at least when it comes to Tommy Triller dying."

"Is Victor happy?"

"I wouldn't say 'happy.' Very confident, though."

"Not exactly breaking news," I said. "What else?"

"A few speakers went out for lunch—but they all came back."

"Who?"

"Let's see." K.O. thumbed through his notebook. "Hy Jinx headed into Tower City by himself; I think there's a pretty good deli down there. Triller's defensive line went out together, since there's nobody left to protect, but they're in their room now, swilling Heinekens. Gaimari took Nardoianni out for lunch, but they came back in about ninety minutes. Dr. Lorelei sailed out of here on the arm of Reverend Paulin—now *that's* a new twosome! The Mayos—Ben and Christine—went out together, and a few minutes after that, Claire Crane left by herself, looking sad and lonely. As far as I know, they're all back in their rooms now."

"Governor Clary?"

K.O. screwed up his face. "What an asshat he is! He and I had words back in the vendors' room."

"You always have 'words' with him. Who else?"

"How about Siddartha West? My grandma girlfriend?" K.O. grinned. "Haven't seen her all day. Maybe she passed away and reincarnated herself as a rare butterfly."

"Old movie stars don't wander around strange cities alone. Easy to check, anyway. Where's Reeve Fesmire?"

"I didn't notice him leave the hotel, but I might have missed it. He was hanging around the check-out desk this morning, saying goodbye to all the conventioneers."

"Was he smiling?"

"Why not? A lot of bucks from the vendors' room went right into his pocket."

"Then what are we left with?"

Tobe Blaine appeared behind me, so I didn't realize she was there until she said, "You're left with me."

I stood up. I really wanted to hug her, but one doesn't hug homicide detectives when they're on duty. Instead, I said, "Hey— how are you feeling?"

"My jaw hurts," she said, touching the side of her puffy, bruised face with delicate fingers. "I have a headache from you smelling like a Tijuana whorehouse from that men's room soap in your face—and I'm so damn hungry that if you put a halfway decent sauce on it, I'd eat your shoe. Let's get the hell out of here for a while."

The three of us emerged out onto Public Square. The temperature was brisk, somewhere in the high sixties. I like September and October in Cleveland. Summers are sticky hot, the streets are crowded, and there are festivals every weekend. Winters are cold, snowy, and black and white—or worse, gray and slushy. But the fall—ah, the fall gets my blood circulating, and the setting sun makes everything beautiful.

We walked a few blocks to East 4th Street, where there is an amazing array of restaurants, and dropped into Lola Bistro. It was early for Sunday dinner—not quite six o'clock, so we didn't have to wait for a table. None of us chose an alcoholic beverage. Tobe was, for all intents and purposes, still on duty, and I don't like drinking when she isn't. K.O. was not much of an imbiber, anyway.

She said, "I'm hoping either for divine inspiration or for one of you to tell me who killed Triller so I can put him or her away and then go home."

"You don't think it was Owens?" K.O. said.

"I doubt it," I told him. "He was scared when he cold-cocked Tobe—and when he ran. Now he's still scared—but he's no killer."

"Why not?"

"I've read his Columbus record, and I can't come up with a single motive," Tobe said. "I don't think he was sure who Triller was in the first place. Also—when the opening ceremonies began on Thursday night and Reeve Fesmire asked Triller to say a few words, Paddy O wasn't even there."

"You searched his room?" I said.

"One of my guys did—and Owens didn't bitch about it."

"No gun, obviously."

"No—and there was no gunpowder on his hands or clothes."

K.O. said, "You tested all the VIPs, too?"

"Every one of them, and they all bitched that they were being picked on." Tobe smiled, or as much as she could smile with half her face still swollen. "Want to guess who bitched the loudest?"

"Governor Clary," K.O. said firmly.

"Reverend Paulin," I speculated.

"Wrong—and wrong. It was the lovely and talented Lorelei Singleton. She screamed and yelled and flounced around and threw things across the room—a damn good thing she didn't throw them at me—and called me names I never heard come out of a woman before."

"What names?" K.O. asked.

"And sully your virgin ears? Again, no weapon, no residue." Tobe took a deep breath, expelling it slowly. "I've never heard her radio show—and now I'll make a point to avoid it." She glanced over at the door and her eyes widened. "Look who's here, guys."

Claire Crane had entered and paused for a moment, allowing her eyes to adjust to the mellow mood of the restaurant. Tobe rose from her chair. "We need to even things up at this table. You know—boy, girl, boy, girl . . . " She walked over to Claire Crane and asked her to join us for dinner.

Claire seemed stunned by the invitation, and I could see her shaking her head. Eventually, though, she gave in and let Tobe lead her to our table.

Tobe overwhelms without even trying.

"I think you know everyone here, Claire," Tobe said, guiding her into a chair. "We're taking some time off, relaxing, and we thought it'd be nicer for you to break bread with friends, rather than sitting in a corner all by yourself."

Claire Crane didn't know what to do with her hands. She looked self-conscious, and said so. "Isn't this awkward? You're all cops."

"The only police officer here is me," Tobe said. "These two guys are my groupies. Relax. You're not getting arrested—just invited to dinner."

Waiting to order, Tobe asked Claire all about herself—home town, schooling, what had brought her to Hollywood, how she got a producer's job with Dr. Ben. None of us cared about the answers, but Tobe was heading for more direct questioning.

When the waitress had come and gone—coffee for Tobe and K.O., tonic with lime for me, and a Diet Coke for Claire—Tobe said, "I know you're as anxious to get out of town as everyone else, but murder investigations take a while."

Claire said, "I do just as much work here as if I were back in

L.A. I'm on the phone twelve hours a day, calling people who want to get booked on the show, calling those *we* want on the show, arranging transportation, booking hotels." She sucked in a chestful of air and blew it out noisily.

"Do you spend a lot of time with Dr. Ben?" I asked.

"No—although more time here than I would in Century City, where we work."

"Do you spend more time with him here? Or when you're on the road?"

"I see Ben more when we're traveling—but we're not friends or anything. I hardly ever talk to Caroline Mayo—and she has no use for me, either."

"Why's that?"

"I don't know. Ask her. She doesn't like most people who work for her husband."

Tobe asked, "Were you the one who called George Lufton in Columbus?"

Claire nodded.

"How much did he charge Ben Mayo for the limo and driver?"

"I think it was five thousand dollars."

"Wow," K.O. breathed.

She daintily sipped her Diet Coke. "Paddy Owens was to drop us off at the airport and then drive the limo back—but of course it'll cost more, now that we're stuck here longer."

"When's the last time you saw Owens?" I asked.

Her brow wrinkled. "I don't know. Sometime yesterday afternoon. He's just a driver and bodyguard."

"Bodyguard? Is Dr. Ben in danger?"

"Famous TV people always need bodyguards because they're in everybody's living rooms or bedrooms every day, and some nutcases think that gives them the right to force themselves into their realities." Brushing the hair back once again. "Like Triller. You've seen those three bodyguards who worked for him full-time—they look like silverback gorillas."

I nodded. "I've talked to all of them."

"Get back to Patrick Owens," Tobe insisted. "You don't know much about him?"

"Just that he works for George Lufton—so whatever he's getting paid comes out of Lufton's five thousand dollars."

The waitress came back and took our dinner orders.

"Did you know, Claire," Tobe said, "that Paddy Owens ran out of the hotel like a bat out of hell yesterday and took the limo with him, all the way back to Columbus?"

Claire Crane looked flabbergasted. I don't think she was a good enough actor to pull that off so well. She gulped and finally said, "He did?"

"I was asking him questions, I pressed the wrong button, and big and strong as he is, he knocked me senseless with one punch. Then he tore out of the room."

"Are you—all right?"

"I heal quickly," Tobe said.

"But why would he do something so terrible?"

"He ran scared. OSU saved his ass in Columbus after he raped a young woman several years ago . . . "

"Oh, no!" Claire wailed.

"He got kicked off the football team and expelled from of school, so he went to work for Lufton, who apparently isn't the nicest guy in the world, either. After Owens punched me out, he took off and headed for home. Don't worry, they nailed him. Milan and I drove down there this morning and brought him back here."

"Where is he now?"

"In jail. Attack a cop? Not a good idea."

"Claire," I said, "could you do us a huge favor? You don't have to—this is just four people getting to know each other and having dinner."

Now she looked suspicious. "Umm—I guess so. What?"

"Tell us exactly what happened from the time Owens picked you up at the Columbus hotel in the limousine. Every little detail you can remember about him, what he said, about the day, about the ride, and what happened after you checked in at the Renaissance on Thursday, right through the first part of today. Can you do that?"

Claire lowered her chin to her chest and studied the Diet Coke in front of her. "I wasn't paying that much attention."

"Once you start talking, you'll be surprised at how much you noticed."

"What do you say, kiddo?" Tobe said.

Claire made a sound as if someone had loaded the world on her shoulders, like Atlas. Then: "I'll try," she said—and began.

CHAPTER THIRTY

MILAN

On the previous Thursday at about eleven a.m., Patrick Owens had arrived, driving a long, black limousine, at the elegant Ritz-Carlton hotel in Columbus. Leaving the limo running out front in a No Parking zone, he'd called the Mayos on the room phone to tell them he'd arrived. Then he stood by the car, a big-and-tall-shop black suit on his wide, beefy physique—inexpensive and rarely worn. No chauffeur's cap, though.

Ten minutes later, the trio from the Mayo party appeared, along with two bellmen wheeling luggage carts. Dr. Ben was wearing a casual tweed sports jacket with leather patches on the elbows over a white shirt and a boring tie, and sported Ray-Ban sunglasses and slim leather gloves, which, Claire told us, he wore all the time, even in the mild Los Angeles climate, because he frequently bit his nails, and to prevent his hands from looking awful on television five days per week. She said he also used moisturizing cream inside those gloves to keep his hands soft.

If anyone wanted to fire a handgun, though, and didn't want gunpowder residue all over his hands, he might choose to wear gloves instead. Just saying. . . .

Thinking of that, I remembered the first time I met Dr. Ben, up in the members' lounge, there was kind of a sweet smell about him that I hadn't even thought about until now. Moisturizing cream.

Owens had opened the spacious trunk, and Claire Crane supervised loading all the luggage carefully. There was Owens's cheap suit bag already in the trunk, and an unmarked package, the size of a box that had once held a pair of boots, wrapped in brown paper and tied with a slim rope. Three large suitcases for Dr. Ben, three more for Caroline, and two smaller ones for Claire were placed in the trunk atop Owens's bag.

When Ben Mayo had tipped the bellmen, he said to Patrick Owens, "You'll be my chauffeur all the way up to Cleveland. After we get there, you're my bodyguard. That means you don't let anyone get near me to ask for an autograph or to take a selfie with them—*nobody*, unless I say so. Try not to get physical with them, but if that's what you need to do, well—" He held his gloved hands, palms up, and shrugged.

"Yes, sir," Owens said.

As Claire continued, I thought for a moment that if people approached me all the time because I was a big celebrity, I'd tell my temporary bodyguard to protect my wife as well. But Ben Mayo hadn't, at least according to Claire. Something for me to consider later. I said, "Did you stop for lunch between Columbus and here?"

She shook her head. "Just for a quick potty break." Her brow furrowed. "Weird, if you ask me."

Tobe asked, "Potty breaks are weird?"

"Even though I've taken dozens of trips with the Mayos, I'd never been in a ladies room with Caroline before. She didn't say one word to me, even afterwards when we were washing our hands and checking our hair and make-up. Our eyes never met." Claire chuckled. "She wouldn't want anyone thinking she *ever* went to the bathroom. When we're at the office or in the studio, she hardly talks to any of the staff. The men, sometimes, but never the women—unless she wants a cup of coffee. She loves having men look at her. She got married for the money and the prestige, but in my humble opinion, I don't think she likes Dr. Ben any more than she likes the rest of us."

"But she's in the audience for his TV show every day," I said.

Claire nodded. "Dr. Ben loves showing her off as his trophy wife, and she likes everyone else knowing how hot she is."

That answer begged for another question, and I couldn't stop myself. "Was Caroline cheating on Ben?"

"I wouldn't know. I know Ben cheats on her because he hit on several women who worked for him." Her sigh was one of regret. "Not me, naturally—I just keep his TV show running smoothly." A sour note crept into her voice. "I wouldn't have given him a second thought, anyway."

Tobe asked, "When you all arrived here at the hotel on Thursday—at what time?"

"Probably sometime between two and three in the afternoon."

"Okay. Did the bellmen take up all your luggage?"

"Not mine," Claire said, "but then I was the one checking in at the desk. Dr. Ben and Caroline were just standing there, waiting."

"And Paddy Owens?"

"He was there, too, but I didn't really notice where exactly."

"You both carried your own suitcases?"

"Yes."

"Was Owens carrying that package wrapped in brown paper?"

"I can't remember."

"Try," I said.

She scrunched up her face. Finally: "I don't know. But I do remember they got everything out of the trunk."

"You don't know what was in the package, or where it ended up?"

"I don't know where it came from, either. All I know is, it wasn't in my room."

Our food arrived. It was still early for me, dinner-wise, and K.O. and I picked at our meals. Tobe ate slowly and carefully, as her jaw was still hurting. Claire Crane, however, attacked her spaghetti as if it was the first meal she'd had in weeks.

Tobe said, "Thursday, did you and Owens and the Mayos go out for dinner?"

"I had room service," Claire said between bites. "I don't know about anyone else."

"I saw Ben Mayo in the conventioneers' lounge later that afternoon," I said, "scarfing up finger sandwiches. I'd imagine most of the speakers ordered room service."

K.O. mumbled, "No one else could afford room service. Eighteen bucks for a hamburger and potato chips?"

"Plus tip," I added.

"Claire—you don't know if Owens went out for dinner Thursday?" Tobe said.

"I have no idea what he did or where he went."

I said, "I don't remember seeing him at the opening ceremonies that evening—or at Dr. Ben's speech on Friday. I thought his job was bodyguard."

"He collected them at their suite, went down in the elevator with them, and made sure they got into the main ballroom that night. I don't think he hung around to hear what they had to say."

"As far as that goes, Claire," I said, "I don't recall seeing you at either one of those events, either."

Her face paled, and this time she used both hands getting her hair out of her eyes. "I was there," she said. "Both times. But I wasn't allowed to sit with the VIPs. I was in the back making sure everything went off okay with Dr. Ben."

"Did Owens take the Mayos back upstairs afterwards?" Tobe asked.

"I don't know. I left as soon as I could, so I wouldn't have to wait forever for an elevator along with four hundred other people."

"And you went straight back to your own room?"

Claire nodded a yes.

"Did either Mayo call you for any reason later on Thursday evening?"

"No."

"So," Tobe continued, "you don't know if they left their suite after that?"

"I'm sure Dr. Ben wouldn't have gone down to the lobby bar that night—people would've been all over him." Claire Crane sighed and leaned back in her chair. "They might have gone out later to drink, like on West Sixth Street—but they never mentioned it to me."

"How do you know about the restaurants and bars on West Sixth Street?" I said.

"Are you kidding? Two months ago I spent hours on the Internet finding out where the hotels were located in Columbus and Cleveland, what restaurants were within walking distance, which people Dr. Ben knew personally in case we needed anything." She tossed her hair from her eyes without using her hands, snapping her head backwards.

"Did you know Tommy Triller personally?" Tobe wanted to know.

"How would I know him? I put in seventy-hour work weeks for the show and only leave that office when Ben's touring around the country somewhere, like now. I hardly know anyone personally. As for Triller—I'm too much of a nobody for him to bother with, and too plain for him to fuck." She crossed her arms across her chest. "You don't even know what a television producer does, do you?"

"Some people don't know what security guys do, either," I pointed out.

That seemed to touch Claire Crane's sore spot. Her face twisted into a sneer and her voice turned six-shots-of-bourbon ugly. "Whatever it is, you do a lousy job at it, if somebody gets killed under your nose."

"No one knocked on my door first to tell me about it."

"Is that why we're sitting here? So you can interrogate me about your screw-up?"

"You're getting loud," Tobe said.

Claire threw down her fork; I had to duck to avoid the splattering of spaghetti sauce. "Am I a suspect?" she snarled. Everyone else in the restaurant turned to look at her. "Do I look like a murderer to you?"

"What do murderers look like?" I asked.

"Is that why I'm here? So you can question me like a goddamn criminal? Well, fuck you!" She stood up so quickly that her chair fell over. Rummaging in her purse, she yanked out two twenty-dollar bills and threw them on the table. "That's for my dinner!"

"I invited you," Tobe said.

"I don't want your dinner! I make twice as much money as all of you combined!" With that, Claire Crane stormed her way toward the door, roughly shoving aside some patrons who'd just arrived and were waiting to be seated.

Tobe, K.O. and I sat quietly. Finally Tobe said, "She's right. She does make twice as much as the three of us. I'm in the wrong job."

"She also works seventy hours a week," I said.

K.O. finished the last bite of his gnocchi. "Sometimes it feels like we do too." He washed down his food with a gulp of water. "Is Claire a suspect, Tobe?"

"Let's just call her a person of interest."

"Then shouldn't Kylee Graves be a person of interest, too? She had a one-nighter with Triller, and thought he was in love with her."

Tobe said, "One of my detectives interviewed her—at length. He also tested her hands and the clothing she wore Thursday for gunpowder. Nothing going on there."

"Maybe she hired someone to kill Triller, then."

"Kylee's salary is thirty thousand bucks a year. You think she hired some Cleveland killer to ice her ex-lover for a carton of cigarettes and a six-pack of Coors?"

"Stroh's," I said, realizing I no longer drank much beer anymore. "Cleveland beer guys like Stroh's. At least Slovenian guys."

"I hate not knowing about that damn package," Tobe said. "Where did it come from, what was in it, who opened it, what happened to it?"

"That's four questions," I said.

"And nobody has answered any of them."

"Can the Columbus police find out if George Lufton gave Owens the mystery package?"

"They can only talk to Lufton's lawyers—who won't even admit it's October."

I stared off into space, not bothering to eat what was left on my plate. Thinking.

We all get quiet sometimes, don't we? Something we see—on the street or in a public place—or something said to us that trips us off into silent cogitation, even when you're in the middle of a fairly talkative group? It had been a long, tiring weekend, but my mind poked into strange places in my own head.

Finally Tobe said, "You're frowning. Ate something that disagreed with you?"

"Nothing that I ate," I said, and stood up, taking a credit card from my wallet and handing it to Tobe. "Just sign my name when the bill comes—and don't forget a tip."

Heading for the door, I almost smiled. Tobe had given me a different kind of "tip."

Back at the hotel, I went up to the small conference room on the third floor, finding it unlocked and empty; Sunday nights are slow for hotel conventions. It was now about six forty-five in the evening, and I hoped I hadn't picked a bad time as I took out my cell phone and dialed a number I knew by heart.

When it was answered on the second ring, I said, "I hope you're not busy, Victor. It's Milan."

"I'm not that busy, Milan. Even God rests on the seventh day—and this *is* Sunday."

"I just need to run a name by you. A Columbus name."

"I don't know everybody in Columbus."

"Maybe you know *of*. Does George Lufton ring a bell?"

A moment of solemn silence, as if someone had died. "Never met the man personally," Victor finally said, "but I know a little about him. A bad boy—loan shark, runs a few hookers, has connections all over the country, if not the world, and keeps a handful of goons on board in case anyone needs a touch-up. He's probably pushing eighty now, but he still has his fingers in a lot of pots. He's careful as hell and has some of the best lawyers in the state, so the police have never been able to touch him. Nobody else ever touched him, either."

"Did you ever do business with him?"

Another long pause. "No, Milan—I never did business with him."

He'd hesitated because he didn't want to tell me something—and I thought I knew what it was. "Victor, did Don Giancarlo ever do business with him?"

"I don't discuss my family's business with you—or with anyone."

"I don't care what it was. That won't make any difference now. Was Lufton involved in Tommy Triller's death?"

"I don't know," Victor said, "and I don't care. I pay you to watch out for Tony Nardoianni—and I don't think Tony ever heard of George Lufton. The rest is your business, Milan—not mine." His breathing was louder; he was running short of patience.

"Tell me this, then. If one wanted a gun, any kind of gun—and didn't have a license or didn't want it known where he got it—could they obtain one from Lufton?"

"I think Lufton has more guns in a safe somewhere than most legitimate gun dealers have in their stores. I'm quite sure none of them are registered, and none of them have serial numbers because they were filed off." He paused for another moment, then said, "This has nothing to do with Tony. Right?"

"Live in hope, Victor," I said.

Between me, K.O., Tobe, the local police, and hotel security, we had interviewed all the VIP speakers—and many civilian attendees as well. The big shots had been questioned, searched, and tested for gunpowder residue, and there was little evidence to hold them for much longer—besides which, most of their lawyers were heading to Cleveland to pry their clients from the grip of the police.

What bothered me, though, was the package. It was apparently from George Lufton—and *apparently* was the operative word. Who was it for? Who wound up with it? What was it, anyway? It could be the gun used to kill Tommy Triller—but it might have been of gift. A pair of boots, since the package was approximately the size of a boot box? Important papers of some sort?

Patrick Owens brought that package with him But Caroline Mayo must have known about it, too, as did Claire Crane. But one—or more than one—was lying.

Perhaps the package was really for someone else.

For Jonah Clary, who had run for the nomination on an almost completely NRA-based campaign? For Lorelei Singleton, who'd had a weekend liaison with Tommy Triller and then was kicked to the curb? For Hy Jinx, who never mussed up his hair the first time he'd committed murder and probably wouldn't be put out of sorts for doing it again? Reverend Jesse Paulin, who disliked Triller for all sorts of reasons but could have had plenty of time to kill him somewhere else? Even for Siddartha West, who'd probably never even held a gun?

I was sure the mysterious package, whatever it held, was not meant for Tony Nardoianni. Victor Gaimari would have never hired me to protect Tony's good name if Victor had guessed he'd already committed a murder. The Cleveland Mob didn't do that anymore. But even in the wild old days of rampant racketeering in America and in Cleveland, most mob killings victimized too-ambitious mob guys trying to shoulder in on a territory that didn't belong to them, or those very few who turned tail and ratted them out to the authorities.

Ergo—Tony Nardoianni was not on my person-of-interest list. I'm not sure if he was on Tobe Blaine's. But everyone in the Mayo party needed to be talked to again.

I stood up and stretched, groaning as I did so. My hairline had been heading north for decades, but it didn't seem to have gotten any worse, although gray streaks showed at the temples as if I'd actually dyed them that way. (I didn't.)

Tobe and K.O. mounted the curving staircase, returning from Lola looking well-sated.

"I thought you were heading to the Greek Isles to hide for the rest of your life," she said. "The least you could have done was say goodbye." She fished my credit card from her purse and handed it to me. "I left her a three-hundred-buck tip because she was so nice," she teased.

"If her ass was as sexy as yours, I'd've left her a bigger tip than that," I said.

"Where'd you run off to, anyway?"

"To make a phone call—and to get my thinking straight."

"And?"

I checked around to see if anyone was listening—but it was Sunday evening and there were few people in the lobby, none near enough to hear me. "The high-end lawyers will be all over us tomorrow morning to get these speakers out of Cleveland and home."

"I can't wait for that," Tobe said, rolling her eyes. "I just love five-hundred-bucks-a-pop lawyers getting in my face."

"I've pretty much boiled it down to the four people in the Mayo party."

"Dr. Ben," K.O. said, "the Owens guy who's already in custody, Claire Crane, and Mrs. Dr. Ben."

I nodded.

"Where's your crystal ball?" Tobe wondered.

"I don't think anyone in that group actually left the hotel on Thursday to try buying a gun on the street," K.O. said, "but Claire Crane said they wandered down the stairs and into Tower City for dinner or something."

"Together?" Tobe asked.

"The Mayos were together," I said. "Owens and Crane went separately. This is your case, Tobe—we're just along for the ride. But these four people need talking to again." I checked my watch; it was almost seven o'clock. "Owens is your best bet, because he's in custody at your jail."

"I've browbeaten him half to death already," Tobe said. "Should I bring some thumbscrews with me this time?"

"You're the boss. Leaning hard on him might help."

Tobe was visibly annoyed, but she eventually nodded. Once.

"K.O.," I said, "why don't you take one more run at Claire Crane?"

"One more opportunity for her to spit in my eye," K.O. said tightly. "Great idea. What will you do now, Milan? Go home and take a nap?"

"This whole package business revolves around Ben Mayo and George Lufton."

"George Lufton won't give you the time of day," Tobe warned, "and neither will his janissaries of lawyers."

"I know," I said. "But Mayo's lawyer won't be here until tomorrow—and his so-called bodyguard is in the cooler. Nobody can keep me away from him. Not yet."

"What about his old lady?"

I headed toward the elevator. "Even better," I said.

CHAPTER THIRTY-ONE

K.O.

K.O. didn't want to confront Claire Crane again—not such a bad person, really. Most of the attendees—the listeners and the note-takers—were probably very decent people who were hungry for wealth and success. But he'd worked with Milan long enough to know that when a crime has been committed and their job is to solve it, those they ran into most often were, at best, difficult to deal with. At worst? Well . . .

K.O. rotated his head around, making his neck pop as he poked the elevator button. He hoped this meeting with Claire would be the last mission of the evening so he could finally get home to Carli and Rodney-cat.

Claire was probably still fuming from dinner, and he wasn't sure he'd get even one toe over the threshold of her room, but she was one of only four people—as far as he knew—even aware of the mystery package. That package, according to Milan, might have the killer's name written all over it.

His knock was almost timid, but he was ready when she threw open the door and bellowed, "Are you kidding me? *Are you fucking kidding me?*" She put both fists on her waistline. "You've already ruined my dinner! Now you're sniveling around to ruin the rest of my evening? Fuck off! Before I call the police!"

"If you call the police, you'll only get Detective Sergeant Tobe Blaine in your lap," K.O. said. "You're a lot better off with just me."

She sucked in a gasp. "This is blackmail!"

"There's nothing to blackmail you about. I'm just looking for a little help—because I don't know where else to go right now."

"Poor muffin!" she snapped.

"Come on, Claire," K.O. cajoled. "Give me ten minutes—that's all. Then comes the bright side. You'll go back to your glamorous Hollywood job and never see me again." He awarded her one of his most appealing smiles, feeling like a damn fool.

She threw her head back and addressed whatever superior being might be up there near the ceiling. "Why does this happen to me? Why?"

"Okay, I'll make it *eight* minutes."

Sigh. *Big* sigh. Then she stepped aside so he could enter her room.

With the exception of a smallish case on the bench at the end of the bed, it looked as though Claire Crane had arrived ten minutes ago—she was one of those people who put all their clothes away neatly in the hotel closets and dresser drawers. He didn't look in the bathroom, though, where she probably had all her make-up spread out on the counter.

There was only one chair, and a desk holding a phone, a lamp, and an entertainment directory printed for visitors and never read. K.O. managed to slide into the chair quietly.

"I've told you everything I know," Claire announced. "There isn't a damn thing more I can say to you—or your cop friends, either."

"Probably not—but for the next eight minutes, let me ask some more questions to make me feel better."

"Seven and a half minutes now."

"Okay, I'll hurry. Let's talk about that package."

"What package?"

"You know what package. The one that was in the trunk before all the other luggage got put in there."

"It was a package! That's all I know. You get into a rented limo, there's stuff in there you don't know anything about, and you don't bother with it. Get off my ass about that damn package!"

"I've never been in a rented limo," K.O. said, "but I know about unmarked packages. You hear about them all the time. They show up at schools, churches, sporting events, military bases, government offices—even at the Boston Marathon a few years back. Maybe it's a bomb. Maybe it's full of anthrax. Or maybe it's just dirty laundry. But people always call the cops—the bomb squad. Nobody in their right mind takes chances today."

"That was no bomb," Claire protested, "or it would have blown up."

"Maybe a different kind of blow-up, then. It arrived in this hotel on Thursday afternoon. Thursday night—or early Friday morning—somebody got killed." She started to answer but K.O.'s raised palm stopped her. "The package might have nothing to do with the murder—or it might have a lot to do with it. That's what I want to find out."

She looked desperately at her cell phone on the bed. "Jesus! I have calls to make."

"If you wind up in the city jail about four blocks from here, they only allow you one phone call."

Defeated, she sank down onto the bed, her legs out in front of her. "I won't confess to a murder I didn't do."

"You shouldn't. But if you lie to the cops, they can nail you for suppressing evidence. They won't put you to death, naturally—but you'll get to know a lot of interesting people in women's prison."

"Stop!"

"Then talk to me, Claire." K.O. leaned forward, elbows on thighs. "What exactly was your relationship to Tommy Triller?"

"My relationship? I had no relationship with him. My boss didn't like him, so it was easier for me not to like him. But other than Thursday night in the ballroom when he made a big speech, I never spent ten minutes in the same room with him in my life."

"Why didn't Dr. Ben like him?"

"Nobody liked him, as far as I know," Claire said. "In the professional world, anyway. The suckers he milked for money could kiss the ground he walked on, but people like Ben Mayo? Well . . . "

"Why didn't Ben like him?"

"Maybe because he had more hair. How would I know why? Ask him yourself."

"When Paddy got to the hotel in Columbus to collect the Mayo party, that plain-wrapped package was already in the trunk, right?"

"Yes," she sighed. "Hotel bellhops brought all our luggage down—Caroline's, Dr. Ben's, and mine—and nobody had a package then."

"You're sure?"

"There's a Gideon Bible in that desk where you're sitting. You want me to swear on it? Don't bother. I haven't been to a church since I was ten years old."

"I believe you." K.O. sat back. "So your limo arrived here on Thursday—with the package. And it didn't go upstairs with Ben and Caroline's luggage?"

"No."

"Paddy Owens' room is right across the hall from here."

She nodded.

"You never asked what the package was?"

"It was none of my business!" Claire said roughly. "I didn't ask him what he had in his pockets, either—or whether he had tattoos where nobody could see. Jesus, I never laid eyes on the guy before."

"Okay," K.O. said soothingly. "You all arrived here around two-thirty in the afternoon."

"Yes. I went to the reservations desk and signed everything."

"All of you went upstairs right away?"

"Yes. Dr. Ben doesn't like hanging around in the lobby—and he told Owens to keep people away from him. That's the bodyguard part, I guess."

"You didn't stop for lunch on the way from Columbus, so you must have been hungry. Did you go out to eat later in the day?"

"Sure I did."

"Where?"

Claire screwed up her mouth, thinking about it. "It's right down the street from here. Noodlecat? Is that the name of it?"

K.O. nodded. "You went alone?"

"Alone, yes."

"Did Paddy O go out to eat that day? He was staying right across the hall."

"Look—I came up here, unpacked, got on the phone to Los Angeles, and didn't go out to eat until about four o'clock, give or take a few minutes. I didn't pay attention to what he was doing. He might have left while I was out, but he didn't show up in

Noodlecat when I was there." Claire pushed herself up off the bed and went over to the window. "Just before Dr. Ben and Caroline were supposed to be down in the big ballroom, Patrick and I met them backstage."

"Did any of the four of you go out during the day on Friday?"

"I had room service breakfast," Claire said. "Later that afternoon, I went out for lunch alone—to the Tilted Kilt a few blocks away." She did her hair thing again. "It's just like Hooters, except waitresses have their asses hanging out as well as their tits."

"I'm almost done,," K.O. said, "and then I'll leave you alone."

Claire leaned against the windowsill and looked out, eastward, the lake shore curving ahead of her into the distance. "You have three minutes left."

"You made all the arrangements for the limo and driver with George Lufton."

She nodded.

"Set the price and everything?"

"It's not my money, so why should I care?"

"You talked to Lufton directly? Who gave you his phone number?"

"Ben."

"And he knew him personally?"

Claire turned. "I have no idea. I don't think he'd ever been in Columbus."

"Where did *he* get the number?"

"Maybe from an acquaintance in this convention who's *from* Columbus."

"And who's that?"

Another sigh. "Dr. Lorelei Singleton," Claire said.

CHAPTER THIRTY-TWO

MILAN

Why was it me who had to talk once more to Dr. Ben?
I felt as if I'd been stalking him for a month, instead of
three days. I disliked all of the self-anointed speaker lumi-
naries, but Ben Mayo—arrogant, difficult, full-of-himself daytime
TV star—took the cake.

That package piqued the interest of all of us. So Tobe Blaine
strolled over to the Justice Center to further question Patrick
Owens, who apparently had taken the mystery package upstairs
with him—and K.O. was taking a final shot at Claire Crane.

That left me to chat with Dr. Ben before the next morning
when his highly paid lawyer-to-the-stars turned up and fled with
the Mayo party back to Los Angeles.

My dinner growled in my gut as I knocked on the door of Dr.
Ben's suite. Music was playing inside that sounded somewhat
like 1980s rock—a musical genre to which I had no reference.
Someone turned it off, and when the door finally opened, it was
Dr. Ben's better half who stood there.

"You again?" Caroline Mayo sighed. There was no getting
around it—she was gorgeous, this time in a blue dress that
matched her eyes and fell three inches above the knee. Her hair
was loose, and she wore bedroom slippers. "We're going to be out
of here by noon tomorrow. Why don't you just leave us alone?"

"Don't you want to hang around Cleveland and see the sights?"
I said.

Her lips pursed in an grimace of displeasure. "My husband

doesn't like hanging around anywhere—even if it's some sort of paradise, like Bora Bora. Unless he's moving around from one place to the other, he's only happy at home."

"Is Dr. Ben here?" I said.

"Take a look around. See him anywhere?"

I stood on the threshold of one large room in the suite—giant TV set, huge conference table, sofas, chairs, six windows—four of which looked out at Lake Erie. To my left was a spacious bathroom, door open, which also led into the bedroom, which sported another fifty-two-inch TV and two king-sized beds.

"Do you know where he is?" I asked.

"I haven't a clue. He might be walking around, soaking up your Main Square atmosphere."

"It's Public Square," I corrected her.

"Like I give a damn," she said.

"Would you mind if I came in for a few minutes?"

"If I did mind, would you go away?"

"Probably not."

She turned and walked to the conference table, sliding into one of the chairs. "Sit your ass down so you can be comfortable while you give me the third degree."

I closed the door behind me and sat my ass down opposite her. "I wouldn't call it a third degree."

"What would you call it, then?"

"Call it what you like. I just have questions so I can finally put part of this investigation to bed."

"You'll need to talk to my husband," she said. "I don't know anything." Her blue eyes turned more gray. "I'm just the trophy wife. Can't you tell?"

"You're beautiful and smart, which makes you much more than a trophy. You graduated from USC with high honors, then spent a few years in law school before you dropped out to get married."

"You Googled me! I figured you might be too old to operate a computer."

"Doesn't everyone Google everyone else? It saves us saying stupid things like, 'Tell me about yourself.'"

"Should I have Googled you?" she asked.

"That and a buck would get you a cup of coffee at McDonald's."

"I don't give a damn about McDonald's coffee, and I don't give a damn about you."

"I give a damn about you, though," I said, "so help me out."

She shook her head, more in weariness than in anger. "Shall I start with my one-year-old birthday party, when I sneezed all over the cake? Or do you want a later version?"

"Start with your relationship with Dr. Mayo."

She closed her eyes. "Ben was in the second year of his TV show, and it was a huge hit. When he asked me to marry him, give up my law aspirations, and be his on-display wife, I figured the money would keep rolling in for years and years." Her eyes opened, and her voice was dust-dry. "Well, it has—so I guess I made the right decision."

"I wanted to ask you about that package . . . "

"I never even saw the package. I don't know who brought it to Cleveland, I don't know where it came from, I don't know if it was ever brought into the hotel. I don't even know if it existed."

"You didn't notice your chauffeur bring it in with him?"

"I wouldn't recognize the—'chauffeur'—if he walked in here and bit me on the ass," Caroline said. "He's one of a million part-time drivers for hire. So I don't even know if there was a package at all. It was never in this suite—at least not that I saw."

"Okay," I said.

"Is that it?"

"Not quite."

She leaned against the back of the chair and let her head drop backwards with another annoyed sigh.

"Your husband didn't like Tommy Triller," I pointed out. "Why?"

She straightened up and looked at me. "I'm sorry, Security— but you're sitting there in a jacket from Burlington Coat Factory and shoes from Payless, asking questions that are too intimate— and you obviously don't know a damn thing about rich people."

"Just that they don't buy their clothes at Burlington Coat Factory," I said.

"So you don't get why my husband, who pulls in forty million dollars a year—*forty million a year!*—hates the guts of someone like Tommy Triller, who earns a *hundred million* a year."

"I get it—but then why not hate Bill Gates or Warren Buffett or the Sultan of Brunei, who all make lots more money than Tommy Triller?"

"Because they're in a different business! Besides, that's not personal—" She stopped, put her fist to her mouth. Taking a deep breath to pull herself together, she said, "I think we're done here."

"Maybe with me, but not with the Cleveland police. If they have to, they'll put you and Dr. Ben under arrest and keep you here until the arraignment—and maybe not even then could your bigshot lawyer spirit you out of town and back to Los Angeles. So I don't think we're done, Mrs. Mayo—at least not until we discuss this *personal* thing."

Finally she said, "I figured you were too low-class to know anything about people like us."

That moment is going down in my memory book, too. I have several pages filled just from this weekend.

Caroline went on, "Sure, I was in law school—and already I was getting invitations from some of the big Los Angeles law firms, more for the way I looked than for my B-minus grades. I wouldn't be able to go anywhere in those companies, though, unless I fucked the bosses. Even then, I'd eventually hit the glass ceiling.

"When I met Ben at a party, he made no bones about being interested in me. Just before his TV show hit it big, he'd divorced his first wife—who wasn't all that attractive, if you want to know the truth—and he was looking not only for eye candy but for someone who could put two intelligent sentences together in public. As for me?" Caroline shrugged. "I knew he'd be around for decades, on TV or someplace else, making a goddamn fortune. And I like the high life, Mr. Security." She flashed both hands at me, and the diamonds glistened and gleamed. "The clothes, the jewelry, the cars, the house, dinners at elegant Beverly Hills restaurants, the limitless credit cards, and the charge accounts at every high-end store. Who wouldn't want something like that?"

I kept quiet and let her continue.

"So when he asked me to marry him, I said yes—with misgivings."

"Misgivings?"

"I didn't love him. I liked him okay, but this was a business arrangement for me. No passion. No romance."

"Too bad," I said.

"Wasn't it, though?" She pushed herself away from the table and began moving around as she talked. I didn't know whether she was wound up from sharing personal information that had to be embarrassing for her, or was turning into a drama queen. "I know he cheated on me. No relationships, naturally—Ben's a one-night-stand kind of guy. But he keeps me around because I look good hanging on his arm—I'm not exactly chopped liver, am I?" She spun around, glaring at me, angry. "What's sauce for the goose, blah blah blah . . . "

"You cheated, too?"

Caroline's chin touched her chest for just a moment; then she raised her head proudly, her jaw extended like a slab of concrete. "Whenever I felt like it," she said.

"Does Dr. Ben know that?"

"I don't care if he knows it or not, and he doesn't, either—as long as I don't degrade his image."

"By making your affairs public?"

"I don't call *USA Today* to tell them about it."

"You sleep with his friends?"

She shrugged. "He doesn't have many friends—only acquaintances."

"You sleep with his acquaintances, then?"

"I sleep with whoever I want, *when* I want—and so does Ben." Caroline Mayo's face turned glacial. "Are you hitting on me? Is that what this is all about? Forget it—you're not my type."

I nodded. "You only have affairs with men who don't buy their clothes at Burlington Coat Factory."

"You're damn right!"

I said slowly and carefully, "Tommy Triller didn't shop at Burlington, did he?"

The smooth flesh over her cheekbones bloomed scarlet, and she turned away so I could no longer see her face. "Where Tommy shopped is none of your business."

"Caroline," I said quietly, having somehow passed by the *Mrs.*

Mayo etiquette. "Your sex life doesn't interest me—unless it includes an affair with Tommy Triller."

"You think *I* killed him?" In the final three words, her voice sailed higher than a dog whistle.

"I don't think anything. But if Ben found out you were having an affair with his number-one competitor, it makes sense that he'd do the killing himself."

"That's a load of crap!" As I sat at the table she loomed over me, spittle flying. "You're trying to blame one of us, or both of us, maybe, for a murder—all because of some package neither of us has ever seen. We don't have any gun! Don't you know the police tested my hands and Ben's hands for gunpowder residue and didn't find a goddamn thing?"

"Ben," I said, "is the only man I know who wears gloves in early October. I wonder if the police tested Dr. Ben's gloves."

"Christ!" she said, "you're pitiful. You have nothing on either of us—and no matter how much you scratch around at our feet, you still won't find a damn thing."

The door to the suite opened and Dr. Ben Mayo walked in, his electronic card key still in his hand. "What's going on here?" he demanded. Then, to me, "What's the big idea of being in our suite? We've answered all the questions we're going to."

Caroline answered before I could. "He's going to arrest us for killing Tommy Triller!"

"I can't arrest anybody." I stood up. "I'm not a police officer."

"Then," he said, once again getting red all the way up to his bald dome, "get the hell out of here before I throw you out. How dare you accuse us of anything?" And he wrapped his large hand around my bicep and jerked me toward the door.

"Take your hand off me, Dr. Ben," I said.

"Move it!" he said through clenched teeth, tightening his grip.

I chopped the side of my hand down on his wrist as hard as I could, and he yelped and let go. He was a big man, and considering that he and I were close to the same age, surprisingly quick as he threw an overhand punch at me.

Without moving my feet, I turned my body so his knuckles landed on the back of my shoulder rather than my jaw. It hurt.

I don't like to be hurt.

I jerked my elbow back and caught him with the point of it—right in the mouth.

Backing up quickly, he tripped over the chair I'd just vacated, and sat down, hard, his lower lip split, his eyes wild and trying to focus as if I'd knocked all the common sense out of him.

"You son of a bitch!" Caroline almost screamed. "Our lawyer will be here tomorrow and you'll be in jail!"

"Caroline," I said. "Take a deep breath—and then hold it until I wind up in jail. I don't know about your glove-wearing husband, though. You and he and your friend in Columbus might wind up in there, too."

"What friend in Columbus?"

"George Lufton," I said.

Ben pulled himself up to his wobbly feet and wiped at his lip, looking shocked to find blood on his hand. He searched the room for a tissue. Caroline went into the bathroom and pulled out a few sheets and handed it to him.

"Listen," he said to me, blotting his lip, "I never met George Lufton. I didn't even talk to him on the phone. My producer called him and made the arrangements."

"Claire Crane? Is Lufton *her* friend?"

He shook his head. "I asked around—people I know—to see who'd been to Columbus a lot. That's where I got Lufton's number."

"And you gave it to Claire to call."

He picked up the chair he'd stumbled over and eased himself into it. "Yes."

"And who was it gave you the phone number?"

"A Columbus native, as a matter of fact. Lorelei Singleton."

Caroline said, "Don't talk to this bastard. He's not a cop. You don't have to say anything."

Dr. Ben shook his head angrily. "It's all fucked up now, Caroline. Everything is fucked up. If it wasn't for you opening your legs for Tommy Triller, none of this would have happened."

His comment shocked me—but it didn't seem to bother Caroline Mayo at all. Finally I said, "Triller getting killed?"

"No. Not him getting killed." Dr. Ben was having difficulty

talking with a bleeding lip. "But if it weren't for her—" and he gestured toward his wife with his head and eyes, "we wouldn't be in this kind of trouble."

"You wouldn't be in trouble at all," she snapped, "if you'd kept your hands to yourself."

He pushed himself upright. "I'm sorry. Things piled up on me, and eventually there's a breaking point. I lost it. Let's face it, this marriage is in the crapper. It has been for several years now." He looked up at me, half fear and half admiration. "Jesus, security guy—you play rough."

I moved to the door. "You have no idea," I said.

CHAPTER THIRTY-THREE

TOBE

Tobe Blaine enjoyed the quiet Sunday evening as she walked back from the main headquarters of the Cleveland Police Department, a cool wind snapping off Lake Erie at her back. Her jaw was still sore from spending almost two hours questioning the man who made it that way, Patrick Owens.

He had been handcuffed, chained to a table in an interrogation room, and his face was almost as badly bruised as Tobe's, thanks to Milan slamming his head into a men's room stall. He knew that in the morning he'd be indicted for attacking a police officer. He also knew that the officer in question was sitting on the other side of the table from him, frightening him more than anything else.

"You keep telling me you're innocent of everything," Tobe'd said to him. "But unless you tell me what you know about George Lufton and that mysterious package and the murder of Tommy Triller on Thursday night, you're going to wind up in prison. Not jail, Patrick, like the one you're in now. Prison. You have any idea what it's like in prison?"

"I didn't do anything!" he whined.

Tobe ignored him. "Prison is tough—trust me. You won't have to make any decisions there, not a single one. They'll tell you what time to go to bed, what time to wake up, what time to eat, what time to take a shit! Smart off to your guards, and you'll wind up in solitary confinement—maybe for a month, if not more—and it'll take about two days of that before you go completely nuts. Smart off to the warden? Well—wardens have pretty healthy egos you sure don't want to mess with.

"But if they don't toss you into solitary, Patrick," she said, leaning back comfortably in her chair, "you'll wish that you were. Want to know why? You're a young, relatively pleasant-looking white guy—and every hard-time con is going to want a piece of you. You can't hold off eight or ten guys at a time. They'll pass you around that prison like a dirty book—and after six months in the joint, you could drive a convoy of Mack trucks up your ass without touching the sides. Just hope you won't pick up a galloping case of AIDS, because everyone in there will have fucked you dozens of times. When you get out—*if*—you'll look like you're sixty, and feel like you're ninety."

Long before Tobe finished, Owens's face was chalk-white, his eyes twice their size, his hands shaking so badly that his handcuffs chimed like "Jingle Bells."

"Think about this," Tobe went on. "You made a living doing whatever George Lufton wanted you to, down in Columbus—and he sent you up here with that package and warned you not to mention it to anyone. Am I right so far?"

Owens didn't answer.

"I understand you're scared of him, Paddy. I'm just wondering if he's as scary as a long stretch downstate will be for you. You need to think about that—and think fast, because tomorrow when they arraign you, it won't just be for attacking a cop. It'll be for accessory to murder."

She stood up. "I'm going to chat with my boss," she said. "She's a homicide lieutenant. Then I'll go to the john. That means I'll be out of here for fifteen minutes. Use those minutes to think about whether or not you want to talk to me when I get back."

After her second session with Owens, Tobe called Milan's cell phone and asked him to find K.O. and meet with her at the fountain in the Renaissance lobby. Now, walking back to the hotel from the police department, Tobe Blaine actually felt like strutting—except strutting with a Glock at her hip was stupid.

Twenty years carrying a badge, she thought, and things hadn't changed a bit. When she returned, Owen was ready to confess to the Lindbergh kidnapping, the Kennedy assassination, and the treason of Benedict Arnold. It took him less than ninety seconds to tell her about the mystery package.

She nodded at one of the plainclothes officers standing near the front door of the hotel, then went inside and found her way to the marble lobby fountain, where Milan and K.O. waited for her.

"Have a nice walk?" Milan asked.

"Sure," Tobe said. "I'm a homicide cop, there's a murderer floating around loose, and I went for a walk. As for now, someone in Room 609 has a lot of explaining to do."

"Oh, damn!" K.O. said. "I know whose room that is. I've been there before. Dr. Lorelei Singleton."

"I scared Owens so badly that he would've told me what brand of perfume his grandmother used, if I'd asked," Tobe said. "Lufton gave him the package to bring up to Cleveland, but didn't tell him what was in it. At around six o'clock Thursday evening, somebody from Lufton's office—and Paddy didn't know the name—called him on his cell phone and told him to drop that package off at the door of Room 609. He didn't know whose room that was. He was just told to put the package on the floor by the door, knock three times, and leave."

K.O. grimaced.

"Claire Crane told me Lorelei Singleton was a Columbus native. Maybe she knows this Lufton guy and turned Dr. Ben onto him."

"More than possible," Milan said.

"You already have a relationship with Dr. Lorelei, don't you, K.O.?" Tobe said.

"I sure do. The last time I saw her, she squirted me with mace. First she wants to fuck me, then she tries to blind me. Some relationship!"

Tobe considered. "Why don't you hang out at the side door to make sure none of our big shots pull a Great Escape. Milan and I will go talk to her."

K.O. shook his head sadly. "I was hoping to go home."

"Going up there is fine with me," Milan said, "but I'm unarmed. Wouldn't you be better off taking one of your own officers?"

"I'm armed, Milan. Besides, I'm not going to arrest her. I don't have enough evidence." Tobe smiled. "We searched her room and tested her hands for gunshot residue. Nothing—but I like tying up loose ends."

"There are no loose ends yet, Tobe. You don't have a perp."

"The next time you investigate a murder, Milan, tie up your own loose ends."

They stepped inside the empty elevator car, and when the door hissed closed, Milan put his arm around her, his hand on her hip, and hugged her. "It's been a long weekend," he said.

"And it's not over yet. I'm on duty—so don't grope my ass in the elevator."

"I wasn't groping your ass, I was groping your hip."

"Then your aim stinks," she said.

When the elevator doors opened, they walked down the hall and Tobe rapped sharply on the door of suite 609. "Detective Sergeant Tobe Blaine, Cleveland Police Department," she announced loudly, not caring if anyone else ensconced in a sixth-floor room heard her.

A just-a-minute voice came from inside the suite, followed by a thirty-second wait. Then Dr. Lorelei Singleton stood in the doorway, her hair long and flying in several different directions, her face without make-up, her slacks and untucked shirt wrinkled.

Tobe flashed her police badge. "Detective Sergeant Blaine, Cleveland P.D. This is a hotel security op, Milan Jacovich."

"Oh, God," Lorelei said, looking more at Milan than at Tobe, "you really caught me off-guard. I was taking a nap."

"Just a few questions for you, Dr. Singleton," Tobe said.

She put her hands up to cover her face. "I'm so embarrassed. Give me two minutes in the bathroom to put myself to rights. Please?"

"We have all evening," Tobe said.

Lorelei went into the spacious bathroom. Before she closed the door, Tobe spied a large box of Kotex on the floor opposite the toilet and an unimaginable display of cosmetics spread out over the counter next to the sink.

Tobe gazed out the window at the Square, and Milan sat on one of the sofas, waiting. Bathroom sounds—water running, medicine cabinet being opened and closed, finally a toilet flush and another rush of water. Then Lorelei reappeared.

Her hair had been combed and was held in place by two bobby pins, and she had applied some lipstick. "This was the best I could do in two minutes, sorry." To Milan, with a smile and a debutante dip of the head, "It takes women forty-five minutes to pull themselves together after a nap."

"You were speedy. Mind if we sit down?" Tobe said. Lorelei moved to sit next to Milan, but Tobe was quicker. Miffed, Lorelei sat on the opposite sofa.

"What is it you wanted to talk to me about?" she said.

"You know that Tommy Triller was murdered in this hotel on Thursday, correct?"

Lorelei shook her head sadly. "Terrible. Tragic and terrible."

"You're a Columbus native, aren't you?" Milan asked.

"I left there when I was twenty-two or so, when I graduated from college—Ohio State, naturally. I still have family there, so I visit every few years—but I don't really have a feel for Columbus anymore."

"Do you still have friends there, too?"

Lorelei battered her eyelashes, too late realizing she hadn't put on any eyelash makeup. "Yes, I have college friends. Did you go to Ohio State, too, Detective . . . ?"

"Just *Mister* Jacovich. No, I went to Kent State."

"Ah," Lorelei breathed. "So all these years later, you still have Kent friends?"

"I'd rather talk about your friends," Tobe said, finally getting Lorelei to look at her. "Do you have a Columbus friend named George Lufton?"

Dr. Lorelei took too long a moment before she swallowed, licked her lips and said, "Why yes, I do, as a matter of fact. More of an acquaintance. He has an employment agency, I believe—and goes out of his way to find jobs for Buckeyes."

"Buckeyes," Milan said, "like Patrick Owens?"

"I—don't know that name. I don't know who he is."

"He's Dr. Ben Mayo's temporary chauffeur and bodyguard," Tobe told her. "Did Dr. Ben ask whether you knew anyone in Columbus who could supply him with a limo and driver?"

Tobe gave Lorelei time to construct an answer. Eventually, Lorelei said, "Dr. Ben didn't call me, but one of his people did. Some woman who, I think, is one of his TV show producers. I told her to call George Lufton—and that's all I know about it."

"You didn't know who Ben's chauffeur was going to be?"

"I'd hardly know any of Lufton's low-level employees, would I?"

"Well, this particular low-level employee was given a package by Lufton with instructions to drive up here to Cleveland with the Mayos. Shortly after everyone arrived here on Thursday after-noon, this Patrick Owens got a call from someone in Columbus, telling him to deliver that mystery package to someone in Room 609. That would be you, Dr. Lorelei."

Lorelei put a hand up to her throat. "That's very peculiar. I don't know anything about a mystery package, and I certainly didn't get one on Thursday."

"Owens," Tobe said, "was supposed to leave it on the floor outside your door, knock three times, and leave. You don't remem-ber that?"

"It never happened! I might have been in the bathroom when the knock came, or I might have been out of the room—like anyone else, I wandered the hotel for a while, looking at things connected with the convention. Then I walked around the Square. In any event, I found no package waiting for me."

"Owens swore he got the phone call from Lufton, and swore he put the package right on your doorstep, knocked, and ran like hell. That package," Tobe said, "might have contained the gun that killed Tommy Triller."

"Who are you believing?" Lorelei demanded. "Some part-time errand boy, or me?"

"Do you have a quarter, Dr. Lorelei?"

Lorelei looked puzzled. "Why?"

"So I can toss it," Tobe said. "Heads, I believe you. Tails, I believe the errand boy."

"Very funny!" Lorelei snapped. "One of your police officers searched my room first thing Friday morning, and he didn't find any gun. He also did something with my hands—I'm not sure what you call it—to see if I'd fired a gun recently. And he didn't find any of that, either."

"You could have shot Triller," Milan said, "and then wandered outside to dispose of the gun in some wastebasket on the street."

"That's bizarre!" Lorelei said. "After all the commotion, I was up there in the hallway outside Tommy's suite—in my pajamas!"

"I saw you." Milan leaned forward, hands on his thighs. "But no one searched this suite until noon of the next day. You could've floated out of here for breakfast, maybe even taken a taxi somewhere blocks and blocks away from here, and thrown your gun into a dumpster."

Lorelei's frustration, building since they'd walked in the door, finally imploded in her throat. "Why the fuck are you bothering me?" she screamed.

Tobe said, "Let's talk about you and Tommy Triller. You knew each other before this convention, right?"

"Of course we did. Almost all the speakers at this con had met many times before."

"But you and Tommy more than 'just met'."

"We knew each other for several years."

"You two had an affair."

"That's very personal!"

"Murder," Milan said, "is a very personal business. Did you or didn't you have a romantic relationship with Triller?"

"I wouldn't call it romantic," Lorelei said. "About six months ago, Tommy and I had a one-weekend fling. I'm very open-minded, sexually, so don't get shocked."

"I'm a homicide cop," Tobe reminded her. "I don't shock easily. So, you and Triller were—friends with benefits?"

"We weren't friends at all. We didn't even like each other very much."

"Before the affair, you didn't like each other?"

"Not much."

Milan said, "You talked to one of my security people—K.O. O'Bannion—several times, and wound up squirting mace into his eyes. That wasn't very nice, was it?"

She sputtered, "He was going to rape me."

"Bullshit!" Milan said.

"You told him," Tobe said, "that you and Triller had discussed joining forces, becoming partners in various things. That's why you had the shagging weekend with him in New York. Those partnerships, though—they didn't work out so well, did they?"

"People in business discuss partnerships all the time," Lorelei protested. "Sometimes they work out, sometimes they don't."

Tobe stood up easily, hovering over Dr. Lorelei. "Triller grossed about a hundred million dollars a year. You're lucky if you earn eight million by talking on the radio. Why on earth would he want a partnership with you? He'd have nothing to gain."

"You, on the other hand, would've had plenty to gain," Milan said. "That, plus him dumping you after a fuck weekend, would make you pretty mad, right? And this convention is the first time you'd seen each other since the Waldorf affair."

"And maybe you were mad enough to kill him," Tobe said, "and jam his own CD into his mouth after he was dead. Murder's one thing; post-mortem humiliation is something else."

"Jesus!" Lorelei said softly. "Are you actually arresting me for murder?"

Tobe said, "You need to accompany us to the station so we can talk some more."

Dr. Lorelei Singleton was silent for thirty seconds. Then she said, "Is that mandatory?"

"It doesn't have to be, if you come with us—on your own, naturally."

"My lawyer will be here first thing in the morning. You can't keep me."

"I can keep you until morning—or we can talk, and I can send you back to the hotel within an hour."

"Are you going to handcuff me?"

"Once again—not if you come voluntarily."

"Oh my God!" Lorelei put her face in her hands for a moment, breathing hard. Then she looked up and said, "Can you let me go to the john before we leave?"

"When you gotta go, you gotta go." Tobe gestured toward the bathroom.

Dr. Singleton mumbled a thank you and disappeared behind the door.

"What do you think?" Milan said quietly to Tobe.

"I think she went to the john five minutes ago. At least she flushed."

"If she had the gun in the first place, she'd never have kept it after Triller was shot. But she wouldn't have tossed it into the hotel trash—my cops looked through every scrap of it. And she didn't leave the building Friday morning."

"So what am I missing here?"

"Everybody in the joint had a Tommy Triller hate motive, but hers was the strongest of all. In the meantime, what are you going to do with Lorelei at headquarters?"

"In an interrogation room—with an uncomfortable straight chair, a blinding overhead light, and a two-way mirror? Walk all over her head to get her to confess." She smiled. "It's a good thing she went to the john now, because nobody's going to let her get up from that chair for hours and hours."

"Cruel and unusual punishment?" Milan said.

"Only because I misplaced my rubber hose."

He looked at his watch and chuckled. "She's been in there long enough. Maybe she escaped through the window."

"There's no window in that bathroom. If there were, we're on the sixth floor. People have survived a fall like that—but not very often." Tobe arose and walked to the dining table. "Here's her purse with her money, credit cards, and the return plane ticket. She's not going anywhere, Milan."

"Some people," he said, "read in the john. Maybe you should bang on the door and tell her the butler did it." He rubbed his eyes. "I already had hand soap thrown into my face this morning. If she squirts me with mace, I'll—be very angry."

"If she squirts you with mace," Tobe said, "I'll shoot her."

Dr. Lorelei came out of the bathroom and stood in front of the sofa where she'd been sitting, facing Tobe and Milan. "I'm not going with you to police headquarters," she said. "It's not fair. You don't drag all the other speakers over there and beat them up in private so no one else will know."

"Nobody will beat you up, Dr. Singleton," Milan said.

"Why just me, then?"

"Because," Tobe told her, "your story touches more corners

of this investigation than anyone else's. You're from Columbus. When Ben's producer called and asked you for a Columbus name, you gave her George Lufton's number. Lufton sent a package here with Patrick Owens, and Thursday he delivered the package, unopened, to Room 609. That's you."

"So? What if I refuse to leave with you?" Lorelei said.

"Then things will not go well at all."

Lorelei considered that. Then she reached under her untucked shirt and produced what looked like a .38 pistol, pointing it at Tobe. "Things aren't going well for *you*," she said.

"Oh, Dr. Lorelei," Tobe said sorrowfully, shaking her head.

"You're not taking me anywhere!"

"You had the gun all along—hidden in that large box of Kotex." Tobe turned to Milan. "A Kotex box is one of the all-time great places to hide something, even when you're being tossed. One of my guys searched the place thoroughly—but what cop will poke around in a Kotex box?" Back to Lorelei: "Well-played," she said.

"And on Friday morning, before the search," Milan suggested, "you stuffed the package wrappings into your purse and went into Tower City for breakfast, dumping the paper in a trash can. Did you use the one in the women's rest room? I doubt if anyone paws through public restroom trash. How're we doing so far?"

"Pretty good," Lorelei said. "And now you're going to usher me out of this hotel, ride with me to the airport, and make sure I get on a plane."

"We are?" Milan said. "You're just going home like nothing has happened—and we won't call ahead for the Los Angeles police to nail you when you step off the plane because you're going to kill us right there in the airport?"

"The better question," Tobe cut in, "is what will happen if we don't take you to the airport?"

"The same thing that happened to Tommy Triller—except I don't have anything to shove into your ugly mouths afterwards."

"Ah." Tobe nodded thoughtfully. She looked at Milan. "Nice knowing you, pal."

"You, too, Detective Sergeant."

Then Tobe turned back to Dr. Lorelei. "Are you planning on shooting us here? Everyone knows this is your suite."

"No," Dr. Lorelei said. "I'll take you into the stairway and shoot you there."

"Good idea, Lorelei," Tobe said. "K.O. O'Bannion knew we were both coming up here to see you—but don't worry. He won't tell a soul."

Dr. Singleton waved her pistol for her two captors to stand. "Come on," she said. "On your feet."

"Uh—what if we say no?"

"What?"

"Suppose we don't want to go into a stairway? Suppose we want to stay right where we are?"

"You'll get this suite all bloody," Milan said. "*Another* suite bloodied up. Yuck!"

"And then what, Lorelei?" Tobe pressed on. "You leave your bloody, corpse-strewn hotel room, get on a plane, go back to Los Angeles, and do your radio show, and no one will even ask you about two dead bodies in your Cleveland hotel suite?"

"She can't go back to her Los Angeles home, her clothes and belongings and her car," Milan said. "She'll need to disappear where no one will find her."

"Someplace like Kazakhstan. She'll have to learn to speak Kazakh. Are you good with languages, Dr. Lorelei?"

"French, maybe," Milan said. "*Voulez vous couchez avec moi?* Or Spanish. It'd be too tough learning Kazakh, wouldn't it?"

Dr. Lorelei looked poleaxed, stunned, her gaze going from one to the other.

"Dr. Lorelei didn't think this out very well," Tobe said. "She thought she'd get away with killing Tommy Triller—but she didn't foresee us Cleveland cops putting all the pieces together and figuring out who did it."

"You know," Milan said, "if you'd chosen to take a walk around the block, you'd have found someone who'd sell you an unregistered gun for just a few bucks—and there'd be no way of tracing the killing back to you. But you decided to trust your good buddy in Columbus instead, and—well, here you are."

Lorelei's gun hand trembled.

"Shooting us is a terrible idea," Tobe explained, "so, sadly, you're under arrest for the murder of Tommy Triller. You still have two choices, though. You could hand me the weapon and come with us quietly—or I can forcibly take it away from you and shove it so far up your ass that you'll need a team of surgeons to retrieve it. What do you think about that, Lorelei? Time's a-wasting."

Ten minutes later, Tobe Blaine, Milan Jacovich, and a handcuffed Lorelei Singleton emerged from the hotel elevator on the street level, stepped out onto the sidewalk, and waited for a valet to find and deliver Milan's car.

K.O. had been called minutes earlier to meet them, and he sauntered around the corner, beaming. "Is this really over?"

"We're relieved of our duties," Milan said. "Go home—Carli's waiting for you."

Stopping in front of Lorelei, who wore her coat loosely draped around her shoulders, K.O. said, "Sorry it all came down like this, Lorelei. If you hadn't maced me, we might have forgotten about you."

Dr. Lorelei's head had been bowed. Now she raised it, her eyes dancing with fury. "Don't worry," she said through gritted teeth. "I'm not going to forget about *you*."

"Got something for you, K.O.," Tobe said. She took from her pocket a dispenser of mace. "I got this from Lorelei's purse, but she won't need it where she's going. I thought you might want it as a keepsake."

"Thanks, Tobe. I'll hang onto it until I pass by a trash basket."

"She'll be arraigned first thing in the morning—whether her lawyer gets here on time or not. In any case, she'll be tried here in Ohio."

K.O. tried not to smile. "In that case, Lorelei, I look forward to seeing you again."

Her three-word response was an expression K.O. had heard often.

Later, after Lorelei had been locked in a cell, Milan and Tobe climbed back into Milan's car.

"Home, James," Tobe said.

"Shouldn't you come back to my place for one more evening? Until your face doesn't hurt so much?"

"My face won't heal quicker at your apartment," Tobe said, "and you might get romantic on me—which, I guarantee you, isn't going to work tonight. Besides, you'll warn me to be more careful on the job, not getting punched out, not getting in the face of a batshit bonkers woman with a gun." She stretched luxuriously. "All I want is a nice warm bath, a glass of wine, and cuddling up by myself to watch the eleven o'clock re-run of *The Walking Dead.*"

"Strange," Milan said, shaking his head, "because we've been hanging out with zombies all weekend."

EPILOGUE

MILAN

A month later, I still hadn't become rich beyond my wildest dreams, no more successful than before hearing of the Global Motivational Speakers Association. I didn't think I was any better—or worse—of a human being than I'd ever been. I hadn't made any new friends along the way.

K.O. did, though—and a pretty important friend, as well. Two weeks after the GMSA convention ended, UPS delivered two giant boxes to his apartment, packed with every book Siddartha West had written, and nearly sixty CDs of her old films, including the one that had won her an Oscar. They were all signed, "To K.O. With Love."

All three of us decided that unless we were watching a comedy monolog by Louis C.K. or Lewis Black, we never again wanted to hear a speech that ran any longer than sixty seconds—and that definitely includes politicians.

Lorelei Singleton had to appear before a grand jury, and will stand trial for the murder of Tommy Triller. The judge accepted her bail—ten percent of five hundred thousand dollars—but ruled she could not leave the city of Cleveland until the trial date had been set—and that included the many Cleveland suburbs and exurbs. She rented a furnished apartment downtown, and until she has been found guilty or innocent by a jury of her peers, there would be no more Dr. Lorelei radio show, no more public appearances, no more writing monthly columns for a major women's magazine.

Patrick Owens was arraigned in Cleveland for his unprovoked attack on a police officer, and in a much more speedy trial was found guilty and sentenced to three years behind bars. One of George Lufton's attorneys had sped up from Columbus to do what he could for Patrick, but when Lufton himself was charged with accessory to murder, Owens's problems were quickly dropped so all of Lufton's lawyers could take care of the man who supported them. Lufton swore Lorelei said she needed the gun for protection, and that he had had no idea what she planned to do with it.

Jonah Clary went back to the ranch he had purchased through bribes he collected as governor. I have no idea what he'll do with the remainder of his life, but his political career is toast. All over but the shouting—and when word gets around the Global Motivation Speakers Association, so will his invitations to give talks at conventions. Dead in the water.

Jesse Paulin returned to Independence, Missouri, where several citizens there accused him of spending most of the money he collected all over the country from his church followers and disciples on his obscenely expensive home, his luxury cars (including a new Bentley), and the rent and expenses of a "very good friend" who was approximately nineteen years old and worked at Hooters in downtown Independence.

Dr. Ben Mayo continued with his career, books, pamphlets, CDs and DVDs of himself, but it was noticed almost at once that his beautiful wife Caroline no longer appeared in the studio audience when he did his daily TV show. Twitter went ablaze with questions from his viewers who wanted to know why, and eventually Dr. Ben admitted to the *Los Angeles Times* that he and Caroline were in the process of a trial separation. His Nielsen ratings dropped precipitously.

Claire Crane, having decided enough was enough, applied for and won a producership on a major network TV game show, cutting her annual salary in half.

Tony Nardoianni's speaking career moved apace, and he now spends much of his spare time with other retired baseball players who probably had no idea that he had bet on them or against them when he managed the Colorado Rockies.

Victor Gaimari was pleased with K.O. and me for whitewashing Tony's back story, so much so that he invited us and our lady loves to dinner at Giovanni's in Beachwood. He, of course, also had a date for the evening—late twenties, a local model, not even close to being Italian. Knowing his background, Tobe refused to attend at first, but when she relented, she found Victor to be a charming, amusing, and a very pleasant guy . . . for a godfather.

Hy Jinx announced soon after returning to Los Angeles that he had completed his next hip-hop album, to be released right after the first of the year. Within a week, the advance sales mounted to more than six million dollars.

Jarvis Green told the press he didn't plan to write another book in the near future, but preferred concentrating on his business dealings. He was paparazzied at The Four Seasons and at Sardi's several times with a famous Broadway stage actor who was openly gay. His former wife, Bailey DeWitt, was offered a three-year contract to appear weekly on one of the morning network talk shows.

Several of Tommy Triller's companies closed down. The only one left, which will continue merchandising his books and CDs, fired Triller's bodyguards, saying the particular company that had hired them had ceased its operations could no longer honor its contracts.

Reeve Fesmire was demoted at an emergency board meeting of the Global Motivational Speakers Association to being not much more than a travel secretary.

Swati S. Sathe and Tobe Blaine actually became friends, and occasionally had lunch together in the Renaissance Hotel.

Kylee Graves returned to Charlotte and wrote K.O. a letter telling him she was getting over Tommy Triller's death and "moving on," as she was now dating four different men. K.O. told me he hoped she'd also find a new hairdresser.

As for Tobe, she and I haven't changed much. We still see each other three or four times a week, either at her place on the West Side, or at my apartment in Cleveland Heights, just a short walk from Nighttown, for a good dinner and listening to some of the best jazz in Cleveland. Neither of us works Sundays, and we spend the entire day and evening together. In autumn, Sundays are pro football days, but now I find myself watching the Browns games less often, as Tobe and I enjoy each other's company more and more. We laugh. We joke. We zing each other kindly. We make love.

For a guy my age, I have to say—especially in Cleveland—that life is good.

AFTERWORD

BY DAN KENNEDY

With this book, I have, officially, rather viciously, bitten hands that feed me.

In a previous collaboration with Les, the book *Win, Place or Die,* I escorted Les, Milan, K.O. and Tobe into the world I inhabit as an avocation: harness racing. Here, I've taken them behind the curtains of a world I've lived and worked in for forty years as my principal vocation. And frankly, a number of my peers, colleagues, clients, and friends in this world are unlikely to be amused by this book.

My place as an intimate insider in the "success industry" is, in brief, as follows: a professional speaker, I spent nine consecutive years on the number-one public seminar tour in America, essentially a traveling, one-day pop-up store mostly housed in sports arenas, with audiences from 10,000 to 35,000. In Cleveland, we played Gund Arena several times—and created major traffic congestion during the morning and evening rush hours. The speaker line-up mixed the kind of fictional celebrity speakers you met in these pages with business celebrities like CEOs and big-name authors with less famous but still top sales, marketing and business trainers and consultants, like Zig Ziglar, Brian Tracy, Tom Hopking and me. With this as its center, I have had a thirty-plus-year, high-profile career in speaking to trade association, corporate, and public audiences. As a seminar promoter myself, I have had numerous celebrity-entrepreneurs join me at my own events, including Gene Simmons (KISS), Ivanka Trump, Kathy

Ireland, George Foreman, movie mogul Peter Gruber, and Joan
Rivers. As a business success author, I have twenty-three books,
including a popular "NO B.S." series, five newsletters, and an association of entrepreneurs built around me—you can see it all, if
curious, at www.NoBSBooks.com and www.GKIC.com. Finally, I
am something of a "guru to the gurus," launching, assisting, advis-
ing, and providing marketing support to more than five hundred
authors, speakers, seminar promoters, and publishers. In total,
we all directly connect with millions of small business owners,
private practice professionals and sales professionals every year.
I even co-founded one of the three professional associations, the
Information Marketing Association (www.info-marketing.org).

I tell you all this so you know that the world you entered in
this book, right along with Milan and friends, was presented *most
authentically.*

Some in the success industry are going to take umbrage at
this book's portrayal. In their defense, let me say that Les and I
have exaggerated the worst of it, and his opinion of it all, which is
harsher than my own, dominates Milan's and K.O.'s views. He also
admitted to some of the good. As Les has taught me, in a murder
mystery, *everybody* must be villainous.

The truth is that success information, ideas, and techniques
are more complex than Milan's summary—*don't be an asshole*—
and the work of many authors, speakers, consultants, and coaches
positively influences a great many people. As it did me, way back
when I first encountered it. Many of the people doing business in
the success industry are well-intentioned, sincere, and making
meaningful contributions to people's lives. Others, though, are
very frankly egotistical, ridiculously self-important blowhards
and outright charlatans. The trouble is telling them apart!

There *is* irony to all this. As George Carlin observed, there
really can't be a *self*-help book written by somebody else for you.

Of course, the characters you encountered here are entirely fictional, made up with a piece of one person and a piece of another,
and a gross exaggeration here and a totally imagined trait there. If
you read any more into any of the characters, you are wrong. Les
attended one of *my* seminars, met attendees and speakers, and got
a guided our by me of the books, magazines, newsletters, famous

and not-so-famous persons of the industry, past and present—but we did not lift any real person, living or dead, and place them in these pages. The celebrity-speakers in the success or motivation industry are, incidentally, a small microcosm of the entire field. Many are former presidents and would-be presidents, former astronauts, former pro athletes and coaches, and entertainers with fading stars. They are often used, as Fesmire said, as Shamu the Whale, an attraction to draw crowds. Most of the valuable information is delivered by people like me, who I call "famous people nobody ever heard of." To our audiences, to our business niches, we are very well known. But the general public is blissfully unaware we exist, and if you're hanging around me in a hotel lobby where there is no Global Motivational Speakers Association meeting, you have no risk of being trampled by autograph seekers or paparazzi!

Point is, the made-up characters here are fairly representative of the celebrity speakers who take their turns on success industry stages—but they are not actual, accurate versions of any such persons.

Anyway, for my peers or clients or others in the success industry, this adventure created for Milan and his fans was all meant as good, clean fun. Let's not take ourselves *too* seriously. We aren't, after all, curing cancer. And if you *think* you spot yourself in here, relax. Think of it like being skewered on an episode of *The Simpsons* or *Saturday Night Live*. SNL did have its own motivational speaker character: Chris Farley's Matt Foley, who lived in a van down by the river. That, and this, are parody. For everybody else, I hope you had fun with this trip to a special kind of circus. I enjoyed my little part, as Les's guide dog, and as contributor of some ideas about characters and some bits of dialogue.

Oh, and what would an Afterword to this book be without some actual success advice? Here it is, from Coach Nardoianni himself:

"You win some. You lose some. Some get rained out. But you gotta suit up for them all."

ACKNOWLEDGEMENTS

Much appreciation to Dan S. Kennedy. I knew nothing about high-end public speaking until he supplied me with research. Now I know more about it than I ever thought I would. He brought the groceries; I just cooked them.

Thanks to all my Facebook friends. You keep me on my toes.

A deep bow to the Renaissance Hotel on Public Square in Cleveland, one of the all-time great hotels.

And a tip of the hat, as always, to Dr. Milan Yakovich and to Diana Yakovich Montagino, who've inspired me for the past quarter of a century.